This is Katie in your arms,

Louis told himself to counteract his desire. The warning had the opposite effect. It touched off an old memory—the one night twelve years ago he'd taken Katie came back to him with utter clarity.

He cringed with an old and a new guilt, remembering. God, it must have been a terrible experience for her. He'd been in a fever to plunge himself into the sweetness of her virgin womanhood. He felt like apologizing, not just for having taken her when he shouldn't have, but for having been such an inexpert lover.

And for being stimulated now by the memory.

He wouldn't be in a hurry this time. He'd make love to her thoroughly, deeply. He'd satisfy her....

As the music came to a throbbing finale, Louis stopped dancing and held Katie in a steel embrace.

Lord, he hadn't been subconsciously waiting all these years for another chance to make love to her, had he?

D0366898

Dear Reader,

Sophisticated but sensitive, savvy yet unabashedly sentimental—that's today's woman, today's romance reader—you! And Silhouette Special Editions are written expressly to reward your quest for substantial, emotionally involving love stories.

So take a leisurely stroll under the cover's lavender arch into a garden of romantic delights. Pick and choose among titles if you must—we hope you'll soon equate all six Special Editions each month with consistently gratifying romantic reading.

Watch for sparkling new stories from your Silhouette favorites—Nora Roberts, Tracy Sinclair, Ginna Gray, Lindsay McKenna, Curtiss Ann Matlock, among others—along with some exciting newcomers to Silhouette, such as Karen Keast and Patricia Coughlin. Be on the lookout, too, for the new Silhouette Classics, a distinctive collection of bestselling Special Editions and Silhouette Intimate Moments now brought back to the stands—two each month—by popular demand.

On behalf of all the authors and editors of Special Editions,
Warmest wishes,

Leslie Kazanjian
Senior Editor

CAROLE HALSTON
High Bid

Silhouette Special Edition

Published by Silhouette Books New York

America's Publisher of Contemporary Romance

To my father-in-law, the elder Monty, who has read
all my romances. Also to Michael, Charlie, Bruce,
Mel, Don, A.J. and all the other workmen who built
our beautiful house for us and provided a wealth of
background information without knowing it!

SILHOUETTE BOOKS
300 East 42nd St., New York, N.Y. 10017

ISBN: 0-373-09423-X

First Silhouette Books printing December 1987

Books by Carole Halston

Silhouette Romance

Stand-in Bride #62
Love Legacy #83
Undercover Girl #152
Sunset in Paradise #208

Silhouette Special Edition

Keys to Daniel's House #8
Collision Course #41
The Marriage Bonus #86
Summer Course in Love #115
A Hard Bargain #139
Something Lost, Something Gained #163
A Common Heritage #211
The Black Knight #223
Almost Heaven #253
Surprise Offense #291
Matched Pair #328
Honeymoon for One #356
The Baby Trap #388
High Bid #423

CAROLE HALSTON

is a Louisiana native, residing on the north shore of Lake Pontchartrain, near New Orleans. She enjoys traveling with her husband to research less familiar locations for settings but is always happy to return home to her own unique region, a rich source in itself for romantic stories about warm, wonderful people.

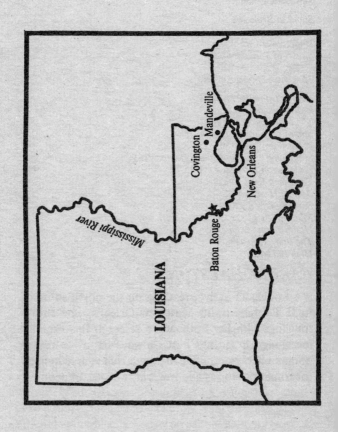

Chapter One

Katie reached for the telephone, drew her hand back and let it hover in space, reached a second time and jerked back to drum her fingers on the scarred surface of her father's large, old wooden desk, to which she'd fallen heir. Stop procrastinating and make your call, she urged herself. You need to know something definite.

It had been a month now since she'd submitted her bid to John Hemphill, an executive with a major oil company. Katie had made a point of asking him to please get back to her, pro or con, but so far she hadn't heard a word. The man was either taking his own sweet time selecting a general contractor to build his new house in one of the more exclusive subdivisions in the Covington area or else he wasn't considerate enough to call and end her suspense.

Earlier in the week Katie had given herself today as a deadline. Now the afternoon was wearing on. She needed to place the call to Hemphill's New Orleans office. She had to know something, either way. She was going out of her mind, wondering, waiting, killing time.

Rocking back in her father's oversize swivel chair, Katie winced at the torturous squeak from the spring mechanism, feeling the sound scrape along her nerves. Although she'd been hearing it as long as she could remember, it had never bothered her until she started feeling desperate. What was she going to do if Hemphill hadn't picked her? she fretted. She didn't have another bid out. No one was asking Gamble Construction for bids now that her father had retired and she was on her own.

The lack of any answer to her own question was making her procrastinate, Katie realized. Normally she was decisive, doing whatever needed to be done. Normally she would opt for disappointment over uncertainty. As a child she'd wanted to know either *yes* or *no* immediately. She hadn't been able to tolerate *maybe* or *let's wait and see*.

Once, in a civics class in high school, she remembered, she'd argued strongly that trial juries should have a time limit for deliberating and arriving at a verdict. "It's cruel to keep the accused person waiting," Katie had stated with utter certainty. "I'd want to know my sentence and either be free or start serving my prison term." That had been in her freshman year, when she was supremely convinced of her own innate innocence, two years before she'd learned her human potential for doing irreparable harm to people she loved.

It would be a strange kind of justice, she thought, if Louis had bid on Hemphill's job, too, and gotten it.

Shoving memory and fateful coincidence aside, Katie fixed her eyes on the phone. She knew perfectly well why she was putting off the call, and she might as well admit it. She hadn't gotten the job. That was why she hadn't heard from Hemphill. Her chances of landing the contract had been slim to none from the beginning.

When Hemphill contacted Gamble Construction, he hadn't been aware, as was the local building community, that Katie's father, Red Gamble, now in his seventies, had suffered another heart attack. Although milder than the one eight years ago, it had put an end to the fiction that he was still building houses. Hemphill hadn't known he was giving a woman contractor a chance to make a bid until his initial conversation with Katie, when the information had come out.

Then her bid had come in too high, through no fault of hers. The same subcontractors who'd worked for her as long as she'd sustained the pretense that her father was in charge had come up with extravagant estimates that clearly made their point. They didn't want to work for a woman. To be in the same ballpark with her male competitors, Katie had severely cut her usual contractor's percentage of the total cost of construction, but she couldn't work for nothing. It was maddening to know that she could eliminate any pay for herself and still not come in lower than the men bidding against her.

Her situation was totally unfair and bitterly frustrating. Katie's only professional shortcoming was her sex. She was a woman trying to compete in an occupation that was a male stronghold in southern Louisiana. It didn't matter that she was competent and would readily have stepped into her father's shoes if she had been the son he'd wanted so badly. Instead she'd been the belated fifth arrival in a series of daughters.

Her father's last hope, she'd tried to be a substitute son for him, proving that she could fish and shoot a gun as well as any boy her age. By the time she entered high school, she'd also known every step of building a house. She'd known too, that her father's occupation was closed to her. A woman simply couldn't be a building contractor.

She'd been twenty-one when her father had his first heart attack. In her junior year of college, she had dropped her studies—temporarily, she'd thought—to take over for him while he was bedridden and then confined to the house for long months. Once he was recovered, she hadn't wanted to go back to school. She'd wanted to continue being his right hand, and her wishes were reinforced by the warning of her father's doctor. Red Gamble needed to slow down and eliminate as much stress as possible.

That had been eight years ago. For the last three years Katie had been totally in charge of building her father's houses. He'd been general contractor in name only. She hadn't minded seeing him get the credit. She hadn't urged him to retire, thinking that the notion that he was still involved in building was good for him. Now she was beginning to perceive the irony of it all. Her father hadn't been hanging on for himself; he'd delayed retirement for her sake, fearing what she would be up against without him as her front.

As soon as she made the call to Hemphill and verified her bleak intuition, Katie would have to face up to humiliation and failure. Failing in her father's eyes hurt most. She'd always striven to make him proud of her, to compensate for not having been a boy.

Finally Katie picked up the receiver and punched out the digits, dread tightening every nerve in her body. She could feel the hard thud of her heartbeat and pulse. It was unbearable, she thought with fierce resentment, being at the mercy of a virtual stranger.

"I'll hold," she told the secretary who explained that Mr. Hemphill was on another line at the moment. "This is a long-distance call," she added to give what priority she could to getting through to him.

Katie's view through the office window offered little relief from the suspense of waiting. She could see the backyard and rear entrance of the two-story Gamble house, her home for the twenty-nine years of her life. The scene she visualized inside would have brought a smile under happier circumstances, but now it brought a painful lump to her throat.

Red and Edna Gamble would be ensconced in their favorite chairs in front of the television set in the family room. One of Edna's soap operas would be in progress. She'd be following the plot avidly, tsking and chattering away as though the characters were real people she knew, her hands busy with a needlework project. Katie's father would be making disparaging remarks, trying to erase any suspicion that he was interested in the daytime serial, too. Yet he wouldn't get up and leave the room until a commercial break.

If Katie appeared at the door, both her parents would look around, love blooming in their dear faces. She'd have to smile and pretend to be cheerful, pretend that she didn't see the deep worry lurking behind the affection in their eyes. It was a terrible strain, trying to be convincing as she claimed she welcomed the free time while she waited for feedback on bids. Lately she'd seen the error of honoring her parents' wishes and not getting an apartment or condominium. She needed her own place, for their sake as well as hers.

The secretary's voice interrupted Katie's musings. "Mr. Hemphill is still on another line, Ms. Gamble. Do you want to continue holding or should I have him return your call?"

"I'll hold," Katie replied, the knots in her stomach pulling tighter until they ached. "It's very important that I speak with Mr. Hemphill this afternoon."

Please, God, let me be wrong, she prayed, closing her eyes on the hot September sunshine so perfect for building houses. Please let him want me to build his house. I can do as good a job as anybody, if I just have the chance.

"Ms. Gamble, very sorry to keep you waiting." John Hemphill's apologetic voice broke into her supplication and brought her eyes open. From his tone Katie knew before he said another word that he had rejected her bid. Prepared as she was for disappointment, the blow was almost overwhelming. She would have cut him short if she could have managed to speak calmly, but instead she listened while he took a roundabout route of disclosing, most regretfully, that he had decided upon another contractor and had not yet found the time to call Katie and tell her.

By the time he finished, Katie had taken hold of herself and was starting to burn with resentment. Not only had he been inconsiderate, but his whole attitude was insulting. He never would have spoken to a male contractor the way he was addressing her, making an obvious effort to let her down gently. He'd have come right to the point, spoken man to man, but with a member of the so-called weaker sex, he couldn't be direct.

Nonetheless, Katie remained outwardly professional and businesslike. "I understand that you're a busy man,

Mr. Hemphill, but I deserved the simple courtesy of a telephone call, which would have taken only a few minutes of your time." She supported her criticism. "It was the least you could do to repay me for my time and trouble. A general contractor doesn't pull a bid out of the air. There's a great deal of legwork and effort involved. I had to get your house plan out to more than half a dozen subcontractors for their estimates, consult various suppliers, study the architect's specifications and figure costs item by item. That's the only way I could arrive at a price that would allow me to build the kind of house you want and get compensated reasonably for the sizable responsibility I would be taking on. In return, all I asked of you was notification of your decision."

Katie paused, taking an utterly joyless satisfaction in his defensiveness as he apologized again, clearly chagrined.

"For the sake of curiosity, may I ask which contractor you did decide on?" she inquired of him when he finished.

As he hedged again, explaining the trouble he'd gone to in making a fair choice, checking out recommendations and so on, Katie gazed out the window, her attention caught by two little preteen girls dashing into view.

They rounded the corner of the Gamble house and headed for the steps to the screened back porch. Watching them, she felt the same odd stirring the sight of the two of them together always awakened. They'd been inseparable this past year and visited the Gamble house often.

The little redhead in the lead was Katie's eleven-year-old niece, Lisa, a near replica of Katie at that age and amazingly like her in temperament as well as looks.

Everyone in the family was fond of pointing out the resemblance. Lisa's companion was Stephanie McIntyre,
a little princess of a girl with long, silky black curls. She
managed to look daintily feminine even running behind the tomboyish Lisa.

Louis McIntyre's daughter. Katie wondered if Louis
ever marveled, as she did, at life's strange twists and
turns. Her niece, so much like Katie at the same age,
and his daughter, a feminine image of him, had become the best of friends. Apparently Louis didn't op-
pose the friendship. He had to know that Stephanie
came and went in Red Gamble's house and encountered Lisa's Aunt Katie frequently.

Today his daughter's timing was uncanny. With the
screen door slamming behind Stephanie's back, leaving Katie with a vision of dancing black curls, John
Hemphill finally got to the point and named the general
contractor he had chosen over Katie to build his house.
Louis McIntyre.

Katie fought down an eerie sensation of fate, reminding herself that the two little girls made a habit of
dropping by after school at about this time to visit Lisa's
grandparents and snack on Edna Gamble's homemade
cookies. And there was nothing surprising, really, in
John Hemphill's choice of Louis McIntyre to build his
house. Louis was fast gaining a reputation as one of the
finest builders in the area.

Because the job meant what it did to her, though,
losing out to Louis took on overtones of retribution,
especially with his daughter appearing as a reminder of
the wrong Katie had done to Louis when he was acting
honorably. Whether Louis realized it or not, he was
getting his revenge. Still, Katie thought her punishment was too severe.

"I take it you're acquainted with Mr. McIntyre," Hemphill prompted, making Katie aware of her absorbed silence.

"Yes, of course. Louis and I grew up together. He worked for my father summers when he was in high school." Katie heard the note of sadness in her voice and suddenly was too deeply discouraged to carry the conversation any farther. "I'm sure Louis will build a fine house for you, Mr. Hemphill," she said quietly. "He's very well thought of in this area, as you're no doubt aware. Good luck to you."

She replaced the receiver and slumped down in the swivel chair. Before Katie was born her father bought it, the desk and the gunmetal-gray filing cabinets secondhand and set up a rudimentary office here in the small building behind the house. He had needed a place out of the busy traffic of the Gamble household to do the paperwork connected with being a small-town general contractor.

Katie, conceived when Red and Edna were in their early forties and thought they had concluded their family, had always had the run of her father's office. He had carried her there before she could walk, held her on his lap while he sat in this same chair and laughed heartily when she wreaked havoc with the invoices and papers on his desk. In her toddler years, he'd kept the bottom drawers of the filing cabinets full of junk mail because Katie took such delight in opening it and pulling everything out onto the floor.

Once she was in school, she'd had her own small desk there for doing homework while her father added figures and updated records before supper. In junior high school and high school, she wrote assignments sitting at his desk. After she learned to type, he bought a type-

writer for her and installed it in the office for her use.
When he needed a letter written, Katie proudly typed it
for him.

Now the typewriter sat on its stand in a corner, its
plastic cover dusty, obsolete since Katie's freshman year
of college. She had been living at home and commut-
ing to the state university in Hammond. Her parents
hadn't wanted her to go away to school, and she hadn't
minded yielding to their persuasion. By staying at
home, she made both of them happy and was able to
take over more and more of her father's office chores
until she was doing all his paperwork and bookkeep-
ing.

With her first computer course in her general business curriculum, she'd seen immediately the usefulness
of a computer in her father's business. She could con-
vert his records to floppy disks for tax purposes, set up
computer files on houses he was building, keep track of
every penny spent, print out itemized cost statements,
and more. Red Gamble didn't argue or grumble about
the expense. He merely reminded Katie that he was an
old dog who wasn't about to start learning tricks with a
newfangled machine. He would buy a computer, but
she would be in command of it.

One reason Katie had been able to take over for him
so easily when he was stricken with his first attack was
her thorough familiarity, from a business angle, with his
several building jobs that were in progress. But she was
also knowledgeable about house-building, literally from
the ground up.

She knew about concrete slabs as opposed to raised
foundations, about framing up a house, about the
rough-in and finish stages of plumbing and electrical
work and installation of heating and cooling systems.

She knew the whole complex sequence of calling in the numerous "subs." It didn't matter that she couldn't do their jobs. She didn't have to. A general contractor was like an orchestra conductor, who doesn't have to know how to play all the musicians' instruments. The conductor guides the musicians and, if talented, gets the very best out of them. Similarly, a contractor coordinated workers' skills so that a sound, beautiful house emerged out of raw materials, lengths of lumber and pipe and rolls of black electrical wire.

Katie knew the whole process. She knew about making sure that orders from the lumberyard and various suppliers were delivered to the jobsite on time and were the proper grade of materials. She knew about weather delays and having to push to keep on schedule, about coping with owners and architects, about soothing workers' ruffled tempers.

She knew all that and more, but because she was a woman, the knowledge seemed useless now that her father was retired. House-building was man's work in Covington and the surrounding area. Katie had been tolerated, on a temporary basis, for the sake of Red Gamble, who was liked and respected.

She'd gleaned her knowledge from the beginning as a privileged visitor in a man's world. When she rode around with her father in his pickup truck from the time that she could walk, people understood, even if they didn't necessarily approve, that Red was making the best of an unfortunate situation. He wasn't going to have that little boy he'd wanted with the birth of each of his five daughters, so he was turning his last disappointment into a substitute son.

Growing up, Katie had been aware of this mixture of sympathy and criticism, but she had adored her father and valued only his opinion. She wondered now, looking back, if he had really wanted her to be such a flagrant tomboy who tagged along after him or if he'd simply been indulging her. Her driving force had been to please him. He had seemed to love bragging about her.

In high school, Katie had had added incentives to show an interest in his work. After she learned to drive, he would let her take his pickup truck to collect the odd piece of lumber or bag of nails or fitting that was needed on a job. She'd felt so responsible, so grown-up. More important, she'd had an excuse to come around any jobsite where Louis was working, on Saturdays and holidays when school was in session and full-time during the summers.

A year older than she, Louis had dispensed with doing a boy's odd jobs to earn pocket money and moved on to a man's labor. Red Gamble had always managed to find a job for Louis on one of the houses he was building, just as he'd come up with endless chores around the Gamble house. Katie had been infinitely jealous of Louis. He'd been the perfect example of what her father would have wanted in a son, and he'd worshiped the very ground that Red Gamble walked on.

By her teen years, though, added to Katie's old conflict of liking Louis and resenting him was an intense new physical attraction. He was one of the best-looking and best-liked boys in school. Katie had a terrible crush on him. She had given up being mean and spiteful to him in favor of chasing him. With the same gentle stoicism he'd displayed when she was a little spoiled brat, he'd put up with her as a persistent love-struck teenager. All because Red Gamble was exactly what he would have wanted in a father.

Louis. Speaking his name silently filled Katie with a multitude of regrets. He had been such a nice little boy, just as nice an adolescent and a fledgling young man—hardworking, sincere, easygoing, polite, liked and admired by everybody. He was probably a nice grown man of thirty now, with all those same good qualities. It hadn't been his fault that he'd brought out the worst in Katie.

Now he was coming into his own as a builder at the very same time that Katie was falling flat on her face. Katie could see a certain justice in that, but that didn't mean she could accept lying there, breathing dirt. Nor was it in her nature to crawl off into the bushes and hide. Somehow or other, she was going to build a house on her own, as Katie Gamble, general contractor, and then she could tell all the good old boys in the building trade in St. Tammany Parish to shove it. It wasn't quitting when she wasn't wanted that she minded so much as being forced out of a job at which she was damned good.

But without a custom-building job, she had only one alternative: building a house on speculation, a highly risky venture. Before she could let all the obvious drawbacks and obstacles come to mind, Katie bolted out of her chair and turned off the air conditioner. Maybe she'd stand a better chance of convincing herself it was a viable idea if she drove to the lot she owned and mulled over the notion of a spec house there.

Leaving the office, Katie closed the door behind her harder than necessary and took heart at the forceful sound. A minute later, though, she wished she'd been quieter. Her path to her Ford Bronco in the driveway took her across the backyard, and when she reached the corner of the house she was hailed from behind.

"Aunt Katie! Aunt Katie! Where're you going? Can we go with you? Please, can we?"

Katie came to a stop and turned slowly, immediately comprehending the ticklish situation confronting her. Although Lisa was fond of tagging along with Katie, much as Katie had loved accompanying Red Gamble, this time Lisa was including her best friend, Stephanie, Louis's daughter. Given Katie's emotional state, the venture was out of the question.

Katie steeled herself for her niece's persuasive efforts. Lisa, like Katie at that age, didn't take no easily.

"I'm only going to look at an empty lot, honey, where I'm thinking of building a house." Katie answered the inquiry on her destination first, laying the groundwork for her refusal. "I'd better not take you two along, since I don't know what time I'll be back. I might be late, and you'll both need to be home in time for supper. Stephanie's grandmother might worry about her."

Katie smiled placatingly at the little black-haired girl regarding her so solemnly with Louis's deep blue eyes. The child's appearance was indisputable proof that Betty Baker *had* been pregnant with Louis's baby. He had done the right thing, marrying her just out of high school, despite seventeen-year-old Katie's hysterical accusation that he was being duped, and despite her vindictive threat, which she'd carried out and deeply regretted afterward.

"But, Aunt Katie, you must be meaning to be back in time for supper yourself," Lisa pointed out reasonably. "Or else you'd have stopped in and told Maw-maw Edna you were going to be late. Steph and me won't be any trouble, will we, Steph?"

Instead of taking her cue and adding her own subtle cajolery, Stephanie McIntyre spoke up with a clear young dignity that made Katie suspect uncomfortably that the child saw right through Katie's refusal.

"I have to go home now. You can go with your aunt by yourself, Lisa."

"But, Steph! Your grandma's not even home from the courthouse yet!" Lisa protested. "You don't have to go! It's Friday! We don't have to do our homework tonight! Aunt *Kay*—tee—" she whined.

Katie pretended to reconsider. "Maybe you girls could be some help to me. You could give me your ideas about the spec house I'm thinking of building." Katie was surprised by the thrill of voicing her desperate plan aloud for the first time. "I guess I could get you both back in time for supper. How about it, Stephanie?"

Katie smiled warmly at the pretty little girl who wasn't in any way at fault for the circumstances of her conception.

"I guess I could go," Stephanie conceded readily.

"Good. Then why don't you two run back into the house and let Lisa's grandma know you're going with me, just in case somebody wonders where you are while we're gone."

Someone like Stephanie's father. Katie completed the thought silently while she stood and waited for the girls. If Louis didn't like Stephanie's accompanying Katie, he would have to deal with it later. She wasn't going to hurt the little girl's feelings.

As for what other people thought, Katie wasn't worried. Who would even remember that she and Louis had dated in high school? Those who did would know they'd never been engaged, hadn't even officially gone steady, despite Katie's determined efforts to that end.

Some of Katie's friends might recall her high-school heartbreak when Louis married Betty in a shotgun wedding, but even they didn't know the whole story. To Katie's knowledge, only three people did: herself, Louis and Red Gamble. Katie couldn't say for sure that her father had ever confided in her mother. Never once had her mother made reference to it.

Did her father still have hard feelings toward Louis after all these years? Katie had no inkling. Once her father had calmed down from his murderous rage that day, which had happened only after Katie had been frightened into confessing the complete truth, he'd never spoken Louis's name again in her hearing. To her knowledge, he had never used his influence against Louis. He had simply X'ed Louis out of existence.

That Red Gamble took Stephanie McIntyre's presence in his house in stride, teasing her and treating her warmly as he treated all his grandchildren's friends, was no true indication of any softening toward Louis. Red had always been kindhearted toward children, and he would have been indignant at the very notion of extending hard feelings against a man to that man's child, who was entirely innocent of the father's wrongdoing.

Except in Louis's case, there had been little wrongdoing, Katie was forced to admit. Stephanie was more proof of Louis's honest, upright instincts than she was a reminder of his young man's lust. One had only to look at Stephanie to understand the high opinion of the community. Louis was a good father and obviously more than a mere provider. Despite having been abandoned by her mother, his daughter was a secure child, with no trace of her father's almost desperate eagerness to please at that age. In fact, Katie noted with interest, Stephanie didn't seem to have inherited her father's personality at all.

As the two girls came bounding out of the house and accompanied Katie to her Bronco, Lisa was all energy and bossy enthusiasm, just as Katie had been at her age.

"Who's gonna get to sit up front with you, Aunt Katie?" she demanded and worked out the problem for herself. "Hey, I know! Steph and me can *both* sit in the front seat. They have to make the seat belts big enough for fat people. It'll fit over both of us. Is it okay, Aunt Katie?"

"You can sit in the front." Stephanie declined the solution before Katie could either agree or object. "I don't mind sitting in the back. The seat's high, and I can see out good."

Suddenly the front seat lost its appeal for Lisa. With some bemusement, Katie found herself playing chauffeur alone in the front. Questioned eagerly about the assistance the girls could render, she explained that a spec house was one a contractor built without a previous commitment, intending to sell it after the fact—ideally during construction, but, if not, afterward. Talking about her venture, even to children, somehow made it more credible to her.

"A spec house has to suit a lot of different people," she pointed out. "Otherwise, you might not be able to sell it. But then, on the other hand, it can't be too ordinary. It needs some special features to make people fall in love with it. Also, it has to be right for the neighborhood."

"Not stick out like a sore thumb, huh?" Lisa chimed in earnestly.

"If it's a neighborhood with lots of kids, the house should be right for a family with children," Stephanie suggested.

"You two catch on fast," Katie complimented them, genuinely impressed as well as amused that they were taking their advisory capacity very seriously.

At the lot they had opinions on everything—where the house should be positioned, whether it should be one story or two. In discussing floor plans, they got into specific detail, not only with size and placement of various rooms, but also with decor. Katie occasionally had to hide a smile. Some of their suggestions were soundly practical and others childish whimsy. She was glad she'd brought them along; they'd definitely lightened her mood.

Close observation of Stephanie McIntyre interacting with her niece was strangely soothing to vague old guilts. History was not repeating itself in the relationship of the two little girls. Louis's pretty daughter was serene and outwardly composed compared to the more volatile and outgoing Lisa, but she was actually the stronger willed of the two. She seldom relented once she'd stated her opinion, whereas Lisa was likely to come around to her friend's point of view.

"Okay, the girl's room can have pink-and-white-striped wallpaper with tiny bouquets of flowers and pink carpet," Lisa conceded after a spirited debate Katie was on the verge of interrupting to announce that it was time to leave. "I guess Steph's right, Aunt Katie. More girls like pink than lavender. But when I grow up and have my own house, my bedroom's going to be lavender with purple carpet. I'm gonna have you build my house for me, Aunt Katie."

Katie fondly rumpled her niece's cap of vibrant rust-red hair, styled similarly to hers, trying not to show how the artless comment depressed her.

"I appreciate the vote of confidence, honey, but Aunt Katie probably won't be building houses by then." With an effort she smiled at Stephanie, who was nibbling her bottom lip, suffering the constraints of politeness. The little girl had made frequent proud mention of her father during the past hour and was clearly dying to name him as her own prospective builder, but she didn't want to offend Katie. "I'm sure Stephanie will want her daddy to build her house when she grows up."

Stephanie nodded gratefully.

"I want my daddy to build me a house exactly like the one he's just finishing. It's the prettiest house I've ever seen." An eager light dawned in her face. "We could go see it, if you wanted to. My daddy's probably there."

"Please, could we, Aunt Katie? Could we?" Lisa danced around enthusiastically, clapping her hands. Her blue eyes, the same bright color as Katie's, sparkled imploringly between long copper-tipped lashes. But it wasn't her niece's animation holding Katie's attention. Stephanie McIntyre was regarding her with quiet suspense, the deep blue of her eyes, so like her father's, tinged violet with hopefulness.

Why not? Katie thought, shocking herself. There wasn't a single good reason to disappoint the child. Why should Katie spend the rest of her life avoiding Louis? It was only a habit, as steering clear of her was probably second nature to him by now. They weren't likely ever to be friendly, but there was no reason they shouldn't run into each other occasionally and act like old acquaintances.

"I guess we have time," she told the two girls, having come to her decision.

With a small girl on either side, Katie walked to the parked Bronco. Lisa skipped and swung her aunt's hand excitedly, overflowing with energy. Stephanie walked more sedately, matching her pace to Katie's, but she held Katie's hand, too, and her clasp was warm and trusting. Shedding some of her earlier reserve, she now competed with Lisa for Katie's attention.

Katie had problems concentrating on what either girl was saying. Before she even got the Bronco in gear, she was having serious second thoughts. On the way to the site, she prayed that Louis wouldn't be there. But a block away from the house Stephanie and Lisa put an end to any such hopes when they spotted a dark blue pickup in the driveway.

"That's my daddy's truck!"

"That's Mr. Louis's truck, Aunt Katie! Oh, boy! He's here, and we can see the house!"

Oh, boy, Katie echoed to herself, panic blooming in her breast. Her foot tensed to step harder on the accelerator and take them right past the house with a burst of speed. She could invent some excuse for an emergency return home and bribe the girls with Cokes along the way.

"There's my daddy now, coming out of the house!" Stephanie announced eagerly.

"There's Mr. Louis, Aunt Katie!" Lisa added, as though Katie needed a footnote.

"I see him. I see him," Katie muttered. She recognized Louis without any trouble as he crossed the front porch that extended the full width of the big two-story house. He took the steps down slowly, moving with the loose-jointed ease that had always suited his personality. He looked tired, Katie noted, as though the day now ending hadn't been a particularly good one. At the bottom of the steps, he stopped to frown at the clipboard he had been carrying under his arm. Oblivious to the Bronco approaching the driveway, he seemed sunk in thought.

Katie had a split second when she could have executed her escape plan. She could have ordered the two little girls into silence and driven on by while they recovered from their surprise. Instead, without slowing down, she wheeled the Bronco sharply into the driveway and braked just behind Louis's pickup. An old devilment sprang to life in Katie as he looked up, first startled and then openly stunned, recognizing the vehicle and then the driver.

Chapter Two

Look how surprised your daddy looks, Steph!'' Lisa giggled, bouncing up and down in an ecstasy of excitement. "I don't think Mr. Louis recognizes your car, Aunt Katie! I bet he's wondering who in the world is coming to see him! Come on, Steph!"

Louis recognized her Bronco, all right, just as she had known the pickup was his without the girls' helpful identification. Two people didn't live ten blocks apart in the same small town, know the same people and work in the same business without generally keeping up with each other.

Katie savored a moment's advantage as she watched Louis's astonishment change to disbelief when both doors of the Bronco swung open and his daughter tumbled out on the passenger side along with her friend, while Katie hopped down from behind the wheel. He shot her a quick, questioning glance before he turned his attention to the two little girls bearing down on him, both giggling and talking excitedly at the same time.

"Hi, Daddy! We came to show Miss Katie and Lisa the house! I told them it was the prettiest house in the whole world and that you were going to build me one just like it when I grow up!"

"Hi, Mr. Louis! You sure looked surprised to see us! I wish you coulda seen your face!"

"I was a little surprised," Louis drawled, smiling in turn at each little girl. When his eyes came back to his daughter's face, they kindled with paternal love. "Hi, sweetheart." He squatted down to kiss her on the cheek and receive her tight hug around his neck. Standing up again, he ruffled Lisa's hair in affectionate greeting. With a hand on the shoulder of each girl, he looked up at Katie, who had walked around the open door of the Bronco and was standing several steps away, watching.

"A couple more minutes and you'd have missed me. I was on my way home." He made a mild general welcome to all three of them out of his disclosure, but Katie could read the uneasy puzzlement in his eyes that would escape the children. He wondered why she was there with his daughter.

"This was Stephanie's idea," she explained in a bland tone. "She insisted that we see her ideal house."

"Steph and me went along with Aunt Katie to her lot, where she's planning to build a spec house. She asked us to help her get some ideas for it. We came up with lots of good ones, didn't we, Aunt Katie? Then we came from there to here," Lisa helpfully filled in.

"You're building a spec house?" Louis asked Katie in surprise.

Katie nodded, torn between wanting to shake her niece and give her a hug for being a blabbermouth.

"I haven't advertised the fact yet, but I am giving it serious thought. Actually, I don't have a whole lot of choice. But I'm sure that comes as no surprise," she added flatly, raising her chin and meeting his eyes squarely.

Louis frowned slightly at her tone but didn't hold her gaze, refusing the silent communication she offered him. Katie watched him move to lean against the cab of his truck, feeling oddly cheated that he hadn't expressed comprehension. He had to know her predicament. He was human and had to feel a *little* glad.

"I'm inclined to envy you," he remarked, cradling the clipboard wearily against his chest. "Right now building spec houses sounds mighty good to me, but I'm not in a financial position to turn down custom jobs."

"I'd gladly change places with you, believe me," Katie retorted, trying without total success to keep from sounding bitter. The two girls were watching and listening with an unusual patience that said they were picking up adult undercurrents. "Stephanie, why don't you take Lisa on a guided tour while your daddy and I talk?" she suggested. "I'll have to get her home soon for supper."

The deliberate mention of a time limitation stirred the two girls into activity, as Katie had intended.

"Okay!" they agreed in unison.

"Daddy, I'll need the key," Stephanie reminded her father, holding out her hand.

Louis dug into his jeans pocket and handed his daughter the brass house key on a loop of leather thong.

"Be careful not to touch any of the white trim. The painter's been here all day, and it might not be dry. The pale yellow trim is okay." He met the question in Katie's face and answered it in a pained voice that matched his expression. "No, the house doesn't have two-tone trim. The lady of the house decided she didn't like the color she'd picked, but she couldn't make up her mind whether to change it until everything had been given the finish coat."

"I hope the doors aren't painted, too." Katie's builder's empathy was instinctive.

Louis winced as he nodded. "They're all solid core and heavy as hell to take down, not to mention that the floors are all finished, the carpet down and the hardwood floors varnished. The painter will have to be extra careful, which will take him longer. Naturally, the owners are raising hell, wanting me to hurry up and finish their house so that they can move in."

"Owners always get impatient at this stage, right at the end," Katie mused sympathetically.

Louis sagged against the pickup cab, surveying the handsome exterior of the house without any pleasure. Despite his relaxed position, there was tension in his voice.

"This job has been a pain in the rear from start to finish. You know the kind. Every contractor has one now and then, where every time you turn your back, there's some kind of foul-up. When something did work out right the first time, the Pearsons decided they wanted to change it. Lord, I'll be glad to see the last of those two people," he said feelingly. Then he added with rueful honesty, "They'll be glad to see the last of me, too."

He looked at Katie, catching her off guard. With his attention on the house, she had been taking full advantage of the opportunity to study him close up and see that he had matured but hadn't essentially changed. A

tall, big-boned man, he hadn't gained weight notice-
ably or gone soft around the middle. He had the same
clean-cut, unassuming masculinity, without a hint of
swagger.

In his jeans, short-sleeved plaid shirt and plain leather
boots, he was neat and presentable, as he had always
been, but not overly fastidious and not vain. His naturally curly black hair looked exactly as it always had,
appealingly unkempt, clean and soft. She remembered
well how it felt.

"You haven't changed," Katie told him, defensive
that she'd been caught looking him over. It came as a
shock to her that she reacted to him with the same instinctive feminine approval she'd felt back in high
school. Since then, though, she'd learned to control her
feelings.

"You haven't changed a lot yourself," Louis replied, smiling faintly as he glanced down at her hands
stuck into the pockets of her jeans. "I see you're still
full of nervous energy."

Katie hadn't been aware until then that she was flap-
ping her thumbs in alternate rhythm against her belt.
Nor was she aware until his gaze dropped still lower to
her feet that she was tapping the pointed toe of one
Western boot.

"I see you're still laid-back," she said, self-
consciously stilling her restless movements.

"I'm not feeling very laid-back lately." Louis brought
his gaze back up to her face via the length of her slim,
leggy form. Katie went taut and knew her surprise must
show in her face as he met her eyes for a brief telltale
moment of a man acknowledging a woman. Then he
glanced quickly away, first at the house and then down
at the clipboard in his hand.

"Sorry. I didn't mean to tell you all my problems," he apologized as he flipped a page. "It's been a long day at the end of a nerve-racking week. There've been a hundred and one little nit-picking details. Personally, this is my least favorite stage in building a house."

His rueful, casual tone suggested that Katie could be any acquaintance in the building trade, man or woman, who had dropped by. It carefully denied the male awareness she had just seen in his eyes. Katie felt a surge of an old exasperation as she watched him scan the pages of his clipboard with frowning absorption. *Nothing has changed*, she thought. He was as nice as he had ever been, and just as frustrating.

"Right now I'd give a lot for your problems." At her irritable tone, he looked up from the clipboard. "If I had any choice, I certainly wouldn't be making plans to build a spec house. As it happens, I don't have a contract on a custom house, nor a prospect in sight."

"I'm sorry to hear that."

"Come on, Louis," Katie scoffed. "Surely it comes as no surprise to you." All at once it seemed a matter of principle to make him admit he had been aware of her difficulties.

"I've been busy. Besides this house..." Louis stopped, perceiving the affront his excuse was likely to contain for her.

"You don't have to spare my feelings," Katie told him proudly. "I've heard that you have people lined up wanting you to build their houses, and I'm glad for you. But do me the favor of being honest with me. Surely you've heard that my father retired and that Gamble Construction isn't in great demand these days now that I'm on my own."

His slow nod was still only qualified agreement. "I heard that Mr. Red had had another heart attack," he said quietly. "How's he getting along?"

Katie's determination ebbed as she stared into his face and saw the same genuine concern she'd heard in his voice, the same sad acceptance. What's the use? she thought. Louis wasn't evading the subject of *her*. She simply didn't matter to him now any more than she ever had. The person who mattered was still her father. What surprised her more than anything else was that *not* being important to Louis could hurt after all these years, when she'd completely gotten over him.

"He's doing fine," she said, looking down at her boots while she coped with her emotions and steeled her courage. Coming here had been a mistake, but she could at least get a load of guilt off her chest.

"Katie, I really am sorry to hear—"

"No, Louis, I'm the one who's sorry." She cut into his uneasy apology, wanting to get her own said before she lost her nerve. "I've wanted to tell you for years how much I regretted what I did."

"Aunt *Kay*—tee! Aren't you and Mr. Louis finished talking yet? Aren't you coming in?"

"Daddy, I want to show Miss Katie the house!"

The youthful demands showered down at them from a second-story window. Katie looked up with deep impatience at the untimely interruption, but Louis apparently welcomed it. Before she could speak, he was shoving himself away from the cab and groaning good-naturedly.

"Okay, okay. Miss Katie and I are coming." He directed his cheerfully grumbling words up to the eager faces framed in the window. "Come on, Katie. We might as well take the guided tour and get it over with."

Katie accompanied him, resenting his evasion of her apology. He obviously didn't want to hear it. He apparently preferred to pretend the past didn't exist, to ignore their personal history together and treat her casually and pleasantly as Lisa's Aunt Katie.

She resignedly played her role. The two little girls had raced down the stairs and were already in the foyer when the adults entered the house. The four of them went through it, room by room, with Lisa and Stephanie primarily in charge. For Katie's benefit, Louis briefly pointed out problem areas and mentioned foul-ups and changes the owners had made until Katie understood why the house was such a sore point with him. His manner implied that Katie was a fully knowledgeable member of the building trade.

Other than these asides and mutual amusement over comments made by the girls, there was no personal communication between him and Katie until the tour had been concluded and Katie and Lisa were leaving without Stephanie, who would ride home with her father. In the driveway, father and daughter stood side by side at the tail of his pickup truck, facing aunt and niece at the front of the Bronco. With the family alignment, the marked physical resemblances were inescapable. Had circumstances been normal, Katie might have made some comment, but circumstances weren't normal, no matter how sociable on the surface.

"Your dream house is very pretty, Stephanie. Thanks for showing it to us." Katie's words and smile brought a flush of pleasure to the black-haired girl's cheeks. Stephanie had warmed considerably toward her best friend's favorite aunt during the afternoon. "Come on, squirt, we have to get home." Katie gave her fidgety niece a playful swat on the rump.

"Bye, Steph! Bye, Mr. Louis!" Lisa shouted her farewells as she skipped around the front of the Bronco, and Katie let them stand for her as well as she turned to walk around the open door on the driver's side.

"Wait a minute, Miss Katie. I have to tell Lisa something." Stephanie followed in quick pursuit of her friend.

Katie stopped agreeably and felt her nerves tighten as Louis surprised her by stepping closer, making private conversation possible. Here was an unexpected chance. She could make quick work of the confession of guilt she'd started and he hadn't allowed her to finish—just state the damning facts and get it over with. *You were right to marry Betty, Louis. I was terribly wrong to turn my father against you. I'm sorry. Maybe—*

"Important secrets, I take it," Louis remarked with humor from distractingly close range.

To hide her reaction to his physical nearness, Katie summoned a benign smile.

"They've only been together all day. There hasn't been much opportunity for filling each other in."

"Lisa looks exactly like you at that age."

Louis's quiet observation took Katie totally by surprise.

"The poor kid hears that all the time, especially around the family," she joked self-consciously, feeling vulnerable under his gaze. He seemed to be confirming the points of resemblance between her and her niece. Besides the hair and eyes, they each had the same short, upturned nose sprinkled sparsely with golden freckles, and a wide, generous mouth that grinned easily or just as easily compressed with stubbornness and displeasure.

"She reminds me of you in ways besides looks, too." Louis smiled as he glanced down at her fingers drumming soundlessly on the Bronco door. "You were always bursting with nervous energy like she is."

"She hears that, too, from all my sisters. They're always telling her she's hyperactive, just like her Aunt Katie." Katie paused. "I wondered—" She broke off, gathering courage. "I wondered if it made you feel strange, too, seeing those two together...."

He nodded and then shrugged to minimize the admission.

"At first it did. But it's been—what, about a year now?—since your sister Trish moved back to Covington from the city."

"It's been a year exactly," Katie confirmed.

"I pretty soon got over the feeling of seeing a ghost," Louis said cheerfully, his tone suggesting that any oddness he'd experienced hadn't been too unpleasant for him. "Lisa's a sweet kid. Underneath all that nervous energy, she just wants to please."

Katie didn't know whether he was extending his comparison or merely changing the subject. Before she could say anything, Louis had taken several steps backward, ending the conversation. Glancing over toward the passenger side, where the whispers and giggles continued, he summoned his daughter authoritatively.

"Your minute's up, Stephie. Miss Katie has been patient long enough."

Combating her sense of letdown, Katie climbed behind the wheel of the Bronco and started the engine. It was ridiculous of her to feel cheated. If she hadn't learned anything else by her past experiences with

Louis, she should have learned not to expect anything of him. What had she wanted from him, anyway?

Not the assurance he'd seemed to offer that their childhood association held no unpleasantness for him. That had to be a lie. Katie *had* been a basically nice child, as her niece was now, despite willfulness and a wearing excess of energy. But she'd often not been nice to Louis. Jealous of him, she'd tried to make his life miserable. Although sweet and gracious on occasion, she'd acted mean and spiteful toward him many a time. It rankled somehow that he would pretend otherwise.

What were his memories of the teenage Katie? Were those bland and pleasantly generalized, too? she wondered. She was disturbed at how strongly she resented the thought that Louis could look back equably at their high-school years. After all, she herself had long ago recovered from her seventeen-year-old's heartbreak. It was her pride that twinged when she remembered.

She had chased him shamelessly from her freshman through her junior year, then made a forced gift of her sexual innocence as his graduation present, thinking that she was trapping him. He had resisted taking advantage of her more than any eighteen-year-old youth could have been expected to resist, especially following a celebration party with ample booze.

Looking back, Katie knew that her main loss of innocence during that difficult period in her life hadn't been giving up her virginity. It had been realizing her capability for doing serious lasting harm to another person. She had wanted to confess her burden of guilt to Louis this afternoon, but he hadn't wanted to hear it.

Louis could at least do her the favor of holding a grudge, Katie thought to herself resentfully, as she drove home, only half listening to Lisa's chatter. She wished now that she hadn't subjected herself to the pointless meeting with him. It had turned out to be a *non*confrontation, awakening old frustrations and giving no satisfaction. If anything, Katie felt more restless and unhappy than she had before.

Louis was extremely unsettled by Katie's impromptu visit, by the shock of seeing his daughter with her. Though he knew Stephanie came and went in Lisa's grandparents' house and must encounter Katie, knowing something and coming face-to-face with the reality were two different things.

Not that he'd felt alarm on his daughter's behalf. Stephanie was in no danger of being mistreated by either Katie or her parents. He was as certain of that as he was of basic human decency.

What the hell is Katie up to? had been his first stunned thought, and then immediately he'd called up old reserves of passivity while he dealt with an equally old and familiar sense of unpreparedness. He'd never felt totally prepared to deal with Katie, even when he knew ahead of time what she wanted and what she was likely to do to get her way. Today her visit had come with no warning whatsoever, when he wasn't feeling his strongest.

The force of her personality had hit him as soon as she stepped down from the Bronco. No, even before that. With his first recognition of the Bronco as she wheeled it into the driveway and slammed on the brakes. She drove a car with the same expert heedlessness with which she'd once ridden her bike.

Had he known about the visit beforehand, he might have viewed it with a measure of complacency. He was thirty years old now, father of a child, a man who was fairly contented with who and what he was. Looking ahead to the meeting with Katie, he would have thought that contact with Lisa, who so closely resembled Katie as a child, would have helped him take in stride talking to Katie after years of separation.

His mistake, he realized belatedly, was that Katie had never grown up in his mind. He had kept her a child and a teenager. Oh, he knew, of course, that she was twenty-nine, a year younger than he was, but he hadn't been prepared for Katie as a woman. It had taken him unawares to be attracted to her sexually.

Instinctively he'd resisted his reflex male interest, knowing from days of old that any uncontrolled response to Katie was dangerous. Right on cue, too, was a ridiculously outdated twinge of conscience from his adolescence. Out of respect for her father he'd done his best not to feel lust for Katie even back then.

He supposed that deep down he'd expected to have a one-on-one talk with Katie eventually. With both of them in the same business, it could easily come about when the time was right, whenever that was. It definitely hadn't been today—not for Louis. He hadn't been ready. He might have known that talking to Katie again wouldn't be comfortable. It would be... *intense.*

She was composed now and had learned physical restraint, but her energy was still there, simmering beneath the surface and breaking out in unconscious nervous movements. Louis had felt it like an electric current. As always, it seemed to be infused into her emotions, making them more powerful. She was so obviously unhappy and discontented.

Louis had had his vindictive moments in years past. He had once consoled himself with the notion that Katie would someday come in for her share of hard knocks. But today he had felt the same way he had as a boy, when he couldn't bear to see Katie cry, not even five minutes after she'd been acting like a brat toward him.

As a child, she had suffered as she did everything else—with total abandon. When harm befell a pet puppy or she was the victim of a cruel prank, she could cry, heartbroken, and Louis would do everything in his power to comfort or divert her. He was naturally soft-hearted, but he also made Katie's happiness and well-being a number-one priority in his life because he wanted to please Mr. Red.

It amazed him that remnants of that old protective attitude remained. However, even without it Louis knew he still would have felt an urge to make things right for Katie today, simply because he was a Southern man and she was a woman. She would spurn his sympathy in a second and call him a male chauvinist. He guessed he probably was a male chauvinist, if being one meant liking the differences between men and women.

Whatever Katie's reasons for coming there today, she hadn't been looking for sympathy. That was perhaps Louis's only certainty about her motives. Why had she come? he asked himself. He didn't doubt the bare facts of her explanation, but there was certainly more below the surface.

On the ride home, he tried to pump Stephanie, searching for a clue. "That was nice of Lisa's Aunt Katie to invite you and Lisa to go with her this afternoon," he observed.

"Miss Katie didn't actually invite us," Stephanie corrected him. "I mean, it wasn't really her idea. It was

Lisa's. Lisa's always trying to get Miss Katie to take us places with her, but she never would before.''

So what made this time different? Louis wondered. His interested silence encouraged Stephanie to continue.

''I figured Miss Katie always said no because she didn't like me. Oh, she was always nice and everything,'' the little girl hastened to add when Louis shot her a scowling paternal glance. ''She just sort of looked at me funny, and she takes Lisa with her all the time when I'm not there. So today when she said we couldn't go 'cause she didn't know what time she'd be back, I said I had to go home. I didn't, but I figured then Lisa would get to go. All of a sudden Miss Katie changed her mind. She said she'd get us back in time for supper.''

Louis could see the scene in his mind, and it wasn't incriminating for Katie. His perceptive little daughter had probably put Katie on the spot. Katie might have done the turnabout to keep Stephanie from going home with hurt feelings.

''On the way, Miss Katie explained to us about what a spec house is so that we could give her ideas for the one she wants to build on her lot.'' Stephanie didn't need any additional probing to continue her narration.

''Where is this lot?'' Louis interrupted her to ask, curious. When she had replied, he remarked, ''That's a good location for a spec house.''

He wasn't surprised that Katie was having problems getting custom-building jobs on her own. Hadn't she known she would? Husbands, not wives, picked out contractors. Subs in the trade were often notorious chauvinists. Local bank officers weren't much more liberal in their attitudes, which brought to mind the question of whether she had bank financing on the spec house. Or was Red Gamble going to foot the bill to save his daughter's pride?

Louis came back to the present. Stephanie was sharing her newfound knowledge about spec houses, with frequent repetitions of "Miss Katie says." Louis listened meekly, without pointing out that he wasn't totally ignorant on the subject of spec houses himself. Next his daughter filled him in thoroughly on how helpful both she and Lisa had been in offering suggestions and how receptive Miss Katie was to their ideas.

Louis conjectured with private amusement that Katie had probably gotten more than she had bargained for in helpful input from the two girls. Certainly Louis was getting more than he had bargained for in pumping his daughter—not only the superfluity of detail, but also an attractive picture of a very tactful and unbiased Miss Katie acting as arbitrator, tongue in cheek.

At one point in Stephanie's narration he would have welcomed a thorough rendering of who said and did what. There, of course, she summarized, explaining only that it was her idea to show Miss Katie and Lisa the Pearson house, where Stephanie thought he would be. They had driven there, and her daddy knew the rest. Wanting the specific details, Louis was forced to question her in a roundabout way.

"You said you thought I would be at the house. Did Miss Katie know that if I wasn't there with the key, she'd be going out of her way for nothing?" Had Katie seized upon the opportunity Stephanie had offered her? That was the question he hoped somehow to answer.

"I guess she knew. I didn't actually *say* the house would be locked." Stephanie looked and sounded vaguely conscience-stricken.

"Honey, she probably guessed from what you said about the house that it was far enough along to be under lock and key," Louis reassured her. He hadn't meant to scold her or make her feel guilty. "So anyway, you invited them to come by and see it, and they both liked the idea." Louis put subtle stress on *both*, counting on his daughter's penchant for accuracy.

"*Lisa* liked the idea. From the look on Miss Katie's face, I felt sure she was going to say no. Lisa started jumping up and down and begging, and I crossed my fingers behind my back and said in my head, 'Please, please, please, Miss Katie.' She took a long time to say yes, but she finally did—and we came." Stephanie's little sigh bespoke her deep satisfaction with the outcome. Her follow-up question took Louis aback with its frank wistfulness. "Daddy, do you think Miss Katie likes me?"

He took one hand off the wheel to chuck her chin tenderly and also to give himself a second's pause before answering.

"She seemed to," he said gruffly. "I take it you like Miss Katie?"

Stephanie looked heartened by his reply and nodded vigorously in the affirmative.

"I hope she takes me with her and Lisa lots more times. Miss Katie is fun to ride with. She starts off and stops real fast." Louis met his daughter's quick measuring glance and read her worry that she'd perhaps revealed too much. "But she's a real safe driver. She made sure we had on our seat belts, and she stopped for red lights and everything," Stephanie added in hasty reassurance for fatherly concern.

Louis smiled with memory as well as fond amusement.

"Honey, I'm not worried about your riding with Miss Katie," he said dryly. "She was driving her daddy's pickup truck when she could hardly sit tall enough to see through the windshield and barely reach the pedals with her feet." For years before that, she had sat on Red Gamble's lap and steered.

"Daddy, I didn't know you and Miss Katie knew each other real good."

"Sweetheart, Miss Katie and I knew each other when we were kids, growing up. Besides, we both build houses, you know. And living in a small town like Covington, everybody knows everybody." Louis didn't feel as casual as he sounded. He wanted to give his daughter just enough truth to kill her curiosity, not feed it. Apparently he was successful, at least for the moment, since her mind moved on.

"Lisa always says she wants to be just like her Aunt Katie and build houses, too, when she grows up," she told him thoughtfully. "But you know what her Aunt Katie told her? She said Lisa should learn by her mistakes and not put a lot of time into learning how to do something she'd have to fight tooth and nail to be able to do. Daddy, what does Miss Katie mean when she says that 'the good old boys' have the business of building houses all tied up?"

Louis cleared his throat, aware of the pitfalls in the conversation. He wanted to be honest and yet not damage himself in her eyes.

"Well, honey, that's just kind of an expression. What Miss Katie meant, I think, is that building houses has always been a man's job, around this area, anyway. Women usually have other kinds of jobs if they don't stay home to be housewives and mothers."

He waited while she mulled over his answer, which admittedly had been more evasion than definition. Her next question was likely to pin him to the wall. If she asked him point-blank if he was a "good old boy," he guessed he'd have to say he was and present her with a contest in loyalty between himself and Miss Katie. At the moment he wasn't too sure of winning. Being a male-chauvinist father to a bright little girl wasn't always easy, and it was going to get tougher as she grew up.

"If Miss Katie knows all about how to build houses, I think they ought to let her." Stephanie voiced her opinion stoutly. Louis looked carefully ahead and worked on a neutral expression, hoping to avoid being pressed for his view on the prickly subject, which might be passed on word for word. "I don't want to build houses when I grow up." Stephanie's thoughts had moved fleetly on.

"No?" He glanced over at her serious, absorbed little face and felt the melting warmth of love. What if she did grow up and want to build houses? Would he bring to bear all his influence and reputation to indulge her, as Red Gamble had done for Katie? Louis could understand now how a man's love for his little girl could overrule his common sense and judgment—even his fairness.

"I don't like houses until they're finished," Stephanie explained. "I think they're all ugly inside until they're painted and have the wallpaper on the walls and carpet on the floors."

"Maybe you'll grow up and want to be an interior decorator," Louis suggested. "Then you can help people pick out colors and wallpaper and carpet for their new houses."

"I think I'd like doing that!" Stephanie pursued the notion enthusiastically for the remainder of the drive home. Her chatter about her current tastes in home decorating required only an occasional absent reply from her father.

Louis was able to mull over his findings, or lack of them, in regard to Katie's motives. It seemed probable that she had given in to visiting the Pearson house, knowing that he might be there, with inner reluctance, just as she had given in to the outing with the two girls in the first place. There was little likelihood of scheming or premeditation. She would probably continue to steer clear of him, and he would do the same with her.

Louis still felt unsettled, stirred up. It was Friday night. He'd go out after supper for a few beers at Back Street, where he'd be sure to run into friends. Katie didn't go to Back Street—because it was his hangout, he presumed. He wouldn't encounter her there tonight. The thought dissatisfied as much as it soothed.

Chapter Three

I'll drop you off at your house," Katie told her niece. Lisa lived just two blocks from her grandparents with her mother and her fourteen-year-old brother, Rich. Katie's sister Trish, at thirty-seven the sister closest to Katie in age, had separated from her husband a year earlier and moved back to Covington, renting a house in the same neighborhood where she had grown up. It had been the first failed marriage in the Gamble family and a deep cause of concern for everyone.

"No, that's okay, Aunt Katie." Lisa blithely opposed her aunt's plan. "I'll walk home in a few minutes. I want to say hello to Mawmaw Edna and Pawpaw Red."

She would more than say hello. Katie knew that taking the little girl into the house with her would be tantamount to bringing along the town crier, with all the news of the afternoon. Her niece would blurt out in eager, artless fashion a full account, with no inkling that the visit to Louis McIntyre's almost-finished house in her Aunt Katie's company was anything to surprise or upset her grandparents.

She could hardly seal her niece's lips without causing puzzled curiosity and prompting questions that were best left unasked and unanswered. Why not let Lisa do the telling? Katie asked herself. It would convey more convincingly than anything else the spontaneousness with which the afternoon had unfolded.

Coward, she accused herself. The truth was that she welcomed her niece's presence as a buffer. Katie dreaded bringing up the subject of Louis McIntyre, whose name she hadn't heard on her father's lips in twelve years. She had no way of knowing whether she would be dredging up memories that could still deeply disturb him or whether ignoring Louis's existence had long since become just a loyal habit for him on Katie's behalf.

The savory aroma of food met her as she entered the house, as usual, from the back porch. Her mother and father were in the big old-fashioned kitchen. Edna Gamble was stirring an oversize pot at the stove, and Red was seated at the kitchen table, which was already set for three. They were awaiting Katie's arrival for supper.

"Mmm. Smells good in here!" Lisa declared, twitching her nose.

"Chicken gumbo." Edna identified the contents of the pot with an indulgent smile. "There's plenty, honey, if you want to stay and eat supper with us."

"Call your mamma, baby," Red commanded with brusque tenderness. "Tell her you're eating supper with Pawpaw Red."

The supper invitation was a matter of course. Edna had never been able to break the habit of cooking in large quantities, even after there was no longer a houseful of daughters and their friends. Any member of the family, any neighbor or friend who happened to drop by at mealtime was more than welcome to sit down and eat.

Lisa was obviously tempted, and her reluctant refusal was clearly a matter of conscience, bringing immediate concern to the faces of her grandparents and an atmosphere of gloom to the homey kitchen.

"I better go home and eat with Mamma. Rich might not be there, and then Mamma would have to eat all by herself."

"Your mamma can come on down and have supper with us, too," Red growled. "I'd like to give that daddy of yours a swift kick—"

"Red," Edna reproved him gently.

Lisa hadn't missed the exchange between her grandparents concerning her father, although she made no direct reference to it. The downcast expression on her young face deepened, and her tone was bleakly resigned as she predicted, "Mamma won't come. She's on a diet. She says she's going to take off ten pounds before she has to go to court if it kills her, and that all she has to do is smell Mawmaw Edna's cooking to gain weight."

"Lisa only came in for a couple of minutes to tell you about our afternoon, didn't you, squirt?" Katie spoke up with determined cheer, any reservations about mentioning Louis McIntyre dissipating with the need for distracting both her parents and her niece from the sad topic of Trish's upcoming divorce. Trish was taking it hard.

"Lisa and her friend Stephanie rode with me over to the Delta Pines subdivision." Katie started the account and paused for her niece to take over.

Lisa's spirits rose within a sentence or two until eagerness to tell everything made the words tumble over each other. Katie tried to act perfectly normal as she helped her mother with last-minute preparations for putting supper on the table. She got down bowls for the gumbo, set them next to the stove, and then put ice cubes into tall glasses for the iced tea, pretending not to notice the shocked undercurrents in the room and her parents' glances at her and each other. The air of gloom and worry in the room that Katie had hoped to ease was suddenly more oppressive than before.

"Run along home, baby," Red told his granddaughter when she had finished. "Pawpaw's been smelling that gumbo cooking all day, and he's ready for his supper."

The heaviness in his voice beneath his gruff kindness brought a pang of dismay to Katie's breast even before she looked at him, and then the sight of his face squeezed her heart painfully. He looked the way he sounded—old and sad and beaten.

"That's right, honey. You run on home now and keep your mamma company." Edna Gamble added her own worried dismissal to her husband's and darted him anxious glances while she placed a generous scoop of steamed rice into a bowl and ladled the thick, stewlike chicken concoction over it.

"Mmm. Looks as good as it smells," Katie praised hollowly as she took the filled bowl from her mother and carried it to the table to set in front of her father. "There you are," she said gently.

She watched with mounting guilt as he sat with his shoulders sloped in a defeated posture, staring down at the bowl. She hadn't dreamed that mention of her seeing Louis today would upset him to this extent. Had her father's hurt and sense of betrayal gone much deeper than Katie had ever suspected? She had a sudden memory of the way Louis's face had looked when he inquired about her father and knew that somehow she had to at least try to undo the terrible damage she had done.

"Louis asked about you today," she said very gently, stepping behind her father's chair to knead his neck and shoulders with light, tender fingers. "He'd heard about your heart attack and wanted to know how you were getting along. He seemed very concerned."

Red picked up his soupspoon and began slowly and methodically mixing the gumbo and rice together. "Sit down and eat," he directed Katie with the same gentle gruffness he used in speaking to Lisa. He took a large spoonful of his gumbo and rice mixture and tasted it. "That's good, woman," he told Edna. "You keep cookin' like that, and I'll keep you around another fifty years."

Katie and her mother mustered smiles that were as halfhearted as Red Gamble's familiar jocose sentiments about his wife's cooking. For several seconds the sounds of spoons clinking against bowls and ice cubes tinkling in glasses were loud in the restrained silence. Red's deep, audible sigh came as a kind of relief, venting the tension for all three of them.

"Did Louis have anything to say about your plans to build a spec house?" he asked Katie, frowning.

Katie held her spoon in midair for a surprised moment and then put it down. It wasn't simply the question coming without preamble that took her aback. There hadn't been the slightest hesitation on her father's part in speaking Louis's name, no telltale inflection to hint that saying it caused him any distaste or pain.

"He sounded a little envious of the idea, but that's only because the house he's finishing up has been nothing but headaches. A lot of things went wrong, and the owners kept calling for changes." Katie picked up her spoon and resumed eating for the sake of appearing casual. "It's just the old 'grass is greener' psychology. Louis doesn't have to build spec houses. From what I hear, he has more custom jobs than he can handle." Unlike me, she finished in her mind. She'd intended to bring her failure out into the open tonight, but now she didn't have the heart.

Once again Red's sigh was long and audible.

"Louis was always a good worker and honest as the day is long," he said, so absentmindedly that Katie gulped down her swallow of iced tea to keep from strangling. His mind obviously wasn't on what he was saying. The grave concern deepening the lines in his face had nothing to do with Louis, she realized with a sinking sensation. It had to do with *her* and her desperate situation. She'd tried to hide her unhappiness from him, but she hadn't succeeded.

"This idea of mine is nothing new," she declared, taking the smallest possible spoonful of gumbo. Her tight throat muscles wouldn't make swallowing easy. "When I bought the Delta Pines lot two years ago, I had it in the back of my mind that someday I could build a spec house on it. By itself, the lot won't be enough collateral for a bank loan, but I can use my five acres between here and Folsom, too."

Discussing the practical details of financing hadn't eased Red's mind one bit. If anything, the worry on his face had increased.

"Katie, have you talked to anybody down at the bank yet?"

"No, not yet. Don't get any ideas about doing it for me, either. This is *Katie's* business, remember? You're retired." She used her spoon for joking emphasis and smiled to soften her warning, not wanting to offend him. "I won't have you worrying about me, either of you." She glanced at Edna, who was looking on with open anxiety. "I know that's asking a lot, because you love me and I'll always be the baby of the family to you. But I'm grown-up. I have to handle my own problems."

Despite her brave little speech, the kitchen still had all the cheer of a funeral. At least her father didn't look hurt, even if his shoulders still sagged and worry made a creased mask of his face.

"Building a spec house can be mighty risky business," he said, shaking his head ponderously. "I've seen more than my share of good men lose their shirts."

"You two are doin' more talkin' than eatin'." Edna spoke up fussily while Katie fought a new, devastating intuition: Surely her father didn't lack confidence in her abilities? "Can I get anybody a little more gumbo?" Edna offered, darting Katie a glance full of pleading and apology. "There's banana puddin' for dessert, too." *Please, honey, for your father's sake, drop the subject for now,* she seemed to beg silently.

Katie didn't resent her mother's protective bias. Edna Gamble adored her children and was a mother to the core, but her husband came first. Her highest praise to her daughters had always been "Your daddy is going to be so proud!'' Her severest remonstrance through the years had been the threat of his disappointment or displeasure. It was long her habit, even before his health had begun to fail, to intercede on his behalf with the children to spare him worry and ensure his peace of mind. Now she sensed danger for him in continuing the conversation, and her youngest daughter accepted her wisdom.

"I think I'll save myself for some banana pudding later on and skip a second helping of gumbo," Katie declared with hollow gusto. She didn't have any appetite left at all. "There's plenty of time to talk about the pros and cons of building a spec house. Right now it's just something I'm thinking about. Nothing more." She took a swig of iced tea and rattled the cubes melting in the glass. "So what happened on the soaps today? Did Rachel decide to remarry? Has Jack discovered that his real mother is also the mother of his bride-to-be? What about the malpractice suit against all the doctors at the general hospital? Has that been decided yet?"

Edna took her cue and prattled artlessly about the happenings in the lives of her soap-opera characters. After a few tense minutes, Red put in a telltale derogatory remark that revealed his own close attention to Edna's stories, and gradually he relaxed. He took a second bowl of gumbo and ate it with relish. Katie longed to excuse herself and retreat to the privacy of her room or office, but she didn't dare break with routine, fearing fresh consternation on her behalf. She sat at the supper table, as she always did, until the meal was finished, and then helped her mother clean up.

Somehow she managed to talk fairly normally and hide the low state of her morale. The more she thought about her father's reaction to the mention of her building a spec house, the more it hurt. The possibility that he might doubt her competence was deeply discouraging, threatening the very foundations of her determination not to give up and admit that she was beaten.

The alternative explanation was hardly more comforting. It could be that Red had reacted so negatively simply because he was anxious for her and frustrated by his own helplessness. Katie couldn't bear being the cause of distress for him because she wasn't happy, yet she couldn't possibly *be* happy with her present situation. What was she to do?

To escape the depressing tangle of her thoughts, she concentrated on what seemed the one positive outcome of a bad day. At least she'd learned that neither Louis nor her father seemed to harbor ill feelings toward each other. Katie believed that she could bring the two men together on amicable terms, if Louis cooperated. She could invite him over for coffee, stay around herself just long enough for the ice to be broken, then leave and let the two of them take it from there. Her part would be done.

The peacemaking mission assumed an importance it wouldn't have had if Katie's mind had been busy with constructive plans for her future. She needed a breather from thinking about herself and her problems, and bringing Louis and her father together gave her a short-range purpose with fairly certain chances for success at a time when her self-esteem cried out for success.

Surprisingly, the prospect of approaching Louis again wasn't terribly daunting. She would simply drive past the Pearson house, where she and the girls had found him today, and stop for a word with him. The following day being Saturday, she mentally postponed her mission until Monday at the earliest.

Just past noon the next day a conversation with Stephanie opened up an unforeseen opportunity.

Red Gamble was napping on the sofa, snoring softly, and Edna was across the street, visiting with a neighbor, when Lisa and Stephanie dropped by the Gamble house for a visit. Shushing the two little girls to keep them from disturbing her father, Katie herded them out to the kitchen and joined them in raiding the cookie jar.

"Your daddy wouldn't happen to be out working today, would he?" she quizzed Stephanie casually.

Stephanie was chewing on a mouthful of cookie. She first nodded, then shook her head. When Katie mimed her humorously, the little girl hurriedly swallowed and made a giggling explanation.

"Daddy's 'out' in his office over the garage, but not 'out working' the way you meant, at a house he's building." She smirked prettily and rolled her eyes. "I think he slept up in his office last night. That's what he does when he stays out real late and doesn't want to wake me and Grandma up, coming in."

How often does that happen? Katie wondered and quickly clamped down on her curiosity. Louis's late-night social habits were of absolutely no interest to her. What was of interest was the information that he might at this very moment be available for a private conversation in his garage office, which Katie hadn't known about. She could go there without feeling that she was barging into his home, and it wasn't likely that she'd encounter his mother, either. Katie could have her say and be gone in five or ten minutes.

On the way over, she fought a mild state of jitters by mentally running through an explanation of her mission. It didn't take long to drive the ten blocks, so there wasn't a great deal of time for rehearsing what she would say. However, she was relying upon the sincerity of her motives, not eloquence, to convince Louis. He should recognize that her purpose was unselfish, other than possibly easing her conscience.

His blue pickup was in his driveway. Katie parked behind it and made for the stairs at the side of the garage. She didn't want to dawdle and attract the attention of Louis's mother if she was home. The house, as well as the garage, was bigger, she noted. Louis must have built onto it, too. The place was neat and well kept now, not run-down looking and needing a coat of paint as it had been when Louis was growing up. Back then there had only been his mother's salary from her clerk's job at the courthouse and what he could earn with odd jobs.

Katie made no effort to climb the steps quietly. They were steep, and her Western boots made clomping sounds on the wooden treads that would give Louis advance warning of a visitor. At the top of the stairs, she paused on the small landing and had serious second thoughts. The top half of the door was glass, and what she could see inside didn't look like an office. It looked more like an apartment.

Louis wasn't in sight, and she didn't hear any sounds of movement within. Undecided whether to knock or go away, she stepped up closer to the door and peered in. Immediately she wished she hadn't.

Louis was headed for the door from the unseen portion of the room—the office area, she could tell now. He came to a dead halt when he saw her, blank surprise blending with annoyance on his face. Katie was obviously the last person in the world he'd expected to be dropping in on him. She felt ridiculous being caught peering in like that, with her nose almost to the glass.

What made matters even worse was the way he was dressed—or *not* dressed. He wore jeans without any shirt and was barefoot. Judging from his wet hair and clean-scrubbed appearance, he wasn't long out of the shower.

This was a mistake. She shouldn't have come, Katie realized in a panic, but it was too late now to retreat. He'd seen her. She drew herself up and tried not to imagine more embarrassing scenes than this one while she waited for him to open the door. She could have peeked in and caught him wearing a towel—or nothing at all. Considering the possibilities did nothing to make her calm or poised.

Louis was in no mood for a visitor when he heard someone climbing the steps to the office. He had a slight hangover. He'd stayed out late and had a few too many beers the night before. His headache, though, was more the result of his labor at his desk. He was trying to come up with some final figures on the Pearson house. His strong point wasn't accounting. He'd known, sitting down to his dreaded task a half hour earlier, that he was going to have to charge the Pearsons extra for the additional labor they'd caused him with all their changes. But the figures were coming up even worse than he'd suspected.

The Pearsons would balk at paying. There'd be a hassle. Louis hated hassles of any kind, but especially over money. He knew he was partly at fault. He should have put the extra cost in writing for them as he went along, but that meant detailed record-keeping. Louis built a damned fine house, but he needed to improve his handling of the business side of things. That was the conclusion he reached too often at the completion of a big custom-building job.

He was feeling down on himself as he got up to see who was at the door. One of his buddies would have pounded on the door and walked in. The footsteps were too heavy to be Stephie's, and she'd have tapped with her special code and sung out a greeting. His mother rang him on the phone when she wanted him. The sight of Katie looking in at him was a shock. Louis felt besieged. *Unprepared*.

For a second or two, he considered making himself more presentable and then dispensed with the delay. She'd already seen him wearing only his pants.

"Katie. This is certainly a surprise," he drawled, opening the door wide. The second such surprise in two days, he implied with his tone and quizzical expression.

"Hello, Louis. I wanted to talk to you about something, and when Stephanie told me you were here in your office, I thought it would be okay to drop by." Katie shrugged apologetically and let her eyes drift over his bare shoulders and chest to complete the statement of her obvious error. She'd seen him naked to the waist numerous times, at various ages. He'd worked without his shirt during the hot summers and gotten deeply tanned. Katie had thrilled to the sight of his bronzed torso in high school, when working on construction crews had hardened and developed his muscles. She wasn't immune to it now, either, with the paler skin contrasting with curly black chest hair.

Tingling under Katie's fleeting scrutiny, Louis suddenly wished he'd taken time to put on a shirt. He shook off the oddly pleasing sensation.

"I'd invite you in," he said reluctantly, glancing over his shoulders, "but the place is a pigpen." It wasn't squalid, exactly, just messy, the way it suited him. He could gather up the scattered newspapers, put the empty beer and soda cans into the garbage pail and the used glasses and coffee cups into the sink all in about five minutes, if he was of a mind to.

"What I have to say won't take long, but I can look you up one day early in the week," Katie offered, making no move to leave.

Louis's manners gave him no choice but to invite her in. Besides, he might as well get to the bottom of her visit. He wouldn't have any peace of mind once she'd left, wondering why she'd come. Her presence raised all the same uneasiness and suspicion he'd put to rest about her visit at the Pearson house yesterday.

"If you can stand the mess, why don't you come in and tell me what's on your mind now?" he suggested politely. "I have to admit I'm curious."

His undertone of caution stung Katie's pride, and for a moment she was tempted to abandon her whole effort. But she hadn't expected a friendly welcome, had she?

"I won't take more than five minutes of your time," she promised him crisply, striding past him into the room, her chin at a proud, determined angle. She waited, tapping her foot, while he closed the door.

"Don't bother," she told him as he went to the sofa and began clearing it. She averted her head so as not to look at the smooth play of muscles in his shoulders and back. "I don't need to sit down. I don't plan to stay that long."

"It won't take a minute." Louis ignored her objection and kept right on collecting the sections of newspaper and making a haphazard pile of them at the far end of the sofa. He straightened when he was finished and saw that she was looking around. "There. Have a seat."

Katie met his eyes for a rebellious moment and then did as she was told. She had taken in Louis's so-called office with a few glances. It was obviously his retreat. This end was a minimal living area, with a man-size sofa, a long coffee table, and a television set on a stand positioned so that the best vantage for seeing the screen was lying on said sofa. The small kitchen area had a wet bar, a sink, a coffee maker and a full-size refrigerator. She assumed the latter would be well-stocked with beer when he hosted poker games with as many as eight or nine of his friends, judging from the number of mismatched chairs jumbled around the large felt-topped game table.

The bathroom was a partitioned cubicle at the opposite end, cutting into Louis's office space, which was furnished with a large wooden desk, a swivel chair and filing cabinets. Katie was facing that end of the room as she sat down on the sofa and couldn't help mentally shaking her head as she compared the disorderly condition of his office to the neatness of her own. His desk was so littered with mail and invoices that she could just glimpse portions of his telephone and answering machine. Filing cabinet drawers were half open, with folders sticking out haphazardly. Rolled-up house plans were tossed helter-skelter everywhere. They served as a reminder to her of how busy he must be, making bids on custom houses.

"I was doing some paperwork," Louis explained on his way to get the clean shirt draped over the back of his desk chair. He gave his desktop a pained glance as he slipped on the shirt. On his return he buttoned it, leaving the tails hanging loose.

Katie was biting her lip to keep from speaking envious thoughts. She wished she had paperwork to do for a building project. But she shouldn't think about herself now, she remembered, while Louis pulled out a chair from the game table and straddled it, facing her and clearly waiting for her to explain her presence.

"I'll come right to the point—" She stopped as his telephone came to life under its mantle of papers.

Louis frowned over his shoulder. "I'll let the machine get that," he said impatiently and looked back at Katie, apparently expecting her to continue. But then, as his recorded message began to play, an engagingly abashed grin spread across his face, and he listened with her. "I didn't have any idea what I sounded like until I bought that thing and heard myself talk. It's weird."

Katie smiled in empathy. "I know what you mean. I couldn't believe my voice, either." She waited, since Louis's caller hadn't hung up and was presumably waiting to leave a message. It would be better to have Louis's full attention when she made her peacemaking proposal.

The signal sounded, and Katie's smile faded as a voice she recognized filled the room, bringing back yesterday's anger and tension.

"Louis, this is John Hemphill calling. I'd like to arrange a time soon when you and my wife and I can get together to make some definite plans. Naturally, we're eager to get a starting date on our house. Give me a ring this afternoon or later in the evening, will you? It's Saturday, about one o'clock."

Louis had been listening, glancing over his shoulder toward the phone, his brow furrowing in irritation.

"That man is a persistent son—so-and-so," he amended, becoming mindful of his language around a woman. "I keep telling him I won't be able to make a start on his house until January at the earliest, but he keeps pressing me."

"I didn't find him persistent at all," Katie said bitterly. She shook her head. "It must be nice, Louis, to have people waiting in line, wanting you to build their houses." She read the uncomfortable question on Louis's face and answered it. "Yes, I put in a bid on John Hemphill's house. He picked you over me."

"I didn't have any idea, Katie," Louis said, feeling awkward as hell.

"I could tell you didn't."

His ignorance seemed to offend her. Louis watched in uneasy suspense as Katie pressed her lips together in an obvious struggle to fight from saying more.

"Katie, maybe things will turn around—"

"Louis, you can't expect me to believe you're not *glad* this is happening to me!" Katie burst out, unable to hear his lame reassurance through. "It wouldn't be human not to gloat! Don't try to make me believe you're some kind of saint and don't hold a grudge!"

Louis stood up and frowned down at the chair as he turned it around and then clutched the top edge of it with both hands to brace himself. The frown stayed on his face as he looked at Katie, who sat tense, waiting.

"What's the point of all this, Katie?" he asked her quietly. "Is this what you wanted to talk to me about?"

Katie stared at him resentfully, then sighed and looked away, feeling utterly defeated. "No point, Louis," she said and didn't feel any better to realize it was true. "No point at all. And no, that isn't what I came here to talk about. I'll tell you, and then I'll go." She looked back at him. "Would you mind sitting down?"

Louis followed her gaze to his hands, which were gripping the back of the chair so tightly that his knuckles were white and the tendons in his forearms were rigid. "Sure," he said and came around to drop down into the chair. He folded his arms across his chest.

"I came to try and get you and Daddy back together again," Katie told him simply. She shrugged in understanding when Louis's eyes narrowed with his surprise. "I know it's sudden after all these years. The idea came to me last night when I got home and told him about seeing you." Katie thought about last night's painful scene in the kitchen, then pushed the memory away.

"Actually, I let Lisa do the telling," she amended with a strained smile. Louis didn't smile back. She wondered uncertainly whether she'd misread his reaction to the mention of her father yesterday. "At any rate, he seemed glad to hear that you were doing so well professionally. I think he'd like to see you. You could drop by and visit him, if you're interested. I thought about inviting you over for coffee...."

Katie stopped. Louis's expression wasn't at all encouraging.

"You're right," he drawled. "This is all pretty sudden."

Katie held his gaze, reading the suspicion in his eyes and trying not to resent it. His reaction was totally understandable.

"Look, Louis, there's nothing in this for me except for easing a guilty conscience," she told him earnestly. "I wanted to tell you yesterday how often I've regretted turning my father against you. I know that there's no making up to either one of you for what I did, but I'd feel better if you and he could be friends again." Katie slid forward to the edge of the sofa, preparing to

get up and go. "That's what I came to say," she concluded, standing.

Louis stood up slowly, obviously not convinced.

"I can see you don't believe me," she said, reading
his silence. "Or maybe you're just not interested."
Sighing her disappointment, she headed for the door.

"I'll give it some thought," Louis said behind her.

Katie stopped and turned around, her mouth open to
state a frank plea. She brought her lips together, the
impulse for speech dying, and stood there, her heart
suddenly squeezed with an unexpected personal regret.
He had been watching her go. He looked perplexed and
disturbed and decent. She had never found him more
masculine or appealing.

"I hope you will," she choked out and hurtled out
the door and down the steps, wishing she hadn't come.

Chapter Four

Katie had pulled the door closed behind her, but Louis walked over to it anyway, cursing softly. He put his hand on the doorknob, gave it an unnecessary push and then stood there, holding it tightly while he dealt with conflicting emotions. He wanted to say no to Katie and yes to what she'd suggested—that was the reason he hadn't made a definite answer.

He'd like nothing better than to visit Red Gamble, who was an old man now. He'd been the most important male influence in Louis's life, the closest thing to a father he'd known. Looking back, Louis was touched, remembering how generous and kind Mr. Red had been to him when he was growing up, and how careful not to damage Louis's pride. He had never outright given Louis money but had found him endless odd jobs, making it seem as if Louis were doing him a big favor, helping out around a household with nothing but women.

But it was the hunting and fishing trips that had meant everything to Louis. He'd have enjoyed them ten times as much if Katie hadn't been along, but he'd had sense enough to realize she was the reason behind them, and he'd counted his blessings for being included. It had tried his patience to put up with her bossiness and needling, but Mr. Red's big, heavy hand on his shoulder and his gruff words of approval in a man-to-man tone were reward enough. Louis had gladly joined in league with the older man in protecting and indulging Katie, since those were the terms of acceptance.

Now, as a grown man, he'd like to thank Mr. Red, not just for the good boyhood memories but for starting him in his profession. Those high-school jobs on building crews had led Louis to where he was now. Louis was grateful. If possible, too—and this was a touchy situation—Louis would like to apologize, to ask the older man's forgiveness for betraying his trust and acting dishonorably with his daughter.

Sure, there had been extenuating circumstances. It was graduation night, he remembered. He was exhilarated, being on the brink of manhood, and slightly intoxicated. Katie had come on to him like a sexy little dynamo, practically begging him to take her. His sex drive was in full force at eighteen, and he'd gotten very aroused, trying all the while to resist her.

Louis resolutely cut off the recollection. What he'd done was without excuse. He should have been stronger. Strangely enough, he felt less a sense of wrongdoing where Betty was concerned, perhaps because she hadn't been a virgin. In fact, she had been more sexually knowledgeable than he was at the time. He'd paid a high price for his pleasure. His brief, loveless teenage marriage had not been a good time in his life. He shuddered to look back on it, but at the same time, he couldn't wish it hadn't happened. Without it, he wouldn't have Stephanie. Life without his little daughter was unimaginable for Louis.

He could put himself in Red Gamble's shoes now and understand the older man's adoration of his youngest daughter. At thirty, Louis was a soft touch for Stephanie. Red had been in his early forties when Katie was born and probably less of a disciplinarian than he had been with her sisters.

Louis had put all of this into perspective before now. Six months ago, when he'd heard about Red Gamble's heart attack, he'd longed to go see him but hadn't dared, uncertain of his welcome. Now he would pay a call, he resolved, but *not* through any prior arrangements with Katie. Either Mr. Red wanted to see him or he didn't. Louis didn't want Katie as his agent. He didn't want her involved in any way. This time she wouldn't be a factor. It would be Louis and Mr. Red, one man to another.

With his mind made up, Louis felt good about his decision. He returned to his desk and the bothersome accounting chore Katie had interrupted, his headache gone. He felt clearheaded and able to cope now. The Pearsons would probably threaten a lawsuit, but let them. The figures would speak for themselves. He'd work up a statement showing the extra man-hours and added expense for materials. If the Pearsons wouldn't see reason, Louis would point out good-naturedly that he had an attorney, too, with the hope that the matter would then be settled amicably.

The immediate problem with Louis's plan was that he couldn't concentrate on the numbers he was trying to add. The scene with Katie today, as well as the one yesterday, kept coming to mind, disturbing him. Finally, he gave up, deciding that he'd wait and start fresh the next day, Sunday.

On the way out of his office, he glanced back at the sofa, where she had sat in her snug-fitting jeans, slim and taut and unhappy. "Go away," he told her vivid ghost. "Go away, Katie, and leave me alone." Then, when he opened the door, he again faced her image as she'd looked on the landing, proud and flustered, slender shoulders drawn back, calling to his attention her small pointed breasts rising and falling under her blouse. Louis felt the hair on his chest prickle with the memory of her blue-eyed inspection of him without his shirt.

He slammed the door hard behind him and took the steps two at a time.

Was that Louis's pickup truck parked in her driveway?

Katie braked sharply out on the street and stared at the vehicle in question. It was either his or one just like it, dark blue with a long wheelbase and double cab. The splattering of red foundation clay along the side provided positive identification.

Louis was inside. He had come to see her father.

Katie tried to adjust to her discovery as she accelerated, pulled past the pickup with inches to spare and parked in front of it. Getting out, she headed briskly toward the office. There wasn't enough money in the world to tempt her to step inside the house while Louis was there. Not for anything would she butt in on his visit. He'd ignored her offer to invite him over and had come on his own instead, with no advance warning to her. She got the message, and she intended to heed it.

By the time she reached the office, Katie's spurt of indignation had subsided. She should be glad, she told herself, that she hadn't totally bungled her attempt to get Louis and her father together after all. She'd left Louis's place on Saturday convinced that she had failed. It was only Tuesday, and here he was. He hadn't wasted much time.

Dropping the broad volume of *The Southern Colonial House* she carried onto the desk with a thud, she sat down to study it. It was a book of house plans, each with numerous variations on a basic design, borrowed from a local firm that specialized in adapting and customizing simple house designs for people who couldn't afford an architect and didn't require something totally unique in a house. One of the partners in the business was a friend of hers. Katie hadn't had the nerve to bring up the subject of her spec house to her father again, but she was proceeding, trying to decide on a house plan.

It was difficult to concentrate on what she was seeing as she turned the pages, knowing that Louis was in the house. She wondered how the visit was going. How had her father reacted? What were they saying to each other? Was there any mention of her?

When one of the plans finally caught her eye, Katie studied it closely, liking it more and more as she noted the layout and the number and size of the rooms. Taking the open book over to her computer table, she sat down, turned on the computer and started up a program she used for making preliminary cost estimates. By entering in dimensions and other pertinent information about a house, she could arrive at sound ball-park figures on materials and man-hours of labor.

Katie had bought the program several years ago and experimented with it until she tested out its reliability. Afterward she'd used it to double-check her own calculations and the estimates worked up by subcontractors. She doubted any other small-time residential contractor in the area used such a tool, but she liked computers.

Red Gamble had shaken his head in bemusement, watching Katie work with the program. "Bunch of newfangled foolishness," he'd said, fascinated in spite of himself at the equations materializing on the monitor screen. Katie thought of her father and smiled, was reminded of the visit in progress and sighed, then forgot about everything else as she got down to work.

Louis had been there approximately a half hour when Katie arrived home. From his point of view, the visit was going most satisfactorily following the initial awkwardness. He had been shocked and saddened to see how much Red Gamble had aged. Fleetingly he'd felt grateful to Katie for giving him the courage to pay the call; then he'd determinedly pushed aside the distracting thought of her.

The conversation had followed a natural course, with Louis first asking questions about the older man's health. Then talk had switched to Lisa and Stephanie's friendship, and he had beamed with genuine pleasure at Red and Edna Gamble's complimentary remarks about his daughter. Edna excused herself and went out to the kitchen to make coffee while Louis responded to Red's comments about how well Louis's business was doing.

So far neither had mentioned Katie. Louis was modestly admitting that he was busy building large custom houses when they heard Katie's Bronco. Louis knew nobody else would come roaring into the driveway like that. He braced himself automatically for the piercing squeal of her brakes and doggedly kept talking while she gave the engine a final rev and seconds later slammed the car door. But he was wasting his breath. He had lost Red Gamble's attention. Giving up, he stopped talking, feeling an old, familiar resentment at Katie's interruption.

His resentment quickly turned to concern, however, as the older man seemed to sag in his chair and get grayer. Louis felt a pang of fear as the heavy-jowled face of the man still so dear to him constricted with pain. Was Red Gamble feeling suddenly ill, having another heart attack?

"Mr. Red, are you okay?" he asked worriedly.

The old man focused with effort on Louis again, his eyes, once as bright a blue as Katie's, dimmed now with age and dulled by sad emotion.

"I'm fine, Louis," he said heavily. Louis waited with a sense of dread while the older man pondered what he would say next. His deep sigh and the sudden kind expression marked his decision not to share what weighed on his mind. "I'm fine, son. I'm real glad you came to see me. It's been too long. Now, where were you?"

Louis swallowed. His throat muscles were so tight that he couldn't speak with the first attempt.

"I hear—" He cleared his throat. "I hear from Katie that she's thinking of building a house on spec."

Louis saw almost immediately that Red had misconstrued his hesitancy, interpreting it as doubt about the wisdom of Katie's venture. The older man's lined face became more deeply etched until it mirrored despairing agreement. Mr. Red was worried sick about Katie's building a spec house, Louis realized and wasn't surprised when Red's reply turned out to be a self-condemning defense of Katie.

"I did wrong by her, Louis, from way back. This is all my fault. Whatever you do, son, don't make the same mistake with your little girl. Don't—" He broke off as Edna came back into the room, carrying a tray with the promised coffee and a plate of cookies. "Didn't I hear Katie drive in just now?" he asked her.

"That was Katie," Edna confirmed. "She went back to the office. I noticed she was carrying something. I'm sure she'll be in to say hello to Louis." Her voice was much too cheerful in contrast to the sharp concern in her glance at her husband's face. "Help yourself," she invited Louis hospitably when he had taken the tray from her and set it on the coffee table. "I seem to remember that those were your favorite cookies. Chocolate chip. Between our Lisa and your Stephanie, I have a time these days keeping cookies in the cookie jar."

"Mmm. These were my favorites, Miz Edna," Louis declared. "You have quite a memory." He took one of the home-baked cookies he'd wolfed down in quantity while growing up and ate it with feigned greediness to please her. His thoughts of Katie killed his pleasure in the remembered taste and texture.

Didn't Katie realize her parents were elderly and shouldn't be worrying about her? he asked himself as he responded to Edna's inquiry about his mother. Katie's apparent self-centeredness made him indignant. She obviously still thought only of herself.

Hoping to introduce a cheerful, distracting subject, Louis asked how many Gamble grandchildren there were now. Red came out of his gloom and readily added his proud rumbling comments when Edna gave the total count as twelve and began a rundown on each grandchild. The older man, not surprisingly, took as much pleasure in his grandchildren as his wife did.

Listening and watching the play of fond expressions on their faces, Louis grew more indignant and more profane in his thoughts. How the hell could Katie be so damned selfish, wrecking their peace of mind? Didn't she have any gratitude, any consideration? By the time he announced he had to go, he was seething with anger.

Edna and Red both thanked him for coming and urged him to come again as they walked with him to the front door.

"I'm surprised Katie hasn't been in," Edna remarked in a concerned voice. "She must not have recognized your truck."

Red didn't say anything, but there was an answering concern in his silence.

Louis knew damned well that Katie had recognized his truck, but he didn't correct Edna's error. He didn't dare mention Katie *period*. He thanked the old couple sincerely, promised that he would visit again soon and walked out to his truck, telling himself he was going to get into it and drive away. Katie was going to worry her father into having another heart attack, but that was none of Louis's business.

With his hand on the door handle and his thumb pressing the chrome button, Louis stood beside his pickup glaring at Katie's red Bronco and fighting with himself. Mind your own damned business, he told himself and promptly ignored the advice, taking off with long strides for the far corner of the house, muttering a curse under his breath.

It wouldn't do any good, but he'd tell Katie she was being a spoiled, selfish brat.

Louis envisioned Katie idle, waiting out his visit in the office. She'd known he was in the house and had chosen for her own willful reasons not to come in, fully aware, he was sure, that she was every bit as intrusive in her absence. She was out here, biding her time, maybe even expecting him. He had no thought of surprising her as he stomped up the steps to the small building, pounded twice with his fist on the door that, unlike his, had no glass, and then shoved it open.

Katie was looking over her shoulder, startled, a frown of concentration on her face. She went wide-eyed with surprise at the sight of him bursting through the door. What the hell was she doing? he wondered, taking in the computer screen full of words and numbers and her hands still resting on the keyboard.

"Louis. You scared me to death," she accused him mildly, both her surprise and her concentration fading as she studied his face and came to pessimistic conclusions about his visit. "I saw your pickup in the driveway. I gather it didn't go as well as I led you to expect."

Louis didn't answer her while he closed the door more gently than he'd opened it and leaned his shoulder against it. He'd lost some of his angry momentum.

"You stayed a good while," Katie pointed out, glancing up from her watch. "I lose all track of time when I'm working with the computer," she added.

"It was a very friendly visit," Louis assured her grimly, ignoring the latter remark. She wasn't going to sidetrack him.

Katie's eyebrows shot up questioningly. "That's good. I'm very glad." So what was wrong? she wondered.

"There aren't two nicer people in the world than your parents," Louis declared sternly.

It sounded oddly like an accusation, not a tribute. Katie suddenly had a glimmer of what was going on here.

"I couldn't agree with you more. Did you come back here to tell me how lucky I am, Louis? How I don't deserve my parents?" Katie read his resentful frown as an affirmative answer. "Well, don't bother. I know I'm luckier than I deserve. I also know that isn't any new conclusion for you."

Louis felt a reawakening of his anger and knew that it was different now. It had a more personal element.

"No, it isn't a new conclusion, Katie." He straightened away from the door, not realizing until her eyes widened that his movement was aggressive. "I would have thought you'd grown up, though, and learned to think of somebody besides yourself. Your father is worrying himself sick about you. When you drove in and he heard your car, he turned gray right in front of my eyes. For a minute I was scared he was having a heart attack."

Louis scowled. "What are you trying to do, Katie, kill him?" he demanded, trying not to soften his harsh tone. She looked stricken, as though his words cut deeply, but he needed to make sure he'd gotten through to her. "Your father is in his seventies. He and your mother both deserve to have a peaceful old age and enjoy their grandchildren. They've done a lot for you, Katie. Now you need to think of them. That's what I came back here to say," he finished up gruffly, addressing Katie's bowed head. He watched, at a loss, while she swiped at her cheeks. She was crying, damn it.

"Katie, for God's sake—"

"I'm sorry, Louis. My nerves are tight as a drum lately." Katie apologized in a muffled voice, then lifted her head so that he could see the teary brilliance of her eyes and the wet smudges on her cheeks. She sniffed and swallowed, composing herself, and forced a humorless smile. "It's not as though you haven't seen me cry before."

Her smile faded, and she went on in a voice so jagged with her emotions that Louis winced and fought in vain against his instinctive sympathy. "Don't you think I feel terrible about worrying my parents, Louis? But what can I do? I'm in a rotten situation that isn't my fault."

Katie rose almost out of her chair and did a twisting stretch to take several snapshots of houses from the bulletin board behind the computer table, giving Louis a view of slim hips, rounded buttocks and trim thighs which he appreciated against his will. Did she have any inkling, he wondered, how the fit of her jeans related to her problems? She wasn't just any female trying to invade a man's world, but a cute, sexy and infinitely desirable one.

"I built all these houses," Katie told him, getting up to bring the snapshots to him. She stood close to look at them with him. "You probably recognize that one." She put her hand on his to stop him from flipping to the next snapshot. "That's in the same neighborhood as the Pearson house."

"It's a nice house. I've noticed it." Louis wanted to look at her, not the snapshot. Her vibrant red hair was a glint in the corner of his eye. He could smell the light, herbal, feminine scent, probably her shampoo. Her hand was warm on his, and she was altogether too close for comfort. "Billy Krauer did the custom mill work, didn't he? I remember hearing him talk about the spiral staircase."

"It was a work of art," Katie declared, dropping her hand. "The whole house is really something." Louis felt it was safe to glance over. She was smiling at the snapshot with a possessive pride he completely understood. In some ways a house—even a problem child like the Pearson house—always belonged to a builder. His empathy made being harshly honest with her more difficult, as did her physical proximity.

"I'm well aware, Katie, that Gamble Construction has built some of the finest houses in this area," he said, handing the snapshots back and moving away from her to perch on the edge of Red Gamble's big old desk. Its surface was neat and tidy, like the whole office, he noted. "Everybody knows your father's reputation. People on the inside, like myself, realize, too, that you took over for your father and did a lot of his work—"

"I did *all* of his work the last three years, Louis," Katie broke in to inform him earnestly. "For reasons of loyalty, I wouldn't say that to just anybody, but it's true." She looked through the snapshots, found one and held it up. "He's never even seen this one. The doctor had told him not to drive, and I was always on the go. When I would think to offer, he would have some TV show on or be expecting company. I realize now that he'd lost interest...." Katie looked away, finishing the rest of the thought in her mind. At the time she'd thought her father was exhibiting confidence in her, but now, with his reaction to her plan to build a spec house, she wasn't sure. Her pride, however, wouldn't let her tell Louis that.

"I wouldn't feel bad, Katie," Louis said with gruff kindness. He empathized with her surprise as she looked back quickly at him; it amazed him, too, to find himself wanting to comfort her. "Mr. Red hung on for your sake because he wanted to. He realized what was going to happen to you after he retired. Everybody—" Louis broke off, warned by the lightning in her eyes of the offensiveness in what he had been about to say.

"What I meant is that anybody familiar with house-building in this area knows that a woman on her own would meet with problems," he amended tactfully, but to no avail. He well recognized the signs of Katie's fury about to erupt: the compression of her mouth, the bright spots of color in her cheeks, the murderous light in her blue eyes. Louis guiltily enjoyed the stimulation despite his chagrin that he'd ruined his chances for reasoning with her.

Katie was as angry with herself for opening up to him as she was at Louis for his male condescension.

"You can spread the news around to 'everybody' that Katie Gamble is going to overcome all those 'problems,' one way or another, and build a house!" she told him hotly. "Now, if you've finished lecturing and insulting me, you can get the hell out of here and let me get back to my work." She turned her back on him and marched angrily to the computer table, where she threw the snapshots down and plumped down in the chair. "I don't hear you leaving, Louis," she said threateningly.

"Throwing a tantrum isn't going to solve anything, Katie," Louis pointed out mildly and felt guilty again at his surge of expectation when she sucked in her breath audibly. "I'm not leaving until we talk this out like two adults," he added more firmly.

Katie's armless secretary's chair squeaked a warning, but she was only crossing her legs and folding her arms across her chest in an attitude of patience, which she emphasized with a deep sigh.

"You're right, Louis. Throwing a tantrum doesn't accomplish anything. It doesn't even get rid of unwanted company." She swung her foot and sighed again. "Okay, since you're not going to leave until you have your say, why don't you just give me the benefit of your infinite male wisdom? What do you suggest I do? Let me guess," she taunted before he could answer. "I'll bet you think I should forget all this foolishness of trying to do a man's work and get myself a feminine job. Or, better yet, maybe I should find myself a nice man to marry, and then I wouldn't have to support myself at all. Which is it?"

Louis didn't know if he'd ever wanted anything more than he wanted to rise to her bait. It pushed his self-control to the limit not to retort that he didn't know a man who was capable of taking on the job of handling her and that he pitied the poor fool who tried.

"Katie, I can understand that you don't want to give up," he managed to say quietly, "but building a spec house is not a solution." Louis felt like the worst kind of bully as he watched her slender shoulders droop and her foot stop its jaunty swing. "Aside from worrying your father, it's not fair to him and your mother to take that kind of risk with their savings."

Katie's shoulders went erect, and she whirled around, the image of indignation.

"Not that it's any of your business, but I have no intention of risking my parents' savings," she corrected him scornfully, rising to her feet. "I'm going to get financing from a bank. I have property for collateral, including the lot I'm going to build on."

"Is your property worth what you'll need to borrow?" Louis asked soberly.

Katie saw where he was leading. If her property wasn't worth enough, he doubted that she would get the money from a bank. Katie doubted it, too.

"I don't know yet what I'll need to borrow," she admitted, her defiance ebbing and leaving her discouraged. She stuck her hands into her jeans pockets and looked disconsolately at the computer monitor and the open book. "I've found a house plan that I like in this book. I was working up some costs when you came in."

"I wondered what you were doing," he remarked, sounding surprised and skeptical. "You don't mean you can figure out what it's going to cost to build a house by using a computer, before you even get estimates from subs?"

Katie smiled fleetingly at the open distrust with which he regarded the monitor screen.

"You sound just like my father. He could never believe it, either. To answer your question, I can come pretty darned close if I calculate what a sub *should* estimate." Her bitter emphasis brought immediate comprehension to Louis's face.

"That's about what I expected," he said gravely. "Your father's old subs don't want to work for you now. Whether you like it or not, Katie, whether it's fair or not, that's what you're going to run into. Don't you see it's not going to be any different with a spec house?"

Katie met his gaze with a downcast, stubborn expression. "Louis, how would you like somebody to tell you that you couldn't build any more houses, for no good reason?''

Louis hunched his big shoulders forward, gripping the edge of the desk on either side of him, plainly uncomfortable with her question.

"Damn it, Katie, of course I wouldn't like it," he admitted honestly. "And I know I have a hell of a nerve trying to tell you what to do. But what's the point of beating your head against a brick wall? You're only going to hurt yourself *and* the people who care about you." Louis got up with an air of weary finality. It was a much-modified, sincere version of what he'd come to the office to say to her. He didn't feel any of the satisfaction he'd expected to get from saying it.

"I know you mean well, Louis," Katie told him with quiet bitterness. "Forgive me if I don't thank you." She was already exhausted from swimming against the current, and his wisdom was like the tidal surge that was going to drown her.

"You aren't going to pay any attention, are you, Katie?" Louis walked to the door, grasped the knob and stood looking at her, exasperated by his prediction. "You're going to go ahead with this spec house idea no matter what, aren't you? You just can't take no for an answer. You never could. When the chips are down, Katie's going to think of Katie and nobody else."

"I took no from you, Louis. Don't you remember?" As soon as she'd said the words Katie wished she could take them back. Their shock value wasn't worth the cost to her pride. She tilted her chin and spoke quickly before he could answer. "You'd love to walk out of here blaming me, wouldn't you? It would make you feel a little less guilty that you're not in my position just because you're a man. I'll decide for myself whether I'm going to build a spec house, and if I make up my mind to build one, by God, I'll manage to do it somehow."

It was desperate bravado. Katie's morale had hit rock bottom. She simply hoped to maintain her dignity until he was gone, and then she'd cry her heart out.

"Katie, that kind of talk doesn't change any—"

"It isn't your problem, Louis," she cut in. "Now, if you don't mind, I have work to do. Good luck on the Hemphill house, when you finally get around to building it," she added sarcastically when he just stood there, frowning at her with as much concern as exasperation.

He jerked open the door and left then, but he didn't slam it behind him. The quiet way he closed it filled Katie with a strange anguish. She moved to the window and watched him cover the distance to the corner of the house with long strides.

When he was gone from sight, she tried in vain to coax tears to alleviate her misery and then walked with leaden steps to the computer. She sat down and closed out the program with rote touches of the keys, not bothering to save her calculations. It had been a futile exercise.

Louis was right. She was beating her head against a brick wall. Her head might be able to take the battering, but she couldn't risk her father's heart.

Chapter Five

I've decided against building a spec house," Katie told her parents that evening. Without seeming to notice the relieved glance they exchanged, she went on cheerfully. "Actually, I'm thinking of getting into some other kind of work, maybe computers."

Before they could comment on either revelation, she changed the subject, having done as much as she could for the time in putting their minds at ease. She simply wasn't up to a discussion of her future, and her parents didn't press.

Nor did Katie have to contend with constant questions from other members of the family. Everyone's concern was focused on Trish and her two children as the day drew near for her appearance in court and the finalizing of her divorce.

With time at her disposal, Katie lent her full support to her sister, niece and nephew. In the effort to keep them and herself too busy to think, she organized shopping expeditions, trips to the movies, suppers out for pizza and a weekend fishing trip with fourteen-year-old Rich and two other nephews. Rich, it turned out, was taking his parents' divorce much harder than anyone had suspected.

The fishing trip backfired on Katie, though, evoking memories of similar outings with her father and Louis that threatened to overshadow the present and her immediate purpose of cheering up her nephew. Vivid images of a younger, vigorous Red Gamble made her sharply nostalgic. It struck her that Louis was the one other person on earth who could understand precisely what she was feeling. If he were there with her, he would be feeling some of the same emotions. Quickly she extinguished the thought of his presence, disturbed by the strength of her longing.

Then, when she returned home with her nephews to a good-natured fuss over her having caught the biggest fish, she found herself wondering if a report on the fishing trip would filter back to Louis through Stephanie. It concerned as well as annoyed her that Louis seemed to be invading her thoughts, after years of seldom thinking about him at all. There was simply no point in thinking about him, she told herself impatiently.

Yet all of a sudden he seemed to come to mind at the most unexpected times, even on the day Trish's divorce was granted and Katie's foremost thoughts were of her sister. She accompanied Trish to court and afterwards stayed with her when Trish readily admitted she didn't want to be alone.

"Please, let's talk about you, not me," Trish pleaded when they'd returned to her house and were having coffee in the living room. "I'm sick of talking about me and my problems, tired of feeling sorry for myself. Tell me, Katie, how you came to be so much smarter than me, not putting your trust in a man. Haven't you ever been wildly in love and wanted to get married and live happily ever after?"

Katie was used to good-natured probing into her love life. Usually she made some joking reply that revealed nothing, but today humorous evasion seemed out of place. Beneath the effort at lightness, Trish's self-contempt was real, and the expression in her eyes was haunted. Katie answered truthfully with the impulse to offer her rare confidence as proof of the two sisters' new closeness.

"I don't think being 'smart' has anything to do with it, Trish. I wonder if I'm not missing something most women have."

The surprise in Trish's eyes at Katie's unexpected candor was quickly mixed with loyal warmth. Before her sister could come to her defense, though, Katie continued, suddenly not wanting to lose her nerve before she'd explained.

"The only guy I was ever crazy about was Louis McIntyre. I was head over heels in love with him and wanted to marry him, but that was way back in high school. It hardly counts." The thoughtful look on Trish's face raised a strange panic inside Katie. "I had steady relationships with a couple of guys in college," she continued hastily. "You must remember Ross Elbert. He was at all our family get-togethers during my freshman year. You all seemed to like him."

"Sure. I remember Ross." Trish's tone was gently abstracted, her mind obviously not on Ross Elbert. "Louis McIntyre. I never once realized..."

"Besides Ross, there was Damon Wheeler in college, too," Katie went on urgently. "He was in premed. He wanted to marry me. Just think, I could be a doctor's wife today. We slept together," she divulged, desperate to wipe the thoughtfulness from Trish's face.

"I didn't think you'd still be a virgin," Trish chided, smiling. "Louis had to get married, didn't he?" she mused. "Stephanie was already on the way. He's been divorced for a number of years, though. And never re-married."

"Louis obviously doesn't feel the need for a wife," Katie pointed out, sounding far too argumentative. "He has his mother to help with Stephanie, who seems to be growing up fine without a mother. Don't go making a romantic tragedy out of what I told you, Trish," she pleaded. "Honestly, I haven't been eating my heart out over Louis for the past twelve years, nor is Louis carrying a torch for me. He never had one lighted." Katie regretted the last statement even as it slipped out, tinged with a faint bitterness.

"Maybe it's not too late to light a flame, Katie," Trish suggested gently. "You're both single. I gather he's unattached, since Stephanie hasn't mentioned a special woman friend, and I'm sure she would have if there was one. Kids that age tell all." She smiled and then turned serious again while Katie was trying to muster an answering smile. "Louis is a very fine man, from all I hear about him. Fine *looking*, too. Even I've noticed that, as down in the dumps as I've been."

"Louis is definitely a decent type, Trish. And, sure, he's good-looking," Katie agreed, trying to sound careless. Her mind flashed fresh attractive images: Louis propped against his pickup; Louis, shirtless, standing framed in his office door; Louis perched on the edge of her father's old desk.

"I can't argue with either of those facts, but you can forget about Louis and me getting together." Katie's smile was humorless. "The last thing I'd ever hope to do is light a fire in him. I used up all my matches in high school and got nothing but burned fingers for my trouble."

Trish reached over and gave Katie's hand a tender little pat.

"They must have been bad burns, honey. I don't think they're completely healed yet. Forgive me if I've been insensitive."

"There's nothing to be insensitive about," Katie protested. "The only thing that's never completely healed is my pride. That's all that was ever hurt."

Trish didn't argue, but as she gently changed the subject it was all too obvious to Katie that her sister was unconvinced. Katie wished she could correct Trish's false belief that Katie was suffering a broken heart that dated back to her futile pursuit of Louis in high school. Katie's heart was intact. Louis had nothing to do with her not having fallen in love since high school and not having married. Absolutely nothing.

Even more of a certainty, Katie definitely had no bearing on Louis's not having remarried. She would stake her life on that.

But she let the whole matter drop, knowing that for all her certitude, she couldn't sound objective. Trish would hear her tinge of bitterness and misconstrue it all over again. Katie, however, knew that the emotion was hurt feminine pride. Nothing more.

She fervently wished she hadn't brought up her old infatuation, and her regret deepened when Lisa came home, accompanied by Stephanie, who greeted Katie almost as enthusiastically as her niece did. Katie could see the wheels of her sister's mind turning. Trish was chalking up Stephanie's obvious affection for Katie as a big plus in favor of Katie and Louis's getting together.

Katie's only comfort was that at least she had gotten her older sister's mind off her own problems. Trish had lost her haunted expression and seemed relaxed and cheerful. Katie left her with the two little girls and fled home, praying that her sister would soon abandon her mental matchmaking. Merely knowing that Trish entertained idle hopes of an adult romance between Katie and Louis made Katie uncomfortable. They would never even be friends, let alone lovers.

When she arrived home, Katie had to wonder if some mean fate was at work, conspiring against her peace of mind. Opening the back door, she heard her parents talking in the kitchen, and she immediately picked up Louis's name. Unable to believe her ears, she paused and listened long enough to surmise that Louis must have come by that day and taken Red for a drive to see some of the houses the younger man had built.

Katie bridled at the animation in her father's rumbling voice as he spoke of Louis with a pride that was paternal. She'd felt the same unpleasant emotion as a child and recognized it now for what it was: jealousy. As an adult, though, she would rise above the feeling, even if she was unable to conquer it.

With her appearance in the kitchen doorway, the conversation between her parents immediately halted, and she was bombarded with anxious questions about Trish and the day's court procedure. After satisfying them that Trish was bearing up well, Katie wrestled with

the temptation to escape to her room and spare herself
an account of her father's outing with Louis. But, unwilling to be cowardly and selfish, she turned to her father with her best effort at an interested expression.

"Did I overhear you saying that Louis McIntyre had
come by to see you today?" she asked him.

Apparently she was convincingly casual, since her
father readily began filling her in. She managed a bland
smile and an occasional comment or question and
somehow kept her resentment hidden. She thought it
damned insensitive of Louis to impress her father with
the younger man's big success as a builder at the very
time that Katie was flat on her face in the same profession, listening to the knockout count. But she would
keep those feelings to herself. She would give Louis a
wide open field with her father, no matter what it cost
her in pride and control.

"That was nice of him to take you for a drive," she
declared when she'd endured as much as she could.
"I'm sure he enjoyed it as much as you did. Now, I need
to get out of these dressy clothes and into some jeans."

Katie fled to her room. Closing the old-fashioned
solid wood door behind her, she leaned against it as
though it were a barricade and took a deep breath. Was
her bedroom the only place where she was safe from
Louis these days? He seemed to be invading her whole
world, encroaching on her private space. She couldn't
get through a day lately without thoughts of him somehow being forced upon her. It might not be so bad if
Louis were being bothered similarly, but she knew
damned well he wasn't.

This distraction had to stop, Katie decided summar-
ily while she undressed, shedding her elegant pleated
slacks and long-sleeved blouse and then perching on the

edge of her four-poster to strip off her panty hose none too gently. She needed to get on with her life. Her whole problem was her indecision about her future; she had no specific goals to occupy her mind. Tomorrow she would get down to the business of living Katie Gamble's life. Once she was productive and happy again, she wouldn't give Louis McIntyre more than an occasional passing thought.

Damn Katie, anyway! He might have known he was in for trouble that first day she showed up! Louis fumed as he scrambled the papers on his desk in search of a telephone number. He finally found it, scrawled on the back of a pink invoice copy. He didn't dial the number immediately, though. Instead, he sat with his elbows propped on the desk, frowning at the invoice gripped tensely in his hands.

"You're crazy as hell for even thinking about doing this," he told himself disgustedly. Calling himself abusive names and repeating them with a kind of dogged desperation, he reached for the telephone, punched out the number and waited for an answer, praying nobody was home. Maybe by tomorrow he would have come to his damned senses.

But no such luck. The man answered, and Louis stated his business bluntly. After a brief conversation, he hung up, appalled at his easy success.

If the phone call and the man's verbal agreement were all that was required, he wouldn't mind. He wouldn't feel so uneasy. But they were just the beginning. The rest was so much trickier, so downright risky. It went against his better judgment and honest nature, but he didn't see any other way.

Or maybe he didn't *want* to see another way. That's what really bothered the hell out of him.

The next morning Katie held on to her firm resolution of the afternoon before. *Today you will get on with your life,* she told herself, braving the office behind the house for the first time in two weeks.

She would put her computer to an entirely new use: to work up a résumé and print out copies. It would be a test of her inner strength to set aside the past and deal strictly with the present once she was in the little building that was chockablock full of memories. Katie was determined to be up to that test.

The strongest memory she had to subdue was the most recent one. Seated at her computer table, her back to the door, she remembered the last time she'd sat there and looked over her shoulder to see an angry, determined Louis bursting through the door. It was the forceful emotion in him, she realized now, that had rattled her even more than the surprise of his presence. Louis had always been so calm, so controlled.

Don't think about him, she ordered herself, and she concentrated fiercely on turning on the computer, starting up her word-processing program, and opening a new file. "R-E-S-U-M-E," she typed, spelling doggedly aloud. She was about to center the heading when the phone on the desk rang, startling her into pressing the wrong key.

Ignoring the query FIND??? on the monitor screen, she got up to answer the call, feeling guilty that she welcomed the interruption. One of her friends must have tried her home number first and was now calling here at her mother's suggestion.

"Hello," she said conversationally, dropping down into the big swivel chair.

"Katie Gamble, please," said a pleasant male voice Katie would never forget. *John Hemphill.* Why would he be calling her?

"This is Katie Gamble."

"Ms. Gamble, this is John Hemphill. Since I talked to you last, I've had reason to reconsider your bid. I wonder if you're still interested in building my house."

Katie clutched the phone in both hands so as not to drop it.

"But—but you'd decided on Louis...Louis McIntyre," she reminded him stupidly.

"Yes, I had decided on McIntyre, but it turns out he won't be able to make a start on the house until the first of the year. My wife and I don't want to wait that long. McIntyre, uh—" John Hemphill cleared his throat "—recommended you quite highly."

"He did?" Katie blurted out incredulously. "That was nice of him," she added in a dazed tone, trying to focus on the truly important aspect of the conversation. This man was opening the door she'd thought was locked and sealed against her. He wanted her to build his house!

"I definitely am still interested, Mr. Hemphill," she told him, speaking as calmly as was possible with a heart that was beating ten times too fast and still picking up speed. "I could get started right away." She could get started five minutes after they finalized the agreement!

"Then there's just the matter of money to be worked out," Hemphill said pleasantly. "Frankly, Ms. Gamble, your bid was high. If you can match McIntyre's price, we've got a deal."

Katie's heart slowed to a dull, thudding beat.

"What was Louis's price?" she asked, hearing the dread in her voice. She winced with real pain when he told her. At that price she'd have to build his house for nothing.

"Well, Ms. Gamble? Do we have a deal?" Hemphill pressed when she was silent, struggling with her overwhelming disappointment.

"I don't know if I can match that...." Katie's voice trailed off as she turned to look at her computer.

If she told Hemphill no, she'd hang up the phone and go back to her interrupted task. Under her title "RESUME" she'd print the pertinent facts about her education and working experience. Then, without much hope, she'd search for some job that even came close to suiting her as much as the one she was being offered— but for no pay.

Still, there was really no contest. She simply couldn't turn down the offer. Here was her chance to build a house as Katie Gamble, general contractor. The full credit or the full blame would be hers and hers alone. If she proved successful, it might even win her a toehold in the profession of her choice.

"All right. I'll build your house for McIntyre's price," she told Hemphill. She felt incredibly elated for someone who'd just agreed to work for no recompense other than personal satisfaction. She reminded herself that the job was an investment in her future.

As she set up an appointment to meet informally with the Hemphills that afternoon, she cautioned herself against unrestrained optimism. Ultimately, the prejudices against a female building contractor might still force her into a different line of work, since she couldn't continue to work for nothing. But even so, she would

feel good knowing that she'd proved herself beyond
question, and afterward, if necessary, she would approach a change in occupation with a more positive attitude.

Her only regret was that Louis had thrown his influence in her favor. She wished Hemphill had picked her
as his second choice entirely on his own.

But she didn't want to dwell on her debt to Louis.
There was work to be done, and she was delighted to be
doing it. During the remainder of the morning she re-
viewed her computer file on the Hemphill bid and was
aghast once again at the discrepancies between her own
calculations of subcontracting costs and the prices she'd
been quoted by subs. If only she could find good subs
to work more reasonably, she could build the house and
make a profit. Either way, though, she would build the
house. She was unshaken in her decision.

At lunch she told her parents the good news and tried
not to feel hurt at the incredulity her father couldn't
hide. At least his reaction put to rest a tiny fear. Like a
dark shadow the thought had crossed her mind that
Louis might have turned down the Hemphill job and
recommended her as a favor to her father. That would
have been too bitter a pill to swallow.

That afternoon she visited building-supply stores and
updated her information on prices and availability of
materials. Then she drove to the Hemphills' and went
over their house plan and the architect's specifications
with them in fine detail. Thoughts of Louis and his recent problems with the Pearsons reminded her to stress
that her obligation was to build the house drawn in the
plans and described in the specifications, not some cre-
ation that evolved with spur-of-the-moment changes.

"You'll probably make *some* changes," she predicted equally. "Most owners do. You should understand, though, that if your changes add to the overall cost, you'll have to pay the extra. I'll keep you informed as we go along, and that way we'll part on friendly terms."

"You certainly sound like you know your business," John Hemphill remarked, looking genuinely impressed.

"I do know my business," Katie declared confidently, getting up to leave. It was difficult to keep her smile businesslike and to act calm and composed. Her adrenaline was flowing, filling her with elated energy. She felt so competent, so damned eager, so *happy* that she could hardly stand it. On the way home, she turned up her favorite country and western radio station until it was blaring and sang along gustily.

When she walked into the kitchen she found, as usual, her father sitting at the table and her mother standing at the stove. They both smiled broadly at the sight of her.

"What a day!" Katie complained happily, giving her mother an exuberant hug and peeking into the pots. "Mmm. Red beans and rice!" She sniffed. "Do I smell corn bread baking, too? I'm starving," she declared. "I could eat enough to feed an army."

Edna Gamble's face was radiant with a mother's happy smile. "That's good to hear! I've been worried about you just pecking at your food lately. You're nothing but skin and bones."

"Ain't that the God's truth," Red put in with grumbling cheer.

Supper was a homey celebration. If Katie hadn't felt so good, she wouldn't have been able to fend off her self-recrimination at realizing how much her low spirits had cast a pall over her parents' household the past months. Soon, she promised herself, she would broach the subject of moving and be firm about it, but not tonight. She didn't want to upset them and spoil the general happy mood.

After supper she felt too pumped up to settle in front of the television. Deciding to call some friends and share her news, she was perched on a stool at the kitchen counter and was reaching for the wall phone when it rang.

"Hello." She answered with a lilt, expecting one of her friends.

"You sound happy," Louis's deep voice drawled in her ear.

"Louis!" Katie exclaimed. "I am happy. I gather you already know why."

"Hemphill called me a few minutes ago to give me the bad news that he was picking a better contractor," Louis admitted. Then he dropped the pretended grudging note and added, "Congratulations. I guess this means you're back in the house-building business."

"Thanks. I—" Katie bit her lip, conquering the impulse to pour out everything to him—what the job meant to her, how it was paying her nothing because she had to match his price, and yet how much she looked forward to the work. The canned laughter coming from the television set in the family room, mixed with her father's guffaw, reminded her that anything she told Louis might be discussed between the two men. The prospect was highly unappealing. "I appreciate your putting in a good word for me with Hemphill," she thanked him stiffly. "That was nice of you."

"Don't mention it. I was glad to do it."

Louis's geniality sounded slightly forced, and he didn't seem to know what to say next. It occurred to Katie suddenly that maybe he hadn't been calling *her*.

"Did you want to talk to my father?" she asked, trying to sound neither as disappointed nor as resentful as she felt. "If you'll hold on, I'll go get him."

"No," Louis denied quickly. "I didn't want to talk to Mr. Red. I was calling you."

"Oh." Katie's cheeks burned with feminine satisfaction. "I'm glad you called," she added quickly. "I was feeling too good to sit still. I was just about to call everybody I know to announce the good news."

"I won't keep you on the line, then. I'll get right to the point," Louis declared with the same forced quality she'd already noticed. "Seems you owe me something for stealing my job. So how about going out with me tomorrow night?"

"Tomorrow night?" Katie echoed, fully as stunned as she'd been that morning when Hemphill asked her to be his contractor. Louis was asking her for a date?

"If you're not busy, why not? We can go somewhere to eat and then maybe drop by Back Street and have a few drinks. On Friday night there'll be a band."

"Sounds nice." Katie tried to sound offhand, but her voice was as strained as his. "Really, it does sound like fun, Louis," she went on, dropping the pretense that she didn't find the idea of a date with him difficult to get used to. "You took me more than a little by surprise."

"It took some courage to ask you," he came back honestly. "But there really isn't any reason we shouldn't go out and have a nice evening together, is there?"

"No reason at all," Katie agreed. "What time?"

"Why don't I pick you up at seven? We can decide then what we're in a mood for eating."

Katie thought he sounded relieved, and the possibility that he'd been afraid she would turn him down was oddly gratifying.

"I'll be ready at seven, then," she promised, thinking the conversation was concluded. She was going on a date with Louis. It was hard to believe.

"Good enough." Louis cleared his throat. "Hemphill mentioned that you'd come down to my price. If you don't mind my asking, what was your bid?"

Katie hesitated, her gaze once again on the open door to the hallway. The sounds of the television in the family room conjured a clear picture of her parents. Her father would be surprised that she was going out with Louis . . . *or would he?*

"I don't mind, as long as what I say doesn't go any farther," she told him in a menacing tone that brought startled silence from his end of the line.

"What do you mean?"

"I mean that whatever I want my father to know about my business, I'll tell him myself," Katie replied bluntly. "I don't want him worrying about me, for one thing," she added.

"I won't repeat anything you tell me to Mr. Red," Louis promised without hesitation, and Katie didn't have a further qualm about confidentiality. Louis would keep his word.

When she told him her bid, he whistled softly.

"Quite a difference between your price and mine," he remarked mildly. "You must be cutting out all your profit."

"I won't be making a dime," she admitted. "My only hope is to find some more reasonable subs, but I'm pressed for time. I promised Hemphill I'd start right away."

"Now that you've definitely got the job, maybe you can reason with your subs and get them down on their prices," Louis suggested hopefully. "Or maybe you'd like to check with the subs I was planning to use on the job. I could give you their names and the prices they gave me. They wouldn't have to work up new estimates."

"Louis, I couldn't use your subs!" Katie protested, overwhelmed by the generosity of his offer. "They're probably busy. Besides, they gave those prices to you, not me. I'd feel awkward approaching them. Thanks, but I'll have to work all this out for myself."

"Sorry, I didn't mean to be sticking my nose into your business," Louis apologized humbly.

"I appreciate your wanting to help," Katie assured him quickly, wishing she hadn't spoken so sharply. She hadn't meant to hurt his feelings. "It's nice of you to offer," she added gently.

But she had offended him, she could tell. In a chastened tone he reconfirmed their plans for the following evening, said goodbye and hung up, leaving Katie totally unsettled. You'll have to be more careful, she admonished herself, and then she wondered at the urgency of the advice.

It bothered her, too, that she no longer had any desire to telephone her friends and tell them her good news. Getting the Hemphill job was temporarily eclipsed by what had just happened, and there wasn't anyone to whom she would confide that she was thrilled that Louis McIntyre had asked her out on a date. That was high-school stuff.

Had Trish been right about her? Katie wondered uneasily, looking down at her hands and remembering her recent conversation with her sister. Was she still infatuated with Louis after all these years?

His physical appeal for her remained undeniably strong. During the telephone conversation, she'd responded to the slow, deep cadence of his voice. The several times she'd seen him recently, the circumstances had been strained and unpleasant, yet she'd been drawn to Louis's looks—his face, his hair, his build. She liked his physical presence. With no effort, she could conjure up a dozen sensual little details about him that made her shivery and warm inside.

Katie guessed it was just one of those strange accidents of life that Louis McIntyre happened to have a powerful, and apparently lasting, masculine appeal for her. She was no less susceptible to it now than she had been in high school. But she was older and, she hoped, smarter now. She had those invisible scars to remind her not to expect anything from Louis. Then she wouldn't be disappointed.

It was that simple.

Louis hung up the telephone after verifying the date with Katie, literally in a sweat.

Actually it had gone surprisingly easily, like the phone call the previous evening. He'd never really realized his talent for telephone negotiation.

There were safety factors in carrying out a transaction over the telephone. You didn't have to worry about transmitting messages with your face and eyes or risk being sidetracked by the other person's mannerisms or expressions. Ending an exchange was clean and definite, too. You just hung up the phone and cut off the connection.

Tomorrow night would be a different proposition. Thinking about it made Louis get up and turn the air conditioner to a cooler setting.

Chapter Six

Katie tried on half a dozen outfits before she decided on a slim-fitting denim skirt and a fancy Western-style blouse with a ruffled yoke and elaborate embroidery. She wanted to look her best for her date with Louis and yet not give the impression that she'd dressed up for a big occasion. For a Friday night out on the town in Covington she could wear nice jeans, but the skirt was more feminine.

And Katie wanted to be feminine tonight....

Standing in front of the full-length mirror on her closet door, she tried various shoes with the outfit, starting with her prize Western boots. Made of alligator, they were outrageously expensive. Next she tried flats, then low-heeled pumps and then the boots again. Finally she settled halfheartedly on the pumps, knowing she could still change her mind after she'd finished getting ready.

Her makeup took time because she was guided by the same conflicting concerns. She wanted to look pretty yet natural, not as if she'd been primping. Taking care to apply mascara and eye shadow with a light touch, she still thought her eyelashes looked artificially long and her eyes startlingly large. She'd smoothed on glossy lipstick, only to blot off most of it.

Her hair was almost dry from her shower. After a few minutes with the hand drier and brush, it settled sleekly into place, a short, brilliant cap of rust red shooting out healthy glints.

Ready, she looked herself over critically in the full-length mirror and went to join her parents while she waited for Louis. Her mother's reaction would give her an accurate reading on her appearance.

"You look very nice, dear," Edna told her warmly. The motherly approval was genuine and yet perfunctory enough to ease Katie's fears of looking too decked out. She felt deflated, though, rather than reassured.

Her letdown dissipated quickly, though, when she opened the door to Louis. He repeated her mother's compliment, minus the endearment, but added an appreciative once-over that was completely male.

Katie smiled at him, feeling not in the least short-changed by the mild praise.

"Do you want to come in and say hello to my folks?"

As he accepted the invitation and strode in, she left her own admiration for his appearance unspoken.

He definitely looked "nice" himself, and all the more masculine for the simplicity of his attire. His blue-and-white-checked Western shirt fit snugly across his broad shoulders and chest, but it had no fancy piping or ornamentation. The shirt was tucked neatly into jeans, which were belted with a wide, plain leather belt with a

functional brass buckle. His calfskin boots were plain,
too. At six feet plus, he didn't need the extra height of
fancy Western boots, and the unadorned style suited
him.

Katie was pleased that Louis refused her parents' invitation to sit down, using his eagerness to get to a restaurant as a joking excuse. She was embarrassed,
though, that her parents were transparently approving
his decision, treating it as a welcome sign of Louis's
preference for being alone with her. She wished they
wouldn't act so tickled that he was taking her out.

"You'd think I was their ugly duckling daughter who
never got asked on a date," she complained dryly as
soon as she and Louis were out of the house. "The truth
is that one of their favorite TV shows comes on in five
minutes. They were just dying to get us out of the way."

Louis chuckled. "I noticed nobody insisted I sit
down," he drawled, accompanying her down the porch
steps.

Katie wasn't surprised to see his pickup parked in the
driveway. Since his mother, like hers, had never driven,
he would have little use for a second vehicle.

"It sure is nice to see an older married couple like
your folks," Louis remarked, his tone fond and reflec-
tive. "They're crazy about their kids and the grand-
kids, too, but they still have a special feeling for each
other after all these years, don't they?"

"Yes, they do," Katie agreed. The awkward moment had passed easily, and yet she was somehow more
irked than relieved that his thoughts had shifted away
from her entirely.

"That's rare, you know," he went on. "So many
older couples really can't stand each other. They stay

together out of habit and convenience, I guess, and live out their time."

"At least they have company," Katie pointed out pragmatically. "And they have a lot of memories in common. That's worth something." She thought of the recent fishing trip and her realization that he was the only person who could share certain special memories with her. "It's almost the same with the two of us."

The words were out before she thought about the embarrassment of comparing herself and Louis to an incompatible old married couple. He'd made sure he wouldn't have to endure marital disharmony with her.

"What I mean, of course," she hastened to add, "is that two people like us, who've shared a lot of experiences and have a background in common, don't have to explain things as much. Whether they like each other or not, they have a special communication. All it takes is the mention of a person or place or incident, and they both have the same thought."

They had rounded the front of the pickup and reached the passenger door. Louis opened it and waited for her to get in, but Katie hesitated, wanting his understanding.

"What you're saying makes sense," he said, sounding uncomfortable.

Katie felt foolish. Still, whether he liked it or not, she wanted to tell him his past was intertwined with hers. They had countless memories in common.

"For example," she said stubbornly, hiking her skirt up for the high step into the pickup, "I thought about you recently when I took three of my nephews fishing."

She took the long step without expecting any assistance. It took her totally by surprise when Louis clasped her elbow and splayed his other hand across the small of her back to give her a light boost. She lost her balance for a moment, and Louis took her full weight. For the brief instant that he supported her, she savored her helplessness and his strength and reveled in the feel of his hands through her clothing.

"Guess I'm not used to doing this in a skirt," she apologized breathlessly as he lifted her easily to the broad bench seat.

"It's a good thing you don't weigh much," Louis replied good-naturedly, but he didn't seem in a great hurry to withdraw his hands.

As she straightened her skirt and settled herself more comfortably, her foot struck something on the floor. "I kicked something down there," she remarked, bending forward to see what it was.

"Probably an empty can," Louis predicted philosophically. He leaned into the cab to search the area around her feet.

Katie swung her legs away to accommodate him, but his shoulder grazed her thigh, and the contact felt incredibly intimate.

"It's not hurting anything," she protested weakly.

"It'll roll around and drive us crazy."

His deep voice seemed to vibrate through Katie, creating an odd, delicious tension, and then his shirt was again brushing her legs as he reached.

"Here it is," he announced with satisfaction, easing backward out of the cab. Straightening, he smiled ruefully at the empty soda can he held. "And I thought I'd gotten them all."

"My favorite brand," Katie said weakly, aware of her heart beating fast and her pulse hammering.

"You don't know the trouble I went to clearing out this dump on wheels for your benefit." Louis grinned as he tossed the can into the back of the big double cab. Aluminum struck aluminum, and Katie glanced over her shoulder and saw the accumulation of debris. Along with numerous empty soda cans, there were cartons, newspapers, crumpled bags and candy wrappers, along with the inevitable rolled-up house plans.

"What do you do when it fills up completely back there?" she inquired with pretended horror.

He shrugged. "By then it's time to buy a new truck."

Katie spoke the last four words in unison with him and returned his broad smile.

He slammed her door and came around to the driver's side.

"I heard about that fishing trip with your nephews," he surprised her by remarking as he slid under the wheel. She'd completely forgotten the interrupted conversation. He started the pickup and looked over his shoulder while he backed out. "I gather you must still be as lucky as ever, catching the biggest fish."

"What do you mean *lucky!*" Katie jeered. "I just haven't lost my knack for fishing. You can't account for all those times I caught the biggest fish on those trips with you and my father as *luck*. Sounds like sour grapes to me."

He glanced at her with an amused smile as he shifted gears and started forward.

"I don't guess it was altogether luck," he drawled, accelerating slowly. "You helped out your odds by casting your line in any spot where either Mr. Red or I had just gotten a strike."

"That's not true!" Katie's protest was sheepishly halfhearted. "Or at least not when I got a little older," she amended honestly.

"Besides," Louis went on imperturbably, "I reckon the fish must have known the rules, too. We weren't going to leave until you caught the biggest fish. They probably named some big old sucker as a sacrifice and pointed him to your lure just to get rid of us."

Katie's giggle joined his low, rich chuckle.

"Those were good times, weren't they?" she said wistfully. "Even though I was so jealous of you that I could hardly stand it, and you didn't like me very much." She met his quick glance and went on lightly, not wanting to destroy the companionable mood. "This is the sort of thing I meant a minute ago about people sharing memories they can't explain to somebody else. It occurred to me on that fishing trip that nobody but you could appreciate how happy and yet how sad looking back and remembering our fishing trips with my father made me feel." Katie swallowed, some of those same mixed emotions coming back now. Apologetic yet hopeful, she looked over at Louis, waiting for his reply.

"You're right. Those were good times," he said, not meeting her glance.

Katie was crushingly disappointed. His thoughtful agreement, tinged with reluctance, locked her out of his memories and left her with nothing to say. Why, she wondered, had he asked her out tonight? He probably didn't like her any better now than he had back then on those fishing trips.

"I can't understand why you'd be jealous of me."

Louis spoke hesitantly into the silence that had fallen between them. It took Katie a second or two to make sense of the remark and realize he was continuing the lapsed conversation.

"Why, I always assumed you knew that," she said, surprised. "Everybody knew my father wanted a boy more than anything, and there you were, the perfect example of the son he'd hoped for." She studied his profile and saw the doubtfulness in his frown. "How else would you explain the way I treated you when we were kids?" she inquired with a touch of impatience. "I know I was spoiled, but I didn't behave that way with anyone besides you."

He looked over at her, the frown still in place. "I knew you wanted all of your father's attention and that you resented my hanging around, but I never thought in terms of your being jealous of *me*." Louis shook his head. "I was certainly never a threat. Mr. Red thought the sun rose and set in you. He still does."

Louis's inflection on the last three words didn't escape Katie. She sighed, thinking how little things had changed. With her father, whom they both adored, between them, they would forever be at odds with each other.

"Well, I was jealous. Actually, I still am." She shrugged defensively, meeting his sharply questioning glance. "Come on, Louis," she chided. "The other day, when you were out giving my father the grand tour of the houses you'd built, didn't you stop to think that hearing about it would be like salt rubbed into a wound for me? There you were, the big successful contractor, and me without a single house to build. Don't tell me the subject of 'poor little Katie' didn't come up. Don't bother to answer that," she implored quickly.

She sighed in self-disgust. "I was so determined not to get off on my problems tonight, and here I go, first thing, bringing them up. Why don't we discuss something cheerful, like where we're going to eat?"

Katie held her breath, waiting for him to answer. His big hands were clenching the steering wheel hard, and she wasn't sure he was going to accept her change of subject. If they could just get past this difficult moment, she would keep the atmosphere light if it killed her.

"We'll eat wherever you say," Louis replied finally, sounding resigned.

"How about seafood?" she asked brightly. "I've been hungry for oysters lately. But I could be talked into a steak. What are you in a mood for?"

"Seafood sounds fine."

They decided on a popular seafood restaurant on the outskirts of town, and Katie made cheerful, determined conversation, using sights along the way as inspiration and mentioning bits of local news and gossip. Louis's responses seemed token efforts at first, but then he made a droll remark about a common acquaintance and joined Katie in her delighted laughter. After that, he relaxed and entertained her with one humorous anecdote after another. Katie's problem soon became hiding how incredibly attracted to him she was.

There wasn't anything about him she didn't like. She was pleased by his clean-cut good looks; his deep, quiet, lazy voice; his laid-back manner; his whole good-natured outlook on people and life in general. Katie wasn't surprised that he seemed to know everything going on around town. People would like him and warm to him now that he was a grown man the same way they always had, the way *she* always had, despite her sense of rivalry.

By the time he pulled into the gravel parking lot at their destination, her response to Louis was a pleasurable ache inside her. There was simply no point, she knew, in trying to make the ache go away. It was stronger than ever after twelve years of willing it dead.

So why worry about it? She would enjoy the evening in his company, be a companionable date, and maybe he'd ask her out again. After all, there had to have been some spark of interest behind tonight's invitation. Beyond that, she refused to think, refused to hope. If past experience hadn't killed his appeal for her, it *had* taught her a lesson: not to expect anything from him.

When Louis got out of the pickup and immediately came around to open her door, Katie prepared herself for the courteous contact of his touch, determined to be the perfect lady. Before tonight was over she would impress upon him that he didn't have to worry about her being pushy and forward as she'd been in her teens.

The restaurant was crowded. Katie and Louis spotted quite a few familiar faces among the diners, including several old friends from high school, and acknowledged friendly greetings all the way to their table.

Louis held her chair for her, and she gracefully accepted the courtesy. When their waitress arrived and asked if they'd like to order drinks, Louis looked inquiringly at Katie and she demurely told him, not the waitress, that she'd love a draft beer.

"Make that two drafts," he told the woman pleasantly. "And bring us a dozen oysters on the half shell while we're looking at the menu, will you?" He looked at Katie for confirmation. "You did say you wanted oysters, didn't you? Or would you rather have another appetizer? A shrimp or a crabmeat cocktail?"

"I'd rather have the oysters," Katie told him without hesitation. She smiled teasingly. "Your only problem will be getting your fair share."

"Better make that a dozen and a half," Louis amended to the waitress, warming Katie with his air of indulgence.

As they sipped beer served icy cold in frosted glasses, Katie found it hard to believe the earlier discord between them had actually existed. The oysters, when they came, were fresh and salty and succulent, and Katie ate with undisguised enjoyment, squeezing lemon juice on each and then dousing it in a sauce of catsup, horseradish and Louisiana hot sauce. Louis grinned at her as she made a little sound of satisfaction and sat back, having consumed her last oyster.

"It's a good thing we got here when we did," he drawled. "You must have been on the verge of an oyster attack. Then again, I seem to recall that you always did eat as though you were putting down your last meal."

"I'm better now. Most of the time," she added, smiling and feeling utterly contented. Happiness, she decided, was being there with him, sharing pleasant conversation and good food.

She watched him spear his final oyster with his cocktail fork and work it loose from its shell.

"They're gruesome-looking things, aren't they?" she mused, her mouth watering in spite of herself.

"Disgusting, when you stop to look at them," he agreed, dipping the oyster into her cup of cocktail sauce. Up until then he'd been eating his oysters with just a dash of hot sauce. "Open up," he ordered her, surprising her by leaning toward her and lifting his fork to her mouth.

Katie's eyes widened and met his before she obeyed, opening her mouth and letting him feed her the plump, delicious oyster coated with pungent sauce. It was an unexpectedly intimate, sensual experience.

"That was generous of you," she told him when she'd swallowed, looking down and reaching for her beer glass before she remembered that she'd taken the last sip a minute earlier.

"You were eyeing it so hungrily that I knew I couldn't possibly enjoy it." Louis's voice was a shade too hearty. "Here. You might as well have my beer, too. I'll order us a couple more." He quickly poured the remainder of his glass into Katie's, then reared back in his chair and made a production of searching for their waitress.

It didn't bother Katie that her heart had picked up its tempo and her pulse had quickened with the intimacy of the moment, but she sensed that Louis had experienced something similar and *did* mind his own reaction.

Why did he mind? she wondered with honest puzzlement. Why should he object to a perfectly normal flareup of physical awareness between the two of them?

The explanation that came to mind wasn't very flattering. Louis was probably being cautious, afraid to show interest and run the risk that she might chase after him the way she had as a teenager.

She guessed she really couldn't blame him. Their onesided high-school romance was probably an unpleasant memory for him. And he had no way of knowing that he was safe now. She'd never subject herself to that kind of rejection and humiliation again, but he'd have to figure that out for himself.

"Guess who I ran into the other day," she said conversationally. Louis reluctantly gave up his search for their waitress and turned his attention back to her. "Mean old Miss Prentiss who taught third grade. Remember her? You wouldn't believe it, but she looks exactly the same. Her scalp still shows pink through her hair, and she wears it knotted up in that same tight little ball on the back of her head. Her mind is clear as a bell. She looked at me through those wire-rimmed glasses and called my name right off in that same critical tone of voice. I felt like I was eight years old again and she'd caught me passing a note in class. I wouldn't have been at all surprised if she'd told me I had to stay in at recess."

Louis grinned broadly at Katie's humorous rancor. "Miss Prentiss. I'll be darned," he declared, seizing the conversational offering. "She must be a hundred years old by now. I thought she was at least that old when I was in the third grade." He shook his head, and his grin softened with reminiscence. "Lord, I'll never forget how hard that poor old lady tried to teach me penmanship. 'Louis, why do you insist upon writing a whole pageful on a single line?' she used to say to me."

Katie smiled at the accurate mimicry spoken with gentle amusement and no malice whatsoever. He was generous to people even in his memories, she reflected. No doubt he was equally generous looking back at her, though that thought didn't warm her very much. She'd much rather have been special.

"I remember how hard it was to make out your handwriting when I typed papers for you in high school," she recollected lightly. She deliberately looked over her shoulder at the salad bar as though the adolescent memory held no more than passing interest for her. "It looks like the line's thinned out," she remarked with casual interest.

"Why don't we take advantage of the lull?" Louis suggested, pushing back his chair, though without any sense of urgency.

Katie measured her success in his relaxed tone and easy, solicitous manner as he rose and came around to her chair. She'd relieved his discomfort by keeping things light, evidently the way he wanted them.

The salad bar offered an ample meal in itself, with crisp greens, fresh vegetables and fruit, coleslaw, potato salad, olives, cheeses and an array of spicy condiments.

"I always take too much," Katie lamented when they reached the end of the line. "They should put out smaller bowls."

She wrinkled her nose in distaste as Louis served himself from a large crock. He glanced up and grinned at her expression. "Aren't you having a little helping of mustard greens?" he asked teasingly. "They're good for you."

"I *hate* mustard greens," she replied, shuddering. "I'd just as soon eat cooked grass."

The smile lingered on Louis's lips as he accompanied her back to their table.

"I take it you still have definite likes and dislikes," he remarked when they were sitting down. "You always either loved a certain food or hated it. There was never any middle ground."

"I guess I haven't changed much in that regard," she admitted, picking up her fork. She took a quick bite of corn relish, trying to hide the clash of her emotions. "I'm *crazy* about this corn relish, for example," she declared. "And this is the only place I ever seem to get it."

She busied herself opening a packet of crackers, not daring to look at him for a moment or two, afraid he would catch her eyes and see how her insides had melted to have him speak of her in that warm, fond tone of voice. She just wished that he hadn't spoken of Miss Prentiss in almost the same tone minutes earlier.

Louis, fortunately, didn't seem to notice anything amiss, and Katie's turmoil quickly passed. The atmosphere was easy and companionable as they ate their salads and then the fried seafood dinners they had ordered. With at least a hundred impersonal topics they could talk about—people they knew in common, local politics, civic concerns—there was no shortage of conversation, and Katie was perfectly contented not to talk about building houses, which was bound to be a touchy subject.

After they finished eating they both ordered coffee, refusing the waitress's offer of dessert.

Katie took a sip of coffee immediately, since she liked it black and hot enough almost to burn her tongue. Watching Louis empty two packets of sugar into his cup with an absent-minded deliberation, she wondered if he was still planning to take her to Back Street, the local tavern he'd mentioned on the phone last night. So far he hadn't brought it up.

"I guess you were busy today, getting ready to start on Hemphill's house," Louis startled her by remarking. He was concentrating his full attention on thoroughly stirring his coffee. "Have you given any thought to what I suggested last night, maybe giving some of my subs a chance to work for you?"

"No," Katie replied honestly, watching him add cream until his coffee was almost overflowing. "I think you like a little coffee with your cream and sugar," she teased.

He grinned but didn't look up as he very carefully stirred, sloshing the diluted coffee over the sides of the cup.

"Usually I ask for half a cup. It slipped my mind this time." He bent and met the cup halfway as he lifted it, taking a gulp to lower the level of the pale contents. "You don't stand to lose anything," he remarked, looking at her for the first time since he'd started his coffee preparation. "By contacting the same subs that gave me bids on Hemphill's house," he added when Katie was momentarily bewildered.

"I thought for a moment there you were suggesting that I should order half a cup of coffee," she joked, taken aback by his serious expression.

Louis made a halfhearted effort at a smile, but he wasn't distracted.

"I don't mean to be pushy about this," he said earnestly. "I just hate to see you take on a job of that scale for nothing. You're looking at four to six months of hard work, as you well know. What could it hurt to check with my subs?" He took a hurried swallow of coffee, intending to answer his own question. "By making just a few phone calls, you stand to gain as much as some people make in a year."

"I suppose it wouldn't hurt to check with them," Katie agreed, purely to placate him. His intentions were good. What point was there in telling him that his suggestion would cost her more than a few phone calls? Her pride would be on the line again—what was left of it. She would try to get her own subs to come down on their prices, but even if they didn't, she'd stick with them.

"Good. I'm glad to hear you say that." Louis sounded relieved that the matter was settled. He motioned to their waitress, who was passing nearby with a coffeepot. He seemed suddenly impatient to get their cups refilled.

"You forgot to ask her for half a cup again," Katie reminded him with amusement, watching him rip open a sugar packet.

"Darn it all. I sure did," he agreed absently, giving her an abashed grin. After he'd emptied that packet, he reached for another, pursuing his thoughts aloud with utter earnestness. "Peewee Joiner is one of the best plumbers around, and he's very reasonable. And George Tucker can't be beat as an electrician. I had George do all the wiring for me when I added on to my mother's house a few years ago and also when I built on over the garage." Once again he was busy pouring cream and stirring. "W. L. Corkern does a fine job with heating and cooling."

Katie opened her mouth several times to speak as he reeled off names of workmen in the building trade, giving each of them his high personal recommendation. But she wasn't able to get a word in until he finally took a swallow of the coffee he'd doctored to his taste.

"Louis, all those guys you've mentioned are friends of yours, aren't they?" she asked him, puzzled at his insistence that she try to hire them. "I remember most of them from high school," she mused, knowing she'd feel impossibly awkward about contacting them.

"Sure. They're all good buddies of mine," Louis agreed, ignoring the reluctance in Katie's voice. "As a matter of fact, I'm expecting to run into most of them over at Back Street tonight. That is, if you'd like to go.

There's a new country and western band playing there tonight. I hear they're pretty good.''

Katie didn't need to be urged. "I'd love to go," she told him without hesitation, putting her napkin on the table. "There's nothing I like better than country and western music. It'll be a treat to hear a good live band."

She'd gladly have gone on to Back Street with Louis if the tavern had boasted nothing more than a jukebox. She was eager to continue the evening with him, wherever he suggested taking her.

Chapter Seven

To Katie's relief, Louis dropped the subject of how she intended to subcontract the Hemphill job, and she was saved from having to tell him that it was her problem, which she would handle her own way. Given a choice, she much preferred to avoid offending him. He was simply being helpful, not meaning to butt into her business.

On the short drive from the restaurant to the main part of town, they talked about country music and bands they liked. Katie sensed a slight nervousness on Louis's part and wondered if he was having second thoughts about taking her to Back Street, where she knew he was a regular. That was the reason she never went there herself.

During the daytime, the local establishment was a lunch place as well as a respectable bar, catering to a mixed crowd of white-collar workers and laborers. On weekday nights it did a moderate bar business, and on weekends it became a popular night spot, often boasting a band.

"Looks like the place is packed," Louis remarked when he had to cruise several blocks in search of a parking place.

Katie was half expecting him to change his mind about going and was glad when he didn't. She was in a mild, pleasant state of jitters as she walked beside him from the pickup to the tavern. His firm, warm grasp on her upper arm heightened her nervous anticipation. She felt ridiculously young and expectant and told herself she was simply looking forward to the loud music and a crowded, partylike atmosphere. After the pressures of the past six months, it would be good to let off steam and have a good time.

"You're right! The place *is* packed!" she exclaimed when they walked through the frosted glass door and found themselves immediately in the midst of a crowd. She practically had to shout for Louis to hear her. His arm circled her waist protectively, and she huddled close and let him guide her, not really caring where or with whom he found a spot for them.

From the looks of the outer room, there wasn't likely to be an empty table. Louis searched the crowded tables on their left and the long bar on the right, where people stood at least three deep. Farther back was the bandstand and dance floor. Through the dancers Katie could glimpse the open door to the back room. Louis headed them in that direction.

"They must be in the back," he said, bending to speak into her ear.

Katie didn't bother to ask who "they" were. Apparently he was expecting to see some friends. Perhaps he'd even asked them to save some space at a table.

All that really mattered to her was that she was here with him, feeling the springy tempo of the music in her veins and Louis's arm around her waist. As they skirted the dance floor she wished he'd forget about finding a place to sit and just dance with her instead.

But he either didn't read her mind or didn't share her impulse. Katie willed her feet not to drag as he guided her to the back room, which was also filled to capacity. Just inside the door they were hailed by a large group occupying several tables. Katie surmised from the greetings and the two empty chairs at one of the tables that Louis was expected, with a date. She had time for fleeting recognitions before he performed the casual introductions, speaking loud above the din of voices, laughter and pulsing country and western music.

"I think most of you already know Katie Gamble. Peewee Joiner and his wife, Marian, W. L. Corkern and Lisa Scott, George and Jo Ann Tucker..."

Katie had to work at keeping her smile in place as Louis named off the men and their companions. It seemed an incredible coincidence that the majority of the subcontractors Louis had been urging her to contact less than half an hour earlier were among the group. Then she relaxed somewhat as she recalled that Louis had mentioned the likelihood of running into them here tonight. Probably there was nothing unusual about the whole group getting together at Back Street on a weekend night with wives and girlfriends.

"Sit down, Katie," Peewee Joiner urged her hospitably when Louis had finished identifying everyone. He indicated the empty chairs at his table. "Big Mac here can fight his way back to the bar and get you two a drink. Lightning Linda is our waitress tonight," he added cheerfully to Louis, who made a pained face with instant comprehension. "You could build up an awful thirst waiting for her to make it over here and then back again with your drinks."

Katie had little choice but to try to hide her qualms about the situation. Not only was it disappointing to find that she and Louis were joining a party, but it was also damnably awkward for her that all of the men in the group were in the local building trade and undoubtedly knew of her professional difficulties.

"I'll stick with draft beer," she told Louis, managing a bright smile when he asked her what she'd like to drink. It helped that he apologized with his eyes for abandoning her and seated her solicitously before he left.

"I like the band. Especially the female lead," she said enthusiastically.

From the eager chorus of comments, she gathered that she wasn't the only one sensitive to Louis's absence. Amid the noise and general confusion, she took the opportunity to register details about her table companions.

Peewee Joiner was small, as his name hinted, but his wiry build suggested the sinewy strength required in the plumbing trade. His brown eyes and boyish features were full of puckish good humor. His wife, Marian, a heavyset brunette, didn't seem a likely mate for him at all. Katie vaguely remembered her as having been a couple of grades behind in school. She thought Marian had been in the school band.

W. L. Corkern, a husky blond man, seemed so shy that it was hard to believe he owned and operated his own heating and cooling business, managing a number of employees. Katie recalled him as a high-school youth, walking with his shoulders slightly hunched and his hands in his pockets. She had no recollection of his date, Lisa, who looked as though she'd stepped right out of the sixties, with waist-length brown hair parted down the middle and streaming over her shoulders and back. When Lisa spoke up, stating that she thought the lead singer sounded like Emmylou Harris, her Midwestern accent stood out immediately as proof that she hadn't grown up in the Covington area, like most of the others.

"Emmylou Harris!"

Everyone, including Katie, a staunch Harris fan, loudly dissented. Those at the adjoining tables were asked for their opinions. By the time Louis returned, holding two frosted mugs of beer, Katie was totally relaxed, glad to be simply a member of the group with no one paying her any special notice.

But when he sat down next to her and draped his arm around the back of her chair, the spotlight of attention focused on the two of them once more. Katie could understand that his friends were naturally curious; they probably would have been with any new date. She smiled self-consciously at Louis, aware of being under inspection, and saw that he was feeling ill at ease, too. When he lifted his mug to make a toast, she waited, expecting some joking remark to make them all laugh and ease off.

"Here's to Katie," he surprised her by announcing. "She just outbid me on a job I had lined up for all of you guys come January. Better treat her nice, fellas. She could keep you off the unemployment line."

Katie felt the color rising in her face as all eyes switched to her while Louis took a swig of beer. Then he cheerfully elaborated, drawing the attention back to himself and giving Katie an opportunity to collect herself as best she could. Why on earth had he done that? she wondered, too amazed to be annoyed. He might at least have warned her!

"I know the house you're talking about. It has a Jacuzzi in every one of the full baths." Peewee was the first to place the Hemphill house, and then the others chimed in with comments.

"That's a real nice house, Katie," W.L. told her, sounding shy even when raising his voice. "I liked the way it was zoned for heat and air conditioning, but, you know, there are some problems with the way the architect laid out the ducting. The plan needs modifying."

"Yeah, and there's no way there'll be room for that door into the third-floor loft bedroom," Petey Jenkins from the next table called over to her. Petey had his own framing crew and was Louis's choice for handling the first basic stage of construction after the foundation was laid. "Those damned architects just draw pictures and let us guys with the hammers find the space once we start building the house," he complained disgustedly.

Katie nodded, in complete agreement with him. All too often she had discovered that to be the case. But before she could respond, Marian cut in.

"Hey, you guys, no more talking about building houses! You know the rules! Right, girls?"

"Right!" all the women except Katie chorused in support.

"Come on, Peewee." Marian turned to her husband and tugged demandingly at his sleeve. "You promised we were going to keep the floor hot dancing tonight."

Peewee made a pretense of having to be dragged bodily from his chair, and the burly Marian looked as if she had the necessary muscle for the task. In the general hilarity, several other couples got up and went off to the dance floor, too. W. L. and Lisa stayed at the table but put their heads together for intimate conversation, leaving Katie and Louis suddenly stranded in a little oasis of privacy amid the noise and music.

Louis grinned uncertainly at Katie, evidently expecting reproach for the surprise publicity he'd given her new building venture, but she'd already gotten over her initial shock and was more interested in the men's reactions than in Louis's motive. Their insightful comments were too welcome for her to resent having been taken off guard. She would definitely follow up on the criticisms of the architect's plan, which her own subs hadn't made. But what really amazed her was the sincere, helpful attitude that had come across, with no condescension.

"It sounds like your friends go over a house plan with a fine-tooth comb," she observed, leaning close so that she could speak without being overheard. "They seem to take their work very seriously."

Louis looked enormously pleased—and enormously relieved? Katie wondered. Before she had a chance to analyze his reaction, however, his arm, lying carelessly along the back of her chair, closed around her shoulders in a warm hug, raising pleasure inside her like a delicious tide.

"They do take it seriously," he declared, smiling. "They stand behind their work one hundred percent. That's why they go over a plan that carefully in advance." He gave her shoulders a tighter hug, making her catch her breath with the thrill of it.

The more
you love romance . . .
the more
you'll love this offer

FREE!

Mail this heart today! (See inside)

Join us on a Silhouette® Honeymoon
and we'll give you
4 free books
A free manicure set
And a free mystery gift

IT'S A
SILHOUETTE HONEYMOON —
A SWEETHEART
OF A FREE OFFER!

HERE'S WHAT YOU GET:

1. Four New Silhouette Special Edition® Novels — FREE!

Take a Silhouette Honeymoon with your four exciting romances — yours FREE from Silhouette Books. Each of these hot-off-the-press novels brings you the passion and tenderness of today's greatest love stories . . . your free passports to bright new worlds of love and foreign adventure.

2. A compact manicure set — FREE!

You'll love your beautiful manicure set — an elegant and useful accessory to carry in your handbag. Its rich burgundy case is a perfect expression of your style and good taste — and it's yours free with this offer!

3. An Exciting Mystery Bonus — FREE!

You'll be thrilled with this surprise gift. It is a useful and attractive item and will be the source of many compliments.

4. Money-Saving Home Delivery!

Join the Silhouette Special Edition subscriber service and enjoy the convenience of previewing 6 new books every month delivered right to your home. Each book is yours for only $2.49 — 26¢ less per book than what you pay in stores — plus 69¢ postage and handling per shipment. Great savings plus total convenience add up to a sweetheart of a deal for you!

5. More Surprise Gifts!

Because our home subscribers are our most valued readers, we'll be sending you additional free gifts from time to time — as a token of our appreciation.

START YOUR SILHOUETTE HONEYMOON TODAY — JUST
COMPLETE, DETACH AND MAIL YOUR FREE-OFFER CARD

Get your fabulous gifts
ABSOLUTELY FREE!

MAIL THIS CARD TODAY.

PLACE
HEART STICKER
HERE

GIVE YOUR HEART
TO SILHOUETTE

Yes! Please send me my four Silhouette Special Edition novels FREE, along with my free manicure set and free mystery gift as explained on the opposite page.

NAME _____
(PLEASE PRINT)

ADDRESS _____ APT. _____

CITY _____ PROVINCE _____

POSTAL CODE _____ 335 CIC 81XT

Prices subject to change. Offer limited to one per household and not valid to present subscribers.

SILHOUETTE BOOKS "NO-RISK" GUARANTEE

— There's no obligation to buy — and the free books and gifts remain yours to keep.

— You pay the lowest price possible and receive books before they appear in stores.

— You may end your subscription any time — just write and let us know.

START YOUR
SILHOUETTE HONEYMOON TODAY.
JUST COMPLETE, DETACH AND MAIL YOUR
FREE-OFFER CARD.

If offer card below is missing, write to:
Silhouette Books, P.O. Box 609, Fort Erie, Ontario L2A 5X3

**Business
Reply Mail**

No Postage Stamp
Necessary if Mailed
in Canada

Postage will be paid by

**Silhouette Book Club
P.O. Box 609
Fort Erie, Ontario
L2A 9Z9**

DETACH AND MAIL TODAY!

As the band in the adjoining room swung into a popular sad love song, Katie suddenly wanted nothing in the world more than she wanted to dance with Louis.

"I love that song," she said wistfully.

"Would you like to dance?" he asked.

"I'd love to," Katie replied dreamily. She rose with the feeling of being a willing slave to destiny.

The dance floor was packed with couples lured from their tables by the slow love song. Louis threaded a path along the wall, protecting Katie with his body, until he found a small empty space and stopped, staking claim to it.

"There's not a whole lot of room for moving." He stated the obvious humorously, speaking close to Katie's ear as he put his arm around her waist and clasped her hand decorously.

Katie tilted back her head and smiled. Her heart was beating slowly and deeply in time to the throbbing tempo of the music. Slipping her arm up around his neck, she hummed the haunting tune as she eased close, her cheek following an old forgotten habit and seeking the hard haven of his shoulder.

His arm tightened a bit, but he still held her lightly as they started moving in step, restricted from doing much more than simply swaying together in time to the music. Katie's joy grew more intense, mounting with bursts of pleasure, as he drew her closer in stages and finally released her hand to slide both his arms around her waist and freed her to hug him with both arms around his neck.

It was the dance embrace of high school. Memory engulfed her and drugged her senses, taking her on a hazy journey back into time. She was dancing with Louis the way they had danced in the crowded gym, amid weaving teenage couples welded by the passionate strains of a love song. Then, like now, Katie had felt herself alone in the universe with Louis, their rhythmic embrace the only meaningful reality.

She had pressed as close to him as she possibly could, yielding totally to the emotions of the song and the aching sweetness of being held in Louis's arms. Her pleasure had been all the more intense for knowing that the song would have to end and that with the separation of their two bodies would come the jarring reality that Louis was merely a captive in her own romantic spell. Holding her wasn't the rapture of body and soul for him that being held was for her.

Dancing with him tonight, twelve long years after the last time, brought it all back vividly for Katie, but just for an emotional minute or so. Then differences overshadowed the similarities between long ago and now, shattering poignant memory and making her concentrate upon the present.

Louis was no longer a high-school youth with a man's big, strong body. He was a man. And he was holding her with the assumption that she was a woman, not a teenage virgin. The hard strength of his arms and the slow rotation of his hips and thighs against hers communicated an intimate sexual message. He'd taken pleasure from women, given pleasure in return and felt confident about the transaction. *Sample that pleasure with me,* he urged subtly with his body language. The invitation shocked and thrilled Katie, who for so many years had been off-limits for Louis. If he had felt any sexual interest in her before, he'd been careful not to show it, except that once, the night he'd taken her. And then he'd been so remorseful afterward.

This was different.

Here, finally, was something new in their relationship. Everything was not the same, locking them into the old, familiar, frustrating pattern. *Louis wanted her.* The realization filled her with wonder and a vague fear. There seemed no choice with Louis holding her close, just blind destiny.

Louis felt no more control over what was happening than Katie did. So far, so good, he had reflected with strained relief on the way to the dance floor. He was deeply grateful that everything was going so unbelievably well. Manipulating people, even with totally unselfish motives, simply didn't come naturally to him.

He felt like a damned undercover movie director, hoping like hell that everybody somehow did and said the right things. So far everybody had. Even Katie. No, especially Katie. In fact, she was making the whole crazy scheme seem worth the trouble and mental anguish.

He had to remember that Katie had always been able to play the angel when it suited her. And when she did, she was irresistible: fun-loving, sweet, eager to please.

Tonight she was definitely on good behavior. Once they'd gotten past the initial awkwardness of going out together and established the unspoken premise of letting bygones be bygones, Louis had found himself enjoying her company. Several times during dinner he'd even wished that this was simply a date, with no purpose other than having fun, and he and Katie were two normal people, a man and a woman, open to a mutually enjoyable relationship.

You and Katie? Don't be crazy, man. His common sense had awakened to warn him.

When he'd first put his arm around her on the dance floor, his main sensation was a nice familiarity that didn't seem threatening. She was slim and pliant in his arms, swaying gracefully to the music, just the way he remembered.

It brought back high-school days of dancing among a crush of other teenage couples in the gym. Her cheek nestled in precisely the same spot on his shoulder. Her arm circled his neck in the remembered way.

There was no keeping her at a safe distance now any more than there had been then. Louis was half amused as he tightened his embrace, holding her close, and then closer. Before he knew it, he was taking the next inevitable step, letting her hand go and holding her with both arms around her waist, just as he had in high school.

Then suddenly he wasn't amused anymore. The man in him was fully, rudely awake, reminding him that this wasn't a high-school dance. It was now. What he was feeling wasn't nice familiarity. It was desire.

He wanted Katie.

In all honesty, his lust should come as no surprise. He'd had fair warning on the three occasions recently when he'd been in her company and experienced a disturbing awareness of her as a woman. He had approached the date with her tonight prepared to combat his basic male instincts, expecting Katie to supply some inadvertent aid by simply being herself and reminding him of the necessity for resisting her.

He hadn't expected her to open the door to him, looking feminine and cute and shyly anxious that her appearance pleased him. Except for the one flare-up of emotion when she'd claimed she was jealous of him, there had been no antagonism to protect him, no element of confrontation. Katie had been a pleasant, delightful date, a model of ladylike behavior, and the physical attraction had been as strong as before for

Louis, but different. If she'd been anyone but Katie, he'd have enjoyed the undercurrents of interest between them.

But she was Katie. All evening it had taken that firm reminder of her identity to keep him levelheaded. He tried desperately to fall back on it now as an emergency measure.

This is Katie you're holding in your arms, he told himself to counteract his desire, without any premonition that the warning would backfire on him and have the opposite effect. With total unexpectedness it touched off an old, shameful memory, something he never thought about. The night he'd taken Katie came back to him with utter clarity.

He cringed with an old and new guilt, remembering. God, it must have been a terrible experience for her, all pain and no pleasure. He felt as if he should apologize to her, not just for having taken her when he shouldn't have, but for having been such an inexpert lover.

And for being stimulated now by the memory.

The intimacies he'd taken with Katie's body that night came back in devastatingly sensual detail, making Louis want her even more tonight. He hadn't taken off all her clothes, but his greedy hands had managed to find her warm, supple bare flesh. Her breasts had been tender little mounds against his palms and fingers. Her inner thighs had been satiny smooth and warm, exquisitely responsive, but he'd been in too great a hurry to savor stroking them apart. He'd been in a fever to plunge himself into the sweetness of her virgin womanhood.

He wouldn't be in a hurry now. He'd make love to her thoroughly, deeply. He'd satisfy her. . . .

As the music came to a throbbing finale, Louis stopped dancing and held Katie in a steel embrace during the last few notes, exerting his control and trying to recover from the combined erotic effects of dancing with her and remembering the one time he'd made love to her. An uneasy thought helped more than anything else to cool him.

Lord, he hadn't been subconsciously waiting all these years for another chance to make love to Katie, had he?

He dismissed the notion scornfully and concentrated on not looking as nakedly vulnerable as he felt as he took Katie back to their table.

She seemed to be in a daze of her own. He could well imagine the thoughts going through her mind, and he braced himself for the first direct meeting of their eyes. His face would tell a guilty story, he was sure.

But to his surprise, the test gaze didn't come. Katie almost seemed to avoid looking at him. As soon as they got to the table, she grabbed her purse, excused herself hurriedly and made for the ladies' room. By the time she got back, Louis had recovered and was ready with his jocular manner and a good-natured smile.

He finally got the searching glance from her he was expecting, but it was quick and uncertain, almost shy. Then she sat down and joined immediately in the repartee among the several tables. Louis picked up a forced note in the friendly animation in her voice, and it disturbed him to know that she was making an effort to be sociable.

Fighting an absurd feeling of suspense, he added his own joking comments and tried to act perfectly normal. But he was tuned in to every nuance in Katie's voice, aware of her slightest movement. He was certain that he was the only one around her who sensed her tension and felt it tighten when the band swung into another slow love song after a series of livelier numbers.

When members of their group started getting up to dance, creating a general turmoil, Louis could see her swallowing and struggling to keep a smile on her face. Before she could turn to look at him, he stood up with a pretense of laziness and declared, "Well, Katie, I guess we might as well get out there with the rest of them and push and shove. What do you say?"

She got up at once, with no reluctance. Louis felt a lurching sensation at her expression. She was already anticipating the moment when they would reach the dance floor, find a spot among the throng, turn toward each other and slip again into the close intimacy of their old high-school dance embrace.

God help him, he was anticipating it, too, so much that he ached.

"This brings back old memories, doesn't it?" he demanded with loud cheer over the noise.

Katie nodded and smiled, giving him a quick upward glance. Louis read her combined disbelief and wonder and knew his effort to wreck the mood had been wasted.

His hands felt possessive, guiding her. His body wanted to protect her, shield her from being jostled while he found a tiny spot for them on the dance floor. When she turned to him, his arms closed around her, bringing her home to him at once. He didn't bother with the futile preliminary business of first clasping her hand.

Nor did he waste his time trying to dispel his male pleasure in holding her by reminding himself that she was Katie. So what if she was Katie? Her identity couldn't cancel out the fact that she had slim, girlish curves and was cute and sexy. He was a normal man. He'd love to take her to bed. It turned him on to think of taking off her clothes and caressing her at leisure in advance of making deep, thorough love to her.

The fact was that he wouldn't do any of that. He would simply dance with her. Because she was Katie, it was far too risky to get involved with her. There were bound to be complications.

Chapter Eight

Lord, it's quiet out here after all that noise," Louis declared, breaking the midnight silence of the deserted small-town streets. Katie's shoes made delicate tapping sounds on the pavement as she walked beside him on the way to his pickup. He wondered if she was thinking ahead to what would happen next, now that they were leaving Back Street. *Nothing* was going to happen.

"The band was great," Katie remarked lightly, taking her cue from his hearty tone. "That was lots of fun. Thanks for taking me. I enjoyed meeting your friends."

"They certainly fell for you." Louis was so glad for the reminder of the successful side of the evening that he expressed his satisfaction openly. Katie's quick sideways glance told him he'd slipped up. "Not that I didn't expect them to like you," he added lamely.

"I liked them."

Her thoughtful tone was fair warning to Louis that he was about to face up to inevitable questions about the evening.

"That's good," he said cheerfully, bracing himself.

"I'm trying to imagine what it must be like to have your friends work for you as subs. Doesn't that ever make for problems?"

"Never." Grateful for the reprieve, Louis was almost fervent in his denial. "I can rely on them never to take any shortcuts, to show up when they're supposed to be on the job and to do their best work. That last counts more than anything else. They take as much personal pride in their work as I do in mine."

"I got that impression tonight." Katie hesitated, and Louis thought, *Here it comes now.* He was about to be put on the spot. "Did you happen to hear Peewee when he asked me if I wanted him to do the plumbing for me on the Hemphill house? Of course, he was probably just joking. Tomorrow he'll feel different when he sobers up."

"Hell, no, I didn't hear him!" Louis almost shouted in his exuberance, giving Katie a bone-crushing hug. It wasn't only her news that excited him, but also her manner of telling it, which raised hope that she would cooperate. "That's great news," he added in a calmer tone, realizing that he'd reacted with far too much enthusiasm. Katie's puzzlement was almost tangible. "Peewee won't change his mind," he went on as strongly as he dared. "He'd never have offered if he didn't mean it. I'd bet money on it that the others will work for you, too, if you ask them. I certainly hope you intend to."

"Louis, you had this all arranged in advance tonight, didn't you?"

It was more a mystified statement of the facts than a question. Louis was relieved that she didn't seem indignant.

"I guess it was pretty obvious, wasn't it?"

"Very obvious. You mentioned them all by name before we left the restaurant, and then there they were at Back Street." Katie's steps lagged suddenly as she was struck by a possibility that appalled her. "Louis, you didn't talk to them about me ahead of time, too?"

"No, I swear I didn't," Louis assured her, thankful that he could put the full force of honesty into the denial and into presenting the rest of his case. He was one hell of a bad liar. "I just let things take a natural course, and it worked out exactly the way I'd hoped. You liked them. They liked you. Now it's up to you and to them whether they work for you. You're not upset with me about it, are you, Katie?" he pleaded. "I would have told you what to expect, but I was afraid you wouldn't go along. I just wanted to get you together with those guys and give them a chance to know you. They operate a lot on personal instinct."

He still had his arm around her shoulders, and its warm weight strengthened the force of his appeal. Katie wished with all her heart that she could be angry with him instead of the way she felt, so disappointed that she ached. He had just explained his entire reason for asking her out tonight, and the charitable intent made her want to cry.

"No, I'm not upset with you." The words stuck in her throat.

"I didn't mean any harm. Honestly, I didn't." Louis defended himself with anxious concern for her. He almost wished she'd reacted with more fire. Her subdued mood was disturbing to him.

"I know you meant well. It was nice of you to put yourself out for me." Katie commended him tonelessly, hoping she could say what she wanted to say next with as little emotion as possible. "I just don't understand why you'd go to so much trouble to help me."

"Why, for old times' sake," Louis declared. He lengthened his stride to reach his pickup. "And tonight was no trouble," he went on in the same hearty tone, dropping his arm from Katie's shoulders and digging industriously into his jeans pocket for his keys. "I had a hell of a good time." He unlocked the passenger door, opened it wide with a flourish and smiled at Katie as he gallantly offered her his hand.

Katie couldn't manage a reply at that moment and certainly not an answering smile. Conscious of the cruel light from the streetlamp illuminating her face and the heartsick emotions that must show on it, she took Louis's hand with the least possible contact and sprang up quickly into the truck cab. As soon as she was seated, she immediately freed her hand and smoothed down her skirt, rubbing her palm against the denim to burn away the sensation of his touch. What a terrible fool she was to be so disappointed.

"You are upset with me," Louis accused softly, stepping closer. Katie could hear the distress in his voice.

"Sure, I'm upset," she admitted with a little shrug. "But I'll get over it. It's just my pride." He didn't move, giving her no choice but to glance over at him, and the sight of him standing there, big-shouldered and masculine and concerned, raised a wave of despair. She could only hope that her expression was hidden in the shadows of the truck cab. He was so near, within such easy reach, and yet utterly inaccessible to her, as he had always been. It was heartbreaking.

"I can understand your feelings," Louis said with gruff gentleness. "You'd rather not be in the position of needing any favors from anybody, even me." He made a wry, apologetic face. "Or maybe especially not from me. I only hope you won't let pride get in the way of your best interest, Katie. However you manage to get them to work for you, you won't be sorry if Peewee and W.L. and those other guys there tonight agree to be your subs on the Hemphill job. I can promise you that."

There was no doubting his sincerity or his urgency in convincing her, but even in her emotional turmoil, it struck Katie that he was being oddly persistent in befriending her for "old times' sake."

"It seems to matter an awful lot to you that I make a profit building Hemphill's house," she said uncertainly and could have bitten off her tongue when he stepped back quickly. Lord, she hadn't meant to sound pleading, as though she were begging him for an explanation she wanted to hear. "I think I know your real reason," she stated accusingly to cover up her shame. "You're trying to look out for my interests as a favor to my father, not to me. Isn't that true?"

"Katie, this job means an awful lot to you," Louis evaded humbly. "I hope you'll keep an open mind." Before she could answer, he closed her door.

Katie desperately summoned her dignity while he walked around to the driver's side—taking the long route around the back end of the truck, she noticed. No doubt he was expecting a scene and dreaded it.

"Katie—"

"Louis—"

They spoke in unison when Louis had slid behind the
wheel and closed his door. The reluctant note in his
voice called forth Katie's pride. She spoke sharply before he could make some apologetic explanation.

"I appreciate the trouble you've taken to put me in
contact with your subs, Louis. It wasn't wasted. I'll
check with them as well as with my own subs in the next
few days. I'd be a fool not to. Then, depending on what
kind of answers I get, I'll decide who I want to work for
me on the Hemphill job."

Louis nodded, acknowledging Katie's clear if unspoken message: Her choice of subs was her decision and
hers alone, not his, and she didn't care to discuss it further.

"I'm sure you'll pick the best men," he said earnestly, turning his attention to starting the truck.

Katie didn't answer him. From his hesitant manner
and the inordinately long time it took him to get the key
into the ignition, she sensed that he wanted to say more.
But whatever it was, she was dishearteningly certain that
it wouldn't make her feel any better. At the moment,
she couldn't think of anything that would.

On the few minutes' drive to her parents' house, she
sat as far away from him as possible. She made no effort at small talk, no pretense of being cheerful. With
everything out in the open, there was no point in acting
as though this were really a date.

In retrospect, she felt like an utter fool, taking such
pains with her appearance, agonizing over what she
would wear, trying her hardest to be good company
with the futile optimism that Louis would ask her out
again. There hadn't been the slightest chance that he
would. From the outset all her hopes and efforts had

been in vain. He'd asked her out with no interest in her personally.

The irony of it was that she couldn't even work up a case of righteous indignation against him, not with him glancing over at her guiltily, obviously at a loss for what to say to smooth over the situation. He hadn't meant to raise false hopes or to hurt her. He had simply been acting out of a sense of loyalty to her father, knowing that the best gift he could ever give Red Gamble was to look after Katie.

Why did Louis have to be such a basically nice human being? Katie wondered bitterly. If only he'd been a more despicable type, maybe she'd have gotten over her weakness for him long ago. Instead it had lingered through the years, like a partially banked fire, ready to flare up and cause her a fresh case of disappointment and heartache. She wasn't confident that she would ever recover from the burns.

"Here we are," Louis announced with forced cheer as he pulled into her driveway and turned off the truck engine.

"Safe and sound," Katie added with a hollow effort at answering cheer to let him know she was fully agreeable to getting the parting scene over with as quickly and painlessly as possible.

She was reaching for her door handle, intending to avoid the need for his helping her, when he popped the wheel up out of his way and sprawled sideways toward her. Katie looked at him in surprise and was taken aback by his leisurely attitude.

"It's late," she said uncertainly, glancing away from him toward the darkened house.

"Your folks have probably been asleep for hours," he suggested cheerfully, as if he were following up on her thoughts.

"I'm sure they have. They're lucky if they get through the ten o'clock news."

"My mother's a regular night owl. She stays up to all hours. I was thinking on the way here that neither one of us can offer to brew up some coffee."

Katie looked over at him searchingly, knowing that the drift of the conversation just *couldn't* be what it seemed to be.

"No, but I don't usually drink coffee this late, anyway." She would not leave herself wide open to him again tonight.

"I don't make a habit of it myself," Louis agreed. "My point is that living with parents can be nice in some ways, but at our age, it has certain drawbacks. Don't you find that to be the case?"

Louis was curious about her sex life, Katie reflected, astounded. Then she remembered the way he'd held her on the dance floor. Was he making a roundabout advance? Katie dismissed the notion, but not before it had made her pulse come alive.

"There is the lack of privacy," she agreed, telling herself harshly not to jump to any foolish conclusions. Louis was *not* interested in her personally. "But that can be a convenience as well as a drawback. I don't have to invent excuses not to invite a date in late at night."

The seat crackled under Louis's shifting weight.

"But I imagine there would be some times you wouldn't *want* an excuse," he speculated.

The thought of telling him it was none of his business crossed Katie's mind as she regarded him with open astonishment. The truth was that she couldn't bring

herself to cut him off or to ask him point-blank exactly
what his interest was.

"Living at home with my parents doesn't mean I
can't go to bed with a guy," she pointed out bluntly,
hoping to calm her flustered state as well as conceal it.
Her common sense told her this wasn't a sexual approach, but her body wasn't listening. "Most of the
men I go out with have their own apartments or con-
dos. It's easy enough to have sex. Quite frankly, I'm not
usually all that keen on the idea, if that's what you're
really asking."

Her answer appeared not to please him. He frowned
and looked troubled.

"You mean you don't like sex?" he asked her halt-
ingly.

"I guess that's about the size of it." Katie was flippant to cover her defensiveness and her confusion. His
reaction was baffling. Why on earth should it matter to
Louis whether she liked going to bed with other men or
not?

The answer came and was so painfully obvious that
Katie felt like the biggest possible fool—for the second
time that night. She had been blind not to see the point
of the surprise question-and-answer session from the
very beginning. Louis's conscience was at work. Nothing else.

"Don't worry, Louis. You didn't spoil sex for me for
life. I tried it several times afterward, under much better conditions, and still thought it was overrated."

The contempt in Katie's voice was for herself, not
him. God help her, she was disappointed, despite being
on her guard. "I've had affairs," she went on with less
emotion, seeing the dismay on his face. "There were
two guys in college I was serious about and one after-

ward. Take my word for it, I gave sex a chance." She shrugged to convey her lack of concern at her findings. "I guess I happen to be one of those women who don't find it all that great. But my feelings don't have anything to do with you."

Katie was emphatic in absolving him of blame, but she didn't intend to be more specific. She'd never really analyzed her basic disappointment with the sex act, but afterward she always felt like crying. Lots of women probably felt the same way, she reasoned—empty and cheated. It had nothing to do with physical satisfaction.

Louis didn't look any less burdened with guilt. When he sighed and stirred restlessly, Katie resigned herself to hearing an apologetic confession. If it would make him feel better, she'd listen.

"I know that first time with me had to be a bad experience." Louis's voice was low, chagrined, but the words weren't what she had been expecting. Before she could recover from her surprise and discipline her body's immediate response, he was continuing. "I thought about it tonight while we were dancing together and felt terrible."

"You thought about *that* while we were dancing?" She stared at him, shocked, and then looked away, flooded by the warmth of her embarrassment and a strange sense of intimacy. There was a disturbing seductive element for her in his revelation. She spoke briskly to counteract her loss of composure. "You shouldn't feel bad. It wasn't even your fault. It was mine. I all but forced you, and I've regretted it many times. I'm sure it wasn't the high point of your sexual experience, either."

"It's different for a guy," Louis confessed humbly. "Especially at the age I was then. Sex is good even when it's totally selfish."

"I guess that's just the way nature works. Actually, it makes me feel better to know it wasn't all bad for you." Katie tried to sound flippant to cover up her emotion. She was oddly grateful to Louis for what he was telling her; it pleased her to know that intimacy with her had been "good" for him, at least physically.

"But nature doesn't keep a guy from feeling rotten afterward, and not just from a moral standpoint."

Katie's heart took a wild plunge as Louis slid over the seat toward her. She could hear the friction of his jeans against the textured vinyl, the give of the springs under his weight, and the sounds added to her swell of panic at his approach.

"You mean the male ego?" she asked him breathlessly as he came up close to her.

"You can call it that, I guess." His fingertips touched her face, tracing her cheekbone and then her jawline. "A man can have a lot of regrets, looking back, Katie," he said softly.

"I wish you wouldn't feel bad on my account," she murmured weakly. "What happened was all my doing." The issue of blame seemed so totally irrelevant in the face of the pleasure coursing through her in response to his tone, his gentle touch, his devastating nearness. Gone were all her defenses, such as they were. She was utterly at his mercy.

"No, it wasn't all your doing," he denied huskily. "You couldn't have made me do anything I didn't want to do."

"But you *didn't* want to...." It was all shadowy, insignificant. What mattered was what he wanted from her *now*.

"I knew I shouldn't," Louis corrected her. "I knew it was wrong. I realize it's all water under the bridge now, but I'm sorry it was like that for you your first time, Katie, in the back seat of a car with a guy who was half-loaded. A girl's first time should be...different."

"I guess so," she whispered, willing to agree to anything with him about to kiss her. She let him turn her face toward him and closed her eyes as he brought his lips to hers.

His mouth was tender with remorse, the warm pressure achingly sweet, but the kiss didn't last nearly long enough. Katie made a protesting sound deep in her throat, and her lips tried to cling to his as he raised his head until there was just a feathery contact.

But he wasn't ending the bliss, just making a transition. When he brought his mouth against hers again, it was a different kind of kiss entirely, with no element of remorse, no reference to old deeds and old regrets. It was a kiss of passion, full of a man's promise of pleasure.

Katie responded to the harder pressure of his lips with the same little thrill of disbelief that she'd experienced on the dance floor, when he'd held her close against him and communicated his desire. *Louis wanted her.* It was a primal, satisfying fact at the very root of her existence. Nothing else mattered, not pride or self-preservation.

There was no consideration of holding back, no thought of not wanting to appear forward. Katie had no choice but to respond to his need. She put her arms around his neck because it was her fate to do so and hugged him with all her strength while she answered the demand of his kiss with total ardor. She urged him to bruise the softness of her lips, welcomed his tongue into her mouth, encouraged its masculine seduction and submitted to the intimate union time and time again until she was weak and breathless.

There was no chance to breathe, not with the miracle of his possession taking place. It wouldn't have done to pause, not with his hands caressing her back and shoulders and slipping down to clasp her hips. She didn't have the strength to protest when he pulled his mouth free of hers, muttering "God, Katie," but her instinct was to resist ending the kiss.

Louis wrapped his arms around her and drew her hard against him in a crushing hug. The imprisonment was heavenly. Katie nestled close, absorbing the tremor in his hard muscles and feeling the violent beating of his heart jar his broad chest. It was awesome and thrilling to know that she was responsible for the tumult he was experiencing.

Louis wanted her. No matter what he'd said the entire evening, no matter what he said now, she was certain of this knowledge, and it gave her joy.

"This is the kind of good-night kiss I can do without, at my age," Louis declared unsteadily, drawing in a long, ragged breath. His mind as well as his body was in turmoil. This was sheer idiocy. He couldn't take Katie to bed. But, God, he wanted to.

And she was his for the taking.

"I can see a certain humor in it, though, considering our previous conversation," he remarked, loosening his embrace. "Here we'd just finished discussing the lack of privacy we both have living at home." Which she had claimed she didn't mind, not liking sex. *He could make love to her and give her pleasure.* Louis's confidence was so deep and possessive that it shook him.

Katie sighed and raised her head reluctantly as he pulled away from her. She couldn't resist combing her fingers through the back of his hair before she drew her arms from around his neck. His hair was soft and silky. Then briefly she stroked the strong juncture of his neck and shoulders and felt the muscles bunch before she took her hands away.

"I know what you're thinking," she mused, shy with a new sense of feminine power she'd never had with Louis and never wanted with any other man. "Just now I didn't exactly act like a woman who doesn't get turned on to sex. But kissing and holding don't count." She smoothed her hair and smiled at him.

Louis knew it wasn't a come-on or a challenge for him to take her in his arms again and turn kissing and holding into sexual foreplay and drive her crazy, make them "count," but that's what he wanted to do. He wanted to make Katie *want* him. The situation was a sobering turnaround from anything he'd ever expected, and it scared the hell out of him.

"I guess we'd better call it a night," he said, sliding over behind the wheel. "This brings back high-school days and makes me feel as old as Methuselah, making out in a parked car in a girl's driveway. Here I am without even a decent back seat." He glanced over his shoulder and made a wry face. "If I had one, it'd probably be buried in junk like this one, too. Tomorrow's Saturday. Maybe I can bribe my daughter and your niece into cleaning the inside of this thing out for me."

Katie regretted his retreat, but his strained effort at a light touch added to her warm glow.

"It could be an all-day project with that accumulation you have back there," she teased. "And those two little girls don't work cheap." Katie would willingly help him cheaply, her only price the pleasure of his company. The thought of the two of them in his driveway, cleaning his truck, laughing and joking, was so appealing that it made her wistful. But he wouldn't suggest it, and she had important things to do tomorrow, anyway. She needed to contact subs and get house plans to the ones who would agree to take another look at the Hemphill specs and reconsider their bids.

"You could just drive to the dump and push it all out," she proposed with absent humor, thinking of all the telephone calls she would have to make. "You'd have time in the morning before the football games start." Her thoughts switched back to calling the subs the next day. "At least it's easier to get in touch with workers on weekends during football season. They're usually home in front of the TV."

Louis followed her mental train of thought and the reminder of the building job she was taking on and his own obligation for making it go smoothly for her cooled him off abruptly.

"Just be sure you don't call them during the LSU game tomorrow," he advised. "It's being televised, since it's out of state. You could get a lot of people mad at you by interrupting them in the middle of a play."

"I forgot about the LSU game!" Katie exclaimed and then smiled in agreement with him. "Don't worry. I wouldn't think of calling during the game, which is just as well. I'll want to watch it myself." Like most native south Louisianians, she was a fan of the major state university football team, even though she hadn't gone to Louisiana State University.

"Come over and watch it with me at my office,"
Louis invited. "My mother hates football, and I'll be
out there when it comes on, anyway, trying to catch up
on paperwork. You can use my telephone at halftime," he offered, as though Katie needed inducement.
"I have all the numbers for my subs handy. I could
show you the bid I gave Hemphill with the breakdown
on prices, and you'd have each guy's estimate right
there while you talked to him."

Louis tried to sound casual about being helpful, but
it wasn't easy. He'd feel so damned much better once
she'd lined up the workmen he knew he could trust to
do a good job.

"What time is the game?" Katie asked, as though the
scheduling had some bearing on her answer, when, of
course, it didn't. She was torn, knowing she really ought
to make her position clear to him and risk offending
him. She should tell him that she'd like to come over
and watch the game with him, but she preferred to call
his subs on her own. She should thank him for his
helpful attitude but state firmly that, being perfectly
capable, she preferred to handle her job herself.

"I think kickoff's at eleven," Louis replied, sensing
her hesitation. "That works out perfectly. I can run out
for lunch at halftime. There's plenty of cold beer and
soft drinks in the refrigerator. What do you say?" he
cajoled, now completely sold on the idea. If she didn't
accept, he'd be genuinely disappointed, whether he
could push the business of her calling his subs or not.
He preferred not to analyze his motives too closely,
however.

"It sounds too good to pass up." Katie couldn't bring
herself to make an issue of her independence. Why risk
hurting his feelings and deprive herself of a pleasant

afternoon in his company? She could avoid his generous interference without being outspoken. "I'll bring some snacks," she offered, putting aside the feeling of having compromised herself.

"That'd be nice. And, hey, how about a handful of your mother's cookies for dessert?" Louis smiled sheepishly at his blatant wheedling.

Katie smiled back at him, amused and warmed by the boyish eagerness in the voice of the man.

"I think I can manage to bring those, too, without any trouble. My mother's cookies weren't, by chance, the whole purpose behind this invitation to watch the game with you, were they?" she demanded.

Louis grinned.

"Let's just say you made the right answer." He sighed reminiscently. "Thanks to your mother's cookies, I can't start up a lawn mower without having my mouth water. If you remember, when I cut the grass at your house, your mother would always fix a pitcher of something cold for me to drink and set it inside the back screen door."

"Your favorite was grape Kool-Aid," Katie put in with a little face at his preference.

"I still like grape Kool-Aid," he admitted. "But it didn't matter what was in the pitcher. Your mother used to put the cookie jar alongside it." He shook his head. "I'm embarrassed to remember what a pig I was." He sobered and looked hesitant at sharing his thoughts. "Your folks are such good people, Katie. They were both awfully nice to me all the years I was growing up. I have a real soft spot for them."

"They think a lot of you, too, Louis. Now I'd really better go in. It's getting late."

His honest emotion touched her and yet stirred deep, complex regrets. She was forever bound to him by the past they shared and yet forever held at a distance. Those feelings he confessed for her parents were responsible for her being there in the truck with him. They were behind his invitation for tomorrow. He was trying to do a good deed for her, wanting to help her get subs to work for her reasonably so that she could make a profit building the Hemphill house.

There was an element of guilt involved, too. He had regrets about his teenage lust, apparently a concern for the damage he might have done her. Naturally he took full responsibility. In his conscientious way, he probably had some misguided intention of making restitution to her personally as well as repaying her parents.

It was all too complicated and not at all flattering or satisfying. Katie wished with all her heart that things were different. But they weren't. And never would be.

"It's a date then: tomorrow at eleven," Louis said anxiously, sensing the sudden change in her mood.

"It's a date," Katie confirmed bleakly.

Chapter Nine

Katie was up early, as usual. It was Saturday, and she'd gone late to bed but she couldn't possibly sleep in this morning. She had important things to do; the day was calling her.

It was exhilarating to have the sense of pressure again. She loved being busy, being on the run, having to coordinate half a dozen tasks at one time. With just the Hemphill job, once she had it under way, she wouldn't be too pushed, but, Lord, she was looking forward to the next several months of being involved in building a house again.

She got on the phone as soon as the hour was close to reasonable for calling on a Saturday morning. She hoped to reach Louis's subcontractor friends before eleven o'clock so she could avoid any hassles over conducting—or refusing to conduct—her business in his office later in the day.

Louis. The thought of him made Katie sigh and smile as she got dressed. The several contacts with him over the past few weeks had been like electric shocks, bringing to life a part of her that had been deadened for a long time. She'd fought the awakening until last night and then given in to it completely, with her eyes wide open to the realities.

As it had been when she was in her teens, it was simply impossible for her not to respond to him. His appeal was enormous. She loved a hundred details about his looks and his physical presence. She was charmed by his personality. He was humorous and easygoing and fun to be with. She admired so many of his character traits. He was kind, honest, generous, hardworking, responsible. He was a basically good, decent human being. Katie was hard put to name a serious flaw. Small shortcomings, like untidiness, as evidenced in his truck and his office, only endeared him to her.

After all these years, Katie was still enamored of Louis. It was a weakness she didn't understand, but she had it in perspective. She simply must not *expect* anything from Louis or make demands. Then there couldn't be devastating disappointment or rejection.

The fact that he wanted her sexually was new—and thrilling in its novelty—but it didn't really change anything. Louis was a normal man with normal sexual needs, and Katie wasn't the victim of an inferiority complex. She knew she was reasonably attractive and blessed with a slim, youthful body. She'd had her share of male interest, her share of compliments, her share of passes.

No, she wasn't fooling herself into thinking she was special simply because Louis had taken a man's pleasure in dancing with her and kissing her. Her identity might have added to his stimulation, because of the old taboo and a sense of caution arising out of their past, she realized, but his physical response to her was biological, male. He could have felt the same sensations with any woman.

With Katie it had been different. Her pleasure had been solely a matter of identity. Because he was Louis, she'd loved the feel of his arms around her, loved the intimacy of kissing him, loved having him hold her and touch her. She wouldn't have felt the same with any other man.

But her weakness for him didn't change her feelings about sex, which she'd confided to him last night. She'd tried sex and found it a meaningless transaction.

Katie wasn't expecting Louis to try to have an affair with her, despite his attraction. Katie wasn't expecting *anything*. But going to join her parents in the kitchen, her mood was light as her thoughts skipped through her morning and came to eleven o'clock, when she would go to Louis's office. She smiled, remembering his request for her mother's cookies.

"Don't you look bright-eyed and cheerful this morning!" Edna glanced up from taking a pan of biscuits out of the oven to greet Katie. She smiled coyly as she transferred the biscuits to a plate. "I didn't know if you'd be up in time for breakfast or not. I woke up enough to glance at the clock when you came in last night. It was after midnight. Did you have a nice time?"

Katie inhaled the delectable aromas of hot biscuits and fresh-brewed coffee.

"Mmm. How could anyone sleep with all these good smells circulating in the house?" she demanded before she answered her mother's inquiry. "I had a very nice time last night." She gave her father a loving pat on the shoulder in response to his rumbling "Morning, honey," and then picked up the pitcher of orange juice on the table and started pouring it into the glasses. Edna already had the margarine and an assortment of home-made preserves set out. The table was set for three, de-spite the expressed doubt about Katie's appearance.

"We ate at Seafood World. I'd been dying for oys-ters, and they were delicious. Afterward we went over to Back Street and ran into a bunch of Louis's friends and their wives. We all sat together. There was a really good band, so the place was packed." Katie good-naturedly volunteered all the information she knew her mother wanted to hear.

Edna brought the plate of biscuits and the coffeepot to the table. Red Gamble liked his coffee made the old-fashioned way, in a drip pot. A coffee maker, a gift from one of the daughters, sat on the counter unused.

"It does sound like you had a real nice time," Edna commented approvingly, filling her husband's cup first, then Katie's and her own before she returned the pot to the stove and came to sit down. "That Louis is such a handsome man. And so nice. When your daddy came home the other day and mentioned how Louis kept bringing up your name, I told him Louis was interested in you."

"Edna," Red rebuked her in his deep, rumbling voice. "You talk too much, woman."

"When was this?" Katie asked casually, splitting open a steaming hot biscuit. "The day Louis took you out for a drive?" She addressed her father and then carefully spread margarine on her biscuit, ignoring the silent communication between her parents.

Edna answered, obviously chastened.

"Louis just seemed real interested in what you were going to do in place of building houses, whether you might be thinking of going back to college. That's this year's batch of crab-apple jelly. Be sure and try it. I think I might have gotten a little too much sugar in it."

Katie was making her choice from the several jars of her mother's homemade jellies and preserves. She obligingly spooned a dollop of pale amber jelly onto one half of her biscuit, clamped the two halves together, and took a big bite.

"It's good," she murmured with her mouth full and waited until she'd chewed and swallowed for a fuller commendation. "It is a little sweeter than last year's, but I like it." Edna beamed gratefully, watching Katie take a swallow of coffee. "No wonder Louis thinks you're the world's greatest cook," Katie went on cheerfully, seeing a natural opening. "He raved on about your cookies last night. I had to promise I'd bring him some today. He invited me over to watch the LSU game with him," she added and finished eating her biscuit, pretending not to notice Edna's smug glance at her husband. "Do you think LSU is going to win?" Katie asked her father innocently and kept the talk on football for the remainder of breakfast.

The information her mother had supplied was most intriguing. Katie had been jealous and resentful of Louis and her father going out together, and defensive about being a subject of discussion between them.

But she'd assumed that her father would be the one to mention her, not Louis. Yet apparently Louis had, and in a way that caught her father's attention. Otherwise Red wouldn't have remarked on Louis's interest to Edna. Her father was a down-to-earth man, not the type to make something out of nothing.

Had Louis taken to heart Katie's bitter complaints about the male-chauvinist building community, of which he was a member in good standing? Had he felt bad because she was being treated unfairly?

More than likely that was the answer. Then, when she'd gotten the Hemphill job, thanks to his own heavy building commitments, he'd generously decided to do everything he could to help her. Katie didn't want to make something out of nothing either, but for the first time she could think of Louis and her father together and not be jealous. It was very strange. She couldn't explain it. But Louis's pumping her father about her removed the element of competition.

Katie's morning telephoning went well. She was warmed by the friendly reactions of Louis's friends to her, but she tried to remain pleasantly businesslike. She didn't want to capitalize upon their liking for Louis and make working for her seem in any way a favor to him.

Peewee Joiner didn't hesitate when she asked him if he'd like to give her a bid on the Hemphill house, which she would be starting on immediately.

"Hell, yes. I'll be glad to give you a price. I've already been over the plans. If there haven't been any changes, I can stick with the bid I gave Louis. Why don't you check with him, if you don't mind, and ask him what it was? I'm sure I have the numbers written down somewhere, but it'll save me the trouble of looking." He made a joking reference to his fuzzy head after last night's partying.

"I don't mind. I'll be seeing Louis later today."

Katie hung up, pleased, and approached the next call with more confidence. George Tucker agreed to give her a bid on the electric work, and Petey Jenkins on the framing, although Petey expressed some doubt about being able to get to the job immediately.

"I'll have to check with Louis and see how much leeway he can give me on a job I have lined up for him."

Katie bit her lip and let the comment pass. Realistically she knew Petey wasn't the only man who would "check" with Louis. Probably all his subcontractor buddies would be seeking his opinion.

Both George and Petey saw the same advantage that Peewee had, being already familiar with the house plan and having previously worked up cost figures. They implied that those figures would be the same for Katie as for Louis, and they promised to get back to her by Monday.

Katie got a recorded answer when she dialed W. L. Corkern's number, not really expecting to find him home. He probably spent the night with his girlfriend, Lisa Scott. She left a message.

It had been worth contacting Louis's subs, Katie concluded, just for the sake of morale. She was heartened and encouraged to think that she did have options in the work force. As she set about telephoning her own subs, who'd given her unreasonably high bids, she was determined to be tactful, not wanting to burn bridges, but put some pressure on them to come down on their prices if they wanted to work for her.

When she closed her office door behind her at ten-thirty and crossed the lawn to the house, her step was springy and she hummed a lively country and western tune. She felt good about her morning and was looking forward to the rest of the day. The sun shone brightly, and the temperature was already up to seventy. There would be lots of sailboats on Lake Pontchartrain today, crisscrossing between nearby

Mandeville and New Orleans or just tacking back and forth near either shore. Water-skiers would be out in force on the Tchefuncta River at Madisonville. Weekend fishermen would be buzzing up and down the cypress-fringed bayous in their outboard aluminum flats, with ample coolers of ice for their catch and their beer.

Katie had spent her Saturday morning on the telephone, conducting business. She would be indoors the better part of the rest of the day, watching television, a boring prospect for some. But in her frame of mind, she was exceedingly fortunate in her recreational plans. She wouldn't have considered changing them.

She wore the same clothes over to Louis's that she'd dressed in that morning: jeans with a Western belt and a close-fitting T-shirt with the tail tucked in. She'd never liked wearing loose, floppy clothes. Scuffed Western boots completed her comfortable outfit. Aside from lipstick she didn't bother with makeup, and attending to her hairdo was a matter of running a comb through her vibrant red cap of hair and then giving her head a little shake. She'd feel silly showing up at Louis's to watch a football game looking as if she'd dolled herself up.

Louis's pickup was parked in his driveway. It was easy to see that it hadn't been washed that morning. The streaks of red foundation clay still decorated the sides. Carrying a paper bag with chips, dip and nuts she'd purchased at the closest convenience store and a foil-wrapped packet of Edna's cookies, Katie paused and looked into the back seat of the pickup's cab, a knowing smile on her face.

The debris was all there, undisturbed, including, she knew, the can Louis had tossed onto the collection last night. Before she walked on to the steps at the side of the garage, her eyes rested briefly on the broad front seat, and memory brought warmth to her cheeks and a kind of wondering skepticism. Standing in the bright sunshine, it was hard to believe last night's passion and intimacy or even the deeply personal revelations.

Recollection made Katie's heart beat faster and made her feel even more alive. She had to curb her exhilaration as she climbed the stairs, her boots clomping noisily on the wooden treads. She'd climbed them once before, a few weeks earlier, her heart pumping with dread. What a wonderful difference there was this time, when she was expected!

Louis opened the door before she had a chance to knock.

"Come on in. I'm glad you're here. I was just on the verge of losing my mind. This paperwork is killing me." He stood holding the doorknob with one hand and shoved the fingers of the other hand roughly through his tangle of black curls, obviously not for the first time that morning. He looked frustrated yet sincerely welcoming.

Katie's pleasure in her reception and in the sight of him was intense. He was dressed similarly to her, in jeans and a dark T-shirt, and looked incredibly masculine. Instead of boots, he wore leather moccasins with the thongs loosely tied.

"Cheer up. I brought the cookies," she assured him gaily, aware that her smile was extending almost ear to ear.

"You look like you had a good morning," he remarked.

"I had an absolutely fantastic morning!"

Katie strode jauntily over the threshold past him.

"It looks like Mr. Clean lives here," she declared, eyeing the orderliness. He'd apparently straightened up in anticipation of her visit. The couch was cleared, and there were no dirty glasses and cups or empty bottles and cans to be seen. She smiled without comment as she glanced down at the opposite end, which was unchanged since the last time she'd seen it. His desk was buried under a mountain of papers, filing cabinets were partially opened, the floor a litter of catalogs and samples and rolled-up plans.

"Feel free to go ahead with what you were doing until the game comes on," she offered cheerfully, walking over to the tiny kitchen area. He had the television on, and a pre-game program was in progress.

"Don't be so nice to me," he retorted feelingly, appreciating the back view of her slim, leggy figure as she emptied her paper bag. Her jeans were a perfect fit, not too tight but hugging her pert bottom and encasing her trim thighs. Her hips were delicately curved, her waist small, her shoulders slender. It would definitely be nice to walk up close behind her, fit her to the front of him, reach his hands around to her breasts....

"Do you have a bowl for these potato chips or shall we eat them out of the bag? I brought dip, too, and nuts. Do you have a couple of small dishes for them?"

Katie half turned to look at him and caught him smack in the midst of intimate male speculation. He could feel his face redden.

"I could go over and get whatever you need from my mother's kitchen," he offered apologetically. "Otherwise I'm afraid we'll have to rough it."

"Eating out of the bag and the can is fine with me." Unconcerned, Katie turned back toward the counter.

Louis eyed her with more mild dissatisfaction than relief that she hadn't seemed to notice his embarrassment. She seemed intent on preparing her snacks and sampling them.

"These potato chips are fresh," she reported, crunching noisily. "And the dip's not bad. There wasn't much of a selection." Louis heard the suck of air escaping the nut can as she opened it vigorously and then did a quality check on them, too. "Gosh, everything tastes so good," she declared, still chewing. "I didn't realize I was hungry."

"You certainly are in a good mood," Louis remarked as she turned around and smiled at him, holding the bag of chips in one hand and the dip in the other. "What did you do this morning? Sleep late?"

"Goodness, no. I was up at six-thirty. I just made a lot of telephone calls and had some good results." Katie was busy transferring her snack offerings to the coffee table while she answered him. Then she sat down on the sofa and gestured invitingly. "Help yourself." She took her own advice, scooping out a handful of nuts. "Oh, good, the game's coming on. My timing is perfect. I guess you don't have time to do any work after all."

"It's just as well," Louis replied dryly, coming over to the coffee table and bending down to plunge his hand into the bag of chips. "I couldn't afford to leave you alone with the goodies, anyway."

Katie was chewing and watching the screen. She gave him a quick smile and turned her attention back to the game. LSU had gotten the toss and had chosen to receive. The Alabama team kicked off, and an LSU receiver caught the ball and made an impressive number of yards before he was downed.

Louis followed the action mainly through the commentary. He found himself watching Katie instead, amused by the way she stopped eating in her excitement and strained with the intensity of urging on her team. Then she began to eat double-time, popping her peanuts one at a time into her mouth.

"Don't you want to sit down?" Katie asked him, finally noticing that he was still standing.

"I was thinking that maybe I should go out and get lunch right now instead of waiting for halftime," he drawled, coming to sit beside her.

"I can make it to halftime," she promised, smiling broadly at his good-natured dig at her greediness. "You don't want to miss any of this. It's supposed to be a really close game."

It was a close game, but Louis had a hell of a time trying to watch it. He was distracted by Katie, through no conscious effort of hers, and his vague arousal refused to go away. He was conscious of her every movement, and Katie at her most relaxed, as she was today, was seldom still for long. She reached forward, coming more into his line of vision, helping herself to chips and dip and peanuts, until she took the edge off her appetite.

Then she lounged back, propping her boots on the coffee table and clasping her hands behind her head, declaring that the rest was his. Louis knew that she didn't have any concept of being provocative, but her position lifted her breasts and stretched the T-shirt upward to mold the undersides of the small peaked mounds, making them extremely noticeable. He knew she had no intention of drawing attention to the sleek line of her thigh when she crossed one leg over the other and moved her knee up and down ever so gently.

Louis could feel her energy, even though it was at a low ebb and not a tense force as it could be when she was unhappy. She definitely wasn't unhappy. He couldn't believe the change in her. She wasn't the same young woman of a couple of weeks ago, bitter and on edge and ready to lash out. Getting the Hemphill job had put the old sparkle back into her personality. Having the chance to do her job as a builder meant everything to her. It was a gratifying but sobering realization.

Louis was glad he'd gone out on a limb for her, but the solution to her problems was only temporary. The Hemphill job wouldn't last forever. What then? Though a major success might turn the tide for Katie, it just as easily might not. She might be up against the same stubborn prejudices again, even if the house turned out perfect, and Louis would do his best to see that it did.

"You said you spent the morning making telephone calls and had good results. I assume you were contacting subs." Louis brought up her explanation for her high spirits during a commercial break in the game. He'd have been hard put to tell the score.

Katie couldn't detect anything but hesitant curiosity in his voice. Nor were there telltale signs of foreknowledge in his face.

"I'm surprised you didn't get a report on some of my calls," she remarked with a trace of skepticism. "Do you mean not a single one of your friends got in touch with you this morning after I got in touch with them?"

"You mean you called Peewee and George and the others?" Louis was obviously surprised and pleased. "No, I haven't heard anything from them." Then he glanced toward his desk with a comprehending, sheepish expression. "But then, they'd have had to drop by.

I have the phone unplugged. Have you lined those fellows up to work for you, then?'' he asked her eagerly.

"Peewee was the most positive. By the way, he told me to get his bid on the Hemphill house from you."

Louis nodded. "Sure. I'll be glad to give it to you. What about the others? What did they say?"

Katie reported on each of the conversations and her failure to reach W.L. She found herself feeling twice as glad she'd made the calls because Louis was so obviously pleased.

"W.L.'s probably at Lisa's place in Abita," he conjectured. "She's a back-to-the-earth type and doesn't have a phone. But he'll call you. And don't worry, I'll work it out so that I can free up Petey to do your framing. You're going to be all set, Katie."

In his exuberance Louis ruffled her hair and then smoothed it with big, gentle fingers, much the same way Katie remembered his doing to her niece Lisa's. But Katie's reaction to his affectionate touch was different from her niece's, she knew, and so, she thought, was his. And he didn't take his hand away, but dropped it to her neck.

"Don't jeopardize your own work schedule because of me," she insisted weakly, looking at him. "Petey's your regular sub, not mine."

"I'm not jeopardizing anything." Louis reached with his other hand and brushed away a tiny fragment of potato chip from her bottom lip and then couldn't draw his hand back when her lips parted on a little intake of breath. He stroked his forefinger along the tempting soft fullness, teasing, "You've eaten all your lipstick off."

"I made a complete pig of myself," Katie murmured.

"The game's back on," he pointed out huskily, his thumb playing with her bottom lip.

"I hear it."

She didn't give him any choice but to kiss her. Her eyes were wide and startled with her awakened sensuality, her lips an irresistible temptation.

"You're going to miss something important," he warned softly, moving closer and sliding his hand along her face to keep it uptilted.

"I don't mind."

Katie's deep breath accompanying her admission lifted her small breasts against her T-shirt. Louis glanced down, following male inclination. When he looked back to her face again, he knew from her expression and her faint color that he'd betrayed himself. He wanted to do a lot more than kiss her.

"It isn't that private out here," he warned her and brought his lips to hers before she could answer.

The caution was for himself, and he hoped it would help him maintain restraint. Katie turned toward him and slipped her arms around his neck. Louis could have kept control if he'd contented himself with kissing her, but he couldn't keep his hands from caressing her. He was his own worst enemy, acquainting himself with the slim curves and planes that had enticed him since she'd arrived.

At first he stayed on fairly safe territory as he had last night, stroking her back and shoulders while he enjoyed the softness and the generous shape of her mouth from different angles. She was slender and warm beneath the T-shirt, which stretched and gave under his palms and fingers. But then as the kiss became more intimate and their tongues came into play, he slid his hands lower, shaped the slim curvature of her hips and indulged himself in caressing and squeezing her rounded bottom, which was soft yet resilient, as sexy and pleasing to his man's touch as to his man's eye.

After that there was no stopping the natural progression of taking liberties, especially since Katie made no objection. In fact, her response to the increasing hunger of his kiss incited him and left his hands free to roam. She held the back of his head and took the hard, restless pressure of his lips with the generous softness of hers. Her mouth parted to welcome him into satiny warmth that promised deeper feminine intimacy. Her tongue coupled with his with greater and greater urgency, exciting and not satisfying her either, judging from her breathing, which, like his, was faster and audible, a sound of passion that egged him on.

Feeling the hard burgeoning of his body, it occurred to Louis that he ought to stop, but he didn't heed the glimmer of common sense. He didn't want to, not yet. He kept kissing her and moved on to caress the supple length of her thighs, then came up with delicious anticipation to her breasts, which were rising and falling with her breathing. They fitted his hands perfectly when he claimed them.

By now Louis was fully aroused and couldn't hear any inner alarms.

"Katie, you feel so good to me," he muttered against her lips, pulling her shirt free of her jeans with the blind purpose of feeling her bare skin.

"Louis, you're not going to take my clothes off!" Katie gasped breathlessly. "Remember what you said! It's not private!"

Louis came to his senses unwillingly and slowly let go of her shirt.

"I'm sorry," he apologized in a low, strained voice. Sitting back, he took her arms from around his neck and held her hands, breathing deeply as he concentrated all his efforts on recovering his equilibrium. "After last night, I should have known better than to kiss you. It's a good thing, I guess, that one of us has some self-control." Louis sounded the way he was feeling—frustrated, disgusted with himself and slightly disgruntled at her. In his state, it was hard to be grateful that she hadn't gotten as carried away as he had.

Katie's strongest emotion was regret as Louis squeezed her hands gently and released them. She almost wished she hadn't stopped him.

"I know you wouldn't want Stephanie walking in and catching us," she pointed out pleadingly, tucking in her shirt. She smiled at him tentatively, hesitant at voicing her thought. "You certainly are a lot more passionate toward me than you used to be. The other girls were always talking about their boyfriends wanting to French kiss them and feel their breasts. I thought maybe there was something wrong with me. I was terribly frustrated that you were such a perfect gentleman."

"Well, the tables are turned now."

Katie had her hands up to smooth her hair. She stopped, her arms still upraised, puzzled by his rueful remark.

"What do you mean?" She dropped her arms self-consciously, seeing his eyes directed at the stress her position was putting on the front of her T-shirt.

Louis shrugged, wishing he hadn't said it.

"I'm just naturally feeling a little frustrated." His smile was a pained confession. "A whole hell of a lot frustrated actually, whereas you..." Louis's glance traveled over her body, completing his message. He couldn't understand how she could be so passionate and cool off this quickly. She'd done the same last night. "I have to admire your recovery rate, Katie."

Katie was immediately defensive.

"It's hard for me to forget myself completely when there's no guarantee of privacy," she pointed out indignantly. "Another thing that held me back that may not have occurred to you is that I'm not protected from getting pregnant. I'm not on the pill, and I certainly didn't come over here today prepared to have sex with you." Her caution went much deeper than that, she realized, finishing up on the self-righteous note. It had to do with protecting herself in other ways and not expecting anything from him.

"I wouldn't have let anything actually happen," Louis objected. He heard his own words and made a self-deprecating face. "But then, my record's not too good on that account, is it?"

"You took precautions with me that one time we had sex together."

Katie went back to smoothing her hair, mortified at the slighted note in her voice. She had sounded jealously reproachful, the way she'd felt all those years ago.

"I took precautions with Betty, but they just weren't a hundred percent effective. Stephie's proof of that." Louis shifted his position, still not physically comfortable or comfortable with the conversation. "That was a rough time in my life, graduating from high school and immediately taking on the support of a family. But I got through it, and things worked out, more or less for the best. I wouldn't give anything for Stephie. Because of her, I can't look back and wish I hadn't gotten Betty pregnant."

"I'm sure it makes you feel good to know you did the right thing, marrying Betty." Katie looked over at the television while she answered him, pretending that the football game was suddenly vying for her interest. Neither of them had been paying any attention to it. "Stephanie is definitely your child. Anyone can tell that just from looking at her. Everyone admires you for being such a good father, including me." Katie wouldn't have wished him desperately unhappy all these years, but his complacent acceptance of his past stung her. She couldn't help making her own interpretation and feeling deeply rebuffed.

"Katie, there wasn't any insult to you intended in what I just said." Louis was apologetic. "I just can't help feeling rather grateful that my life turned out as well as it did, considering my mistakes."

He was begging her to drop the subject, but Katie couldn't. She was under some compulsion to slice her pride wide open for him.

"You mean, considering the worse one you could have made. Like being forced into marrying me instead of Betty."

"That's not what I meant." Louis was conscious of his own note of desperation. She had him backed into a corner. He didn't want to hurt her feelings any more than he inadvertently had already, but he couldn't lie either. "To be honest, Katie, I don't think you and I would have made a happily married couple. You were more than I could have handled. We'd be just another divorce statistic now. Besides, all of that was too many years ago to worry about, don't you agree?"

"I agree with you absolutely." Katie looked resolutely at the screen. She hadn't wanted to be "handled." She'd wanted to be special to him. She'd wanted him to love her. "It looks like we've missed the whole first quarter."

Louis was thoroughly dissatisfied, sitting next to her with not one iota of interest in the damned football game. He'd wanted to drop the hazardous probing into their high school relationship, but he didn't want an impasse now, in the present. He needed to be on friendly terms with her. He *wanted* to be on friendly terms with her.

It wouldn't have worked for you and me back then, Katie, he found himself thinking in his frustration. *Back then?* His unconscious word selection came as a shock to him.

"I don't know about you, but I'm starving," he declared, standing. "I think I'll run out and get some po'boys before halftime. What kind would you like?"

Katie stood up, too. She'd been staring at the screen blindly and feeling miserable.

"I think I'll pass on lunch. I was just thinking I have things I should be doing this afternoon." Such as going somewhere private to cry.

"Don't go. Please," Louis said quietly. "I won't be long. I'll call in our order." He glanced down at his desk with a smile meant to lighten the heavy atmosphere. "Of course, I'll have to plug in the phone." The smile lingered and was cajoling as he looked back at her. "You can stay here and have a nice, cold beer."

As though the matter was settled, Louis went to the refrigerator.

"Or would you rather a soft drink?"

"I guess a beer," Katie replied uncertainly. She was overwhelmed by his insistence. She had expected him to present a polite objection but deep down prefer for her to go, sensing, as she did, that the afternoon had been a mistake. But whatever his reasons for putting forth all this persuasion and however mixed her feelings about staying, there was little chance that he wouldn't have his way. If Louis really wanted her to stay, Katie would.

Chapter Ten

He just couldn't let her leave tense and hurt, Louis told himself. She'd been sparkling and sending off happy messages with every word and smile and movement before he'd kissed her and lost control, before they'd had the damned conversation. He wanted her that way again.

From now on he was going to be twice as careful not to hurt her feelings. At age thirty he couldn't bear the sight or thought of a wounded Katie any more than he could at twelve or eighteen. His protectiveness was a habit and had overtones of loyalty to her father, but there were new motives mixed in now in wanting to make things right for her—a strong personal element that Louis was discovering in himself with considerable uneasiness. It cast a disturbing light on his generous instincts to help her.

On the way to get lunch, he thought about how he'd let her believe last night that he'd asked her out because of his feelings for her father and purely for the purpose of putting her in contact with his subcontractor friends. That interpretation wasn't entirely true, he admitted now. There was more than loyalty to Red Gamble involved, more than doing a good deed behind the invitation. Actually, Louis had known that last night and hadn't wanted to admit it.

Damn it, he'd known getting involved with Katie would turn out to be complicated. He'd gone against his better judgment, his die-hard belief that openness and honesty were the best policies. It was too late to turn back now.

But did he sincerely wish he'd kept his distance from the Gambles, from Katie? Would he undo the afternoon visit to the elder Gambles, the drive with Mr. Red when the older man had substantiated Katie's claim that she'd largely built her father's houses for some years and had also given Louis a new picture of her entirely as the one person in her large family that everyone depended on? Would he have last night and this afternoon *not* happen?

Louis had to be honest with himself. His answer to all those questions was no. Part of the reason he was driving her Bronco to get the sandwiches, aside from the fact that she'd parked behind him, was that he didn't want to get back and find Katie gone. Even if she'd left a cheerful, believable note easing any concern about her departure, Louis would be more than a little disappointed to have the afternoon with her cut short.

He could tell immediately on his return that she had relaxed. She'd evidently been watching the game with renewed interest and had drunk most of her beer, which he'd served her in an iced mug from the freezer.

"LSU just scored again," she reported as he came in the door. "And they kicked the extra point, too, so they're seven points ahead. Now if they can just hold that lead until halftime."

"That Alabama team is famous for playing catch-up in the last few minutes of the second quarter," Louis reminded her.

"Did you have any problems with the Bronco?" Katie asked, still surprised that he'd taken it. She felt an odd pleasure thinking of him driving her car.

"Nothing serious," Louis replied, deadpan, moving the coffee table farther from the couch.

"What do you mean, nothing serious? It runs perfectly for me."

Louis emptied his paper bag, taking out two bulging, loaf-shaped sandwiches wrapped in butcher paper.

"I had to drive with one foot on the brake, that's all. It kept trying to go faster." He grinned at her, and she smiled at his teasing reference to her fast driving. "Ready for another beer to go with your sandwich? I've been envying you the whole time I was gone, thinking about that cold beer you were drinking."

Every reservation Katie had about remaining vanished as she sat down on the carpet next to him and unwrapped her po'boy.

Called heroes or submarines or grinders in other parts of the country, and shortened from "poor boys" here, the overstuffed sandwiches made on small crusty loaves of French bread were delicious but messy.

She spread the paper wrapping on the table to catch the overflow. She'd asked for her hot roast-beef sandwich to be "dressed," which meant with mayonnaise, lettuce, tomato and pickle. Picking up half of her sandwich loaf, she bit into it, holding her head over the table. Rich gravy dribbled onto the paper.

"This is good," she told Louis approvingly when she could talk. He was just taking a bite. "I see you decided on shrimp," she commented as a crispy deep-fried shrimp fell out of his sandwich and onto the wrapper. He had been undecided between shrimp or fried catfish.

Louis nodded and made an appreciative sound as he chewed to communicate that he was pleased with his decision. After he'd swallowed and taken a swig of beer, he picked up the fallen shrimp and put it in front of Katie.

"Here. This one jumped right out of my sandwich for you."

Katie ate the shrimp without any argument.

"Mmm. Delicious. You can have this other half of my roast beef," she offered, taking another bite of her sandwich.

Louis was busy eating, but he gave her a teasing glance.

"Is that a hint that you want to go halfsies?" he asked her when he could talk.

Katie hastily swallowed her mouthful so that she could giggle.

"No," she denied, smiling. "That's not what I meant at all. These sandwiches are just too big to eat both halves." She tried to look innocent. "But if you happened to have a knife and wanted to go quarters..."

"I knew you had your eye on my food," he accused her. He switched halves with her over her protests that she'd only been kidding and couldn't possibly eat the second half of either his or her own sandwich. "Eat what you want of it," he ordered her cheerfully. "If you can't eat all the bread, pick out the shrimp. Actually, you've fallen right into my hands. I wanted half your roast beef as soon as I smelled it."

His air of indulgence warmed her. They ate companionably, watching the final minutes of the first half of the game, dragged out by the usual time-outs and strategies for stopping the clock.

Katie picked out the shrimp as he'd suggested, giving him the last two, then slumped against the couch, blissfully content.

"Wake me up when the game comes back on," she told him, closing her eyes and groaning. "I'm stuffed."

"Why don't you lie on the couch and take a nap?" he suggested. He folded up the sandwich papers and stood to put them in the garbage pail. "During halftime, I think I'll tackle that mess on my desk."

Louis was feeling extremely cozy with her there. He was comfortably full and his sexual frustration was gone.

"Maybe I can help you," Katie offered lazily, opening her eyes. The sight of his broad-shouldered build and loose-jointed ease of movement raised a familiar pleasure in her.

"That's the most enthusiastic offer I've gotten in days," he tossed over his shoulder, not taking her seriously.

Katie waited until he had sat down at his desk and then got to her feet and followed him with a sense of luxury.

"What are you doing?"

"The usual. Checking bills against invoices to make sure I'm paying the right amount. Trying to make heads or tails of how much has been spent on each job I've got going." Louis glanced up with a heartfelt grimace as Katie stopped beside his chair. "This paperwork is endless. I absolutely despise it." He sighed and picked up a bill.

Katie watched him as he shuffled through invoices, talking aloud to himself, and then couldn't stand it any longer. She was amused and yet honestly amazed at his lack of efficiency.

"I think maybe I can give you a hand with what you're doing," she suggested tactfully and was soon sitting in the desk chair herself, organizing the invoices. Louis pulled over a chair and sat next to her, theoretically helping but mostly watching. It was an easy matter for her, since she was so thoroughly familiar with the paper-related tasks of house construction. Having him beside her added a new dimension of enjoyment to her expertise.

"You're fast with that adding machine," he complimented her with awe, seeing her fingers fly over the keys. "You don't even look at what you're doing."

"I took business courses in high school," Katie reminded him. "I learned the touch system of using an adding machine as well as a typewriter."

"The third quarter's starting," he murmured.

Katie had to hide a smile.

"I can hear it," she said. "I might as well go ahead and clear up this work for you, now that I'm started. It won't take that long."

Louis didn't argue, and he was visibly grateful when she finished.

"Lord, Katie, you've saved me hours." He regarded his newly neat desk as though she'd performed a miracle. "I wonder if I could talk you into coming over more often on weekends," he teased.

Katie was about to make a light reply as she stood up, not wanting to show him how enormously appealing his facetious suggestion was. But before she could speak, his telephone rang.

"I forgot to unplug the damned thing again," Louis grumbled apologetically.

Regretting the interruption, Katie got out of his way and returned to the other end of the room to give him privacy. But she could hear his side of the conversation and felt extremely awkward. It was George Tucker calling him, berating him for having his phone unplugged all morning.

Katie didn't have to guess why George had been trying to call Louis. The electrician wanted Louis's feedback on working for Katie. Louis quickly apprised George of her presence in his office, and the conversation didn't last long. Katie knew that Louis's "Sure thing" was an agreement to call George back later.

Her flare-up of proud resentment was irrational. She'd known Louis's subs would check with him. She'd known that their working for her was contingent on his approval. It was probably all for the best that George had called while she was there, making her obligation to Louis a distasteful certainty. Katie didn't have to accept his professional favors. She could be independent, use her own subs and say to hell with making a profit on this last house she would build.

But she wouldn't. And it really had nothing to do with profit. With his subs on the job, Louis would come around the job site. She'd see him. Despite the cost to her pride, she couldn't deny herself the contact with him.

* * *

It was a compromise that Katie didn't regret in the coming days and weeks, which flew by for her. With the terms of her building contract finalized, she proceeded with the details involved in a "house start," the building vernacular for the initial stages of construction. There were official permits to obtain, which required dealing with small-town bureaucracy. She had to arrange for a temporary electric hookup and oversee the clearing of trees and underbrush on the heavily wooded site. Culverts and fill dirt had to be brought in to create a driveway for delivery trucks.

The house had to be located precisely on the property, using batten board and string to mark its outlines, with great care being taken to ensure that the corners were square. Katie helped on this crucial step herself and kept a close eye on the foundation work in preparation for pouring the concrete slab. Footings had to be dug and poured with concrete and the whole foundation dug out, leveled and heavily reinforced with steel rods to strengthen the slab.

Plumbing pipes that would be encased in the concrete had to be laid in advance, bringing Peewee Joiner onto the job with his puckish sense of humor. Katie was glad, even before an hour had passed, that she'd hired him, seeing how efficient he was, with everything all worked out in advance in his mind.

With the slab poured and cured, it was time to bring in Petey Jenkins and his carpenters to start raising the skeleton of the house. Petey's crew was a motley bunch, arriving in battered pickup trucks and vans, but they worked together with casual, muscular precision to ear-shattering music from a powerful portable radio, carrying two-by-fours and laying them out to make the plates on which walls and partitions would rest. Petey and his main carpenter marked the plates in codes that indicated placement of doorways and windows and headers, the various solid portions of wall that would give strength and support. Once the plates were accurately finished, the carpenters could raise the first-floor superstructure without scrutinizing the house plan.

"Watch out for Big Mac if he comes around today," Petey warned her gleefully his third morning. "He'll probably be trying to hit somebody up for a loan. We fleeced him last night at the poker game."

"I'll be on my guard," Katie promised gaily, smiling. It was a blatant fiction. All the cash in her possession would be Louis's for the asking.

The carpenter's easy assumption that Louis might be dropping by didn't bother her. Nor did she worry herself about the fact that she'd probably been a topic of discussion at last night's weekly poker game with Louis and his subcontractor friends, who were all committed to work for her.

Katie was too happy and too busy these days to worry needlessly. She'd opted for a friendly association with Louis that Saturday afternoon of the LSU game and gotten much more than she'd bargained for. He dropped by daily on the jobsite, usually in the afternoon about the time the workers were leaving. She loved showing him around, commenting on the day's little problems and soliciting his professional opinion. They were working colleagues, she and Louis.

If she hadn't been so certain of her capability, she might have felt a slight discomfort at his close notice of every single detail, but Katie was securely in her element. It was a source of pleasure to her to share her day-to-day accomplishments with him.

Louis was back in her life, and it was marvelous. When she encountered him now at a building-supply store, they'd go out of their way to chat, not avoid each other. When they passed each other on the street, they'd blow their horns and wave. There was no more ignoring each other's existence.

They'd even had a number of casual dates. He invited her out to eat. They'd gone to Back Street again a couple of times and socialized with his friends. He'd come to supper at her mother's urging. They'd taken Lisa and Stephanie to a movie and her nephew Rich and a friend of his to a Saints game in the Super Dome in New Orleans. Katie's helping him with his paperwork when it accumulated was becoming a regular thing. It was all casual and comfortable and, for Katie, wonderfully different from their high-school dating.

Louis was the one seeking her out this time, not the opposite. Katie had never been coy with him or tried to hide her honest delight in his company, but she didn't suggest dates or issue invitations. Nor was she deliberately provocative, testing his physical control. But it continued to thrill her that he was sexually attracted to her and obviously wanted her.

He tried to keep his hands off her, but he had problems. An affectionate man, touching came naturally to him. He liked to hug and pat and hold hands. When he kissed her good-night, he'd try to restrain himself from intimate caresses, but sometimes he couldn't. They joked about living with parents in a small town, but Louis's humor was strained. Katie sensed an underlying puzzlement and male irritation that she wasn't nearly as bothered by their situation as he was.

Several times he referred lightly to managing a night together in New Orleans or on the Gulf coast, but he didn't make an actual proposal, and Katie let the suggestion slide, knowing her answer would be yes if he asked her. *Yes* was the only response she seemed capable of giving Louis, but her mind veered away from the idea of going to bed with him, even though it was tremendously alluring.

She didn't know exactly why she wanted to put it off. The obvious explanation was that she wanted to keep the spark of sexual interest alive so he'd keep coming around, keep wanting to see her. But there was a deeper reservation, too, that had to do with past sexual dissatisfactions and protecting herself. She never once mentioned to him getting a place of her own, which she'd postponed for the time being.

Then, in late October, when she and Louis had been seeing each other for six weeks, her ambivalence was put to the test. Lucy and Craig Bergeron, friends since she'd built their house for them several years ago, called her to say they were going out of town suddenly because of an illness in the family. Would Katie do them a big favor and look after their pets for a week? They'd welcome having her sleep in the house and make herself completely at home if that would make it easier for her.

Ignoring her panic at the sudden unforeseen opportunity, Katie agreed at once to help them out and drove over to get the house key and instructions for looking after the two cocker spaniels and a Siamese cat.

"It might be better for me to move in for a week," she told Lucy and Craig, meaning to give herself the option.

"That's what we were hoping!" Lucy exclaimed. "But we hated to ask. These dumb animals are so spoiled. They've never been left overnight by themselves. We'll feel so relieved knowing you're sleeping here in the house. Thanks a million, Katie.''

This does not mean you have to go to bed with Louis, Katie told herself over and over that night when she couldn't sleep. She repeated the same desperate wisdom throughout the next day, which was Friday. She was nervous, thinking ahead to seeing Louis. They didn't have a date, but plans usually developed for a Friday evening.

He came by the site later than usual. Petey Jenkins and his crew had been gone for almost thirty minutes, and Katie was about to give up and leave, too. For all her dread and indecision, she was terribly disappointed.

And then the blue pickup came down the street at a slow, steady pace. Louis got out, smiling and looking glad to see her but moving wearily.

"This has been one hell of a day," he announced. "I stopped to get a six-pack." He held up the cluster of cans with one already missing as he headed toward her with his long, loose stride. Katie experienced all her usual pleasure at the sight of him, along with the return of her nervous tension.

"I was about to give up on your coming by today," she told him lightly. "I thought you might be skipping your daily inspection." An odd look crossed Louis's face, almost like regret. Katie wondered if there might have been something in her words to offend him. "I was hanging around, hoping you'd come," she added. "There's something I wanted to ask your opinion on, if you feel like climbing up to the second story."

Katie's heart quickstepped as Louis came up close to her. He put his arm around her shoulders and gave her a hard little hug, then bent to kiss her on the lips.

"That's why I came by," he said quietly. "Not to make an inspection or give you the benefit of my experience."

Katie was nonplussed. Apparently he *had* been offended.

"I'm always glad to have you come by," she assured him. "I appreciate your interest, and your opinion means a lot to me."

He hugged her shoulders again and was plainly considering another kiss when a car cruised by slowly, reminding them that they were in view of the neighborhood.

"My opinion right this moment is that we should find a comfortable place to sit and drink a cold beer."

"That's what I mean about respecting your opinion," Katie retorted lightly.

They sat side by side on a stack of lumber behind the house and sipped their cans of beer.

"What was so bad about today?" she asked him. "Did you have some things go wrong?"

"Just about everything," he replied. "I've evidently been saving up." He elaborated, and by the time he concluded his list of annoyances, he was able to view them with amusement. "So there my roofers were, half the damned day with no shingles, and then the delivery truck finally showed up with the wrong ones, which was just as well, I guess. Those guys had been to the quick-stop store about twenty times and put down twice their weight in junk food and soft drinks. They'd have been off balance walking around on that slanted roof."

Katie laughed appreciatively.

"Roofers are definitely a special breed of characters, aren't they? I can never get over the way most of them

wear just any kind of old shoes. You'd think they went
to the Salvation Army to get them."

"Now that I've done all my complaining, how did
your day go?" Louis inquired, thinking as he listened
to her answer that he looked forward more and more to
talking to her daily and sharing their routines. It
weighed on his mind that Hemphill might make a slip
and ruin the camaraderie. Louis wanted to tell Katie
everything, but so far he hadn't found the nerve, and
with every week that passed it was harder to confess
because there seemed more and more to lose.

"I sure am glad I took your advice and hired Petey,"
Katie ended up. "Not a thing slips by his attention."
She smiled with a hint of sadness. "If I were going to
stay in this business and build more houses, I can warn
you I'd be competing with you for Petey—and Peewee,
too. I haven't worked with the others yet, but I don't
doubt they're as good."

"Don't think I'm not worried," Louis joked gruffly,
reacting to her undertone of regret. It made him feel
powerless to know he couldn't cure the problem he'd
solved for her only temporarily. "Those guys would
choose you over me in a second. They think you're 'it.'
Another job may turn up," he pointed out at the cost
of his conscience. "This house will be a heck of a recommendation by the time it's finished."

Katie patted his knee, touched by his effort to bol-
ster her spirits. He immediately covered her hand with
his bigger one, squeezed it and kept it there.

"People are never satisfied, are they?" she reflected,
finding it difficult to feel gloomy about anything with
Louis holding her hand. "A month and a half ago all I
asked for was one last house to build that I'd have
complete credit for. Then, I told myself, I'd find some-

thing else to do. There's my sign out there facing the
street—Katie Gamble, General Contractor. When this
house is finished, there shouldn't be any doubt in anybody's mind that I know my business. But you know
what I didn't realize, Louis?" Her wan smile was a
confession. "It's going to be twice as hard to quit now
than it was before." Seeing that his concern had deepened into open anxiety, Katie stood up briskly. "But
that's months off. Do you think you can haul yourself
up to that second-floor platform now so I can show you
the problem I was talking about?"

Louis got up slowly.

"I'm sure I'll agree with whatever you and Petey decide," he said heavily. "I have complete confidence in
both of you."

Katie found it difficult to feel rebuffed by his lack of
interest, considering his method of sidestepping her request.

"I shouldn't bother you," she apologized. "You
work all day and then come by here, and I usually try to
get free advice."

"I wouldn't say it's free," he objected, smiling with
an effort. "I'd say I'm in your debt, with all that help
you give me with my paperwork." He ruffled her hair
and smoothed it with big gentle fingers. "What about
tonight? You want to go out to eat? I'm not much in the
mood for Back Street." He heard the resigned frustration in his voice and made an apologetic face. He
wanted to spend the evening with her, but their pla-
tonic relationship was a strain on him.

Katie's heart had started beating very fast.

"I'm kind of obligated to go to the Covington High
football game tonight. My nephew Tommy thinks the

coach may let him play, and he's all excited. He made a point of calling me.''

Louis groaned good-naturedly.

"Okay. I'll go to the game with you." He glanced at his watch. "It'll be pushing it to eat beforehand. You want to just snack at the game and go out afterward?''

Katie nodded, her throat tight.

"What time shall I come by for you?'' Louis inquired. "About six-thirty? The game probably starts at seven, doesn't it?''

Katie wet her lips and swallowed.

"I won't be at my house tonight. I'm staying at some friends' place for a week, looking after their animals. They called me last night and asked me. Lucy's mother, who lives in Florida, is having emergency surgery.''

They both heard the nervous note in Katie's explanation.

"Your friends live here in town?'' Louis asked quietly.

"Over on Sixth Street. Actually, I could stay home and go over periodically to take care of the animals, but my friends were so relieved when I suggested sleeping at the house that I was kind of trapped into doing it. They don't have children, and they dote on their animals.''

"I see. I'll pick you up there, then. What's the address?''

Katie told him and hesitated, embarrassment coloring her cheeks. "I hope I'm not giving you the wrong impression, that I grabbed this opportunity to stay in my friends' house.''

"You didn't give that impression at all,'' Louis replied. His smile was pained. "Quite the opposite, in fact. Katie, I'm not going to force my way in tonight after the game, so don't make a nervous wreck out of yourself.'' He gently pinched her hot cheek and bent to give her a swift, light kiss on the mouth before he walked away, calling over his shoulder, "See you at six-thirty."

Louis had some doubts about his promise. Just the thought that they had a private place to go tonight purged his mental and physical fatigue. God, he wanted to make love to Katie. His desire for her had become an ache that didn't go away. Kissing her and touching her were masochistic pleasures he couldn't do without.

He'd never built up this kind of hunger for a woman before, never had this frustrated yearning for a woman to want him in return. No matter what Katie said, he feared that he had spoiled her for sex, taking her the way he had back in high school, without expertise or sensitivity. She had too much fire and passion in her not to like sex. So mixed in with his physical urgency was the hope that he could change her attitude and open up to her the pleasures of intimacy with a man. Whatever damage he had done, he wanted to undo it.

Later, on the way to pick up Katie, he tortured himself with the fantasy that she would suggest they forget about the football game and spend the evening alone. However, she emerged immediately from the house when he pulled into the driveway, looking cute and feminine in pleated slacks and a pullover sweater. Wearing flats instead of her Western boots, she didn't stand as tall as usual next to Louis as he opened the door for her.

"I may be accused of dating a high-school student," he teased her, picking her up bodily and seating her in the truck over her squeal of protest. Leaning into the cab with his arm still around her waist, he kissed her smiling lips. "You smell good enough to eat," he told her and then kissed her again, this time deeply, and felt his instant arousal as her tongue curled around his, warm and intimate. ''You're driving me crazy, kissing me like that, Katie,'' he said huskily, pulling away.

Katie waited with a sense of fate, her heart beating wildly, but he didn't urge her to forget the game and invite him inside instead. He closed her door and came around and got in on the driver's side. She tried to make herself speak the suggestion, but she couldn't force the words out. Then he had started the truck and was backing out. It was too late, and she was enormously disappointed and enormously relieved that they were proceeding with their plans and postponing the inevitable lovemaking. Because it was inevitable, without a doubt. The time had come, she knew.

They sat in the bleachers with Katie's sister Barb and her husband, Tommy senior, and a sizable party of other parents. Katie chatted with everyone and cheered the local team, but her heart wasn't in it, and she was sorry she'd dragged Louis to the game. He made every effort to be affable and suffered all the parental enthusiasm, but underneath, she knew, he was wanting it to be over, as she was.

During halftime, they left the bleachers to stretch their legs and share a bag of popcorn. Katie was mustering the courage to suggest they make an early departure when several high-school girls passed by, talking fast and eagerly, arresting her attention.

''I know I'd sure go out with him if he asked me. What girl at Covington High wouldn't?''

''I'd *love* to date him. He's the greatest-looking guy in the whole school. But just try talking to him! It's impossible! That Michelle Palmer acts like she *owns* him! She tries to make everybody think they're going steady, and they're really not.''

"Can you believe the way she goes after him? Jenny Anderson and Betty Reasoner are both friends of hers, and they swear that she doesn't just hint around to him. She comes right out and *asks* him to take her out. The girl has no pride.''

"It seems to work for her. He takes her everywhere, even though I swear he doesn't look that happy about it.''

"Hey, maybe we should try asking him out ourselves!''

Amid much giggling at the bold suggestion, the girls swept out of earshot, leaving Katie with warm cheeks.

"I guess things don't really change,'' she remarked, smiling with both amusement and embarrassment. "There were probably lots of remarks like that made about you and me. It makes me blush to remember how forward I was. You'd have had your pick of all the girls in the school if I hadn't hung around you constantly, cramping your style.''

"I doubt that,'' Louis drawled unconcernedly. He fed her several kernels of popcorn. "But even if it was true, I don't see where I had a complaint. You were cute and full of personality. There were plenty of guys who would gladly have stepped into my shoes, you know.''

Katie managed to chew and smile gratefully at him at the same time.

"That's sweet of you to say,'' she told him when she had swallowed. "But tell me honestly. Would you ever have asked me out on your own if I hadn't hinted and bargained and outright begged?''

Louis's grin warned that he was going to evade giving her a truthful answer.

"You were definitely a young lady who knew her own mind back then," he teased. "If you hadn't had your sights set on me, there'd have been some other lucky fellow, and you wouldn't have given me the time of day."

"That's just a nice way of saying you wouldn't have asked me out," Katie accused wistfully. "I knew that at the time, but I just couldn't accept it. I wasn't interested in any other guys. You were the only one I could see." *You still are,* she might have added.

"I ask you out now," Louis pointed out. "Isn't the present what counts?" He wasn't really interested in discussing their past dating, which had little importance to him now but apparently still bothered her.

"But why did you let me monopolize you in high school? I know it was because of my father, but did you really think he would hold it against you if you didn't take me out?" Katie asked with earnest puzzlement. "Didn't you think he'd be fair enough to realize you had the right to date a girl you liked?"

"Katie, that was all ages ago. What does it matter now?" Louis chided, offering her more popcorn from his fingers.

"It doesn't matter, I guess. I've just always wondered." She opened her lips and let him feed her, reluctantly dropping the subject.

Louis sighed, giving in as he knew he was bound to do with Katie.

"It's impossible for me to explain what I don't completely understand myself," he stated reluctantly. "I did always want to please your father, and a sure way to do that was to make you happy. But also I liked seeing you happy myself and hated disappointing you." He tenderly brushed a fragment of popcorn from her bottom lip. "It was certainly no hardship for me to date you, except that of all the girls in the whole school, you were the one I couldn't think of being fresh with. Like most teenage guys, I was horny as all get-out and obsessed with sex."

Katie nodded, finding his explanation wonderfully soothing to old hurt pride.

"I can see your dilemma now, but I couldn't then."

Louis made a guilty face. "It's a shame to say it, considering she's Stephie's mother, but I was interested in Betty primarily because she wasn't a 'nice' girl. Her main attraction for me was her reputation. I figured I wouldn't have to marry a girl if I wasn't the first. Naturally, I didn't plan on getting her pregnant." He shrugged his broad shoulders unhappily. "That period around my graduation was a nightmare. I felt terrible about you, but I had to stand by Betty because of her circumstances. Her parents put her out of the house and would have nothing more to do with her when they found out she was pregnant. She didn't have anyone to turn to, and there was the distinct possibility that she was carrying my baby."

"I remember you explained all that." The words were hard for Katie to get out. The memories still hurt. "You always were conscientious. I was depending on that when I pushed you into having sex with me. I was doing my best to trap you. When it didn't work, I was vindictive, but I was sorry immediately afterward when I realized I'd done something terrible I couldn't ever undo."

"Katie, it all worked out—"

"I took my full share of blame with my father," Katie went on swiftly, not wanting to hear again Louis's optimism that the chain of events in his past had worked out for the best. "Not out of any sense of fairness, but because his first reaction scared me when I poured out my one-sided story. He went into such a rage that I was afraid he might kill you. I had to tell him the truth about what had happened to calm him down. After that day he never once mentioned your name. I always wondered if he'd gone to you and gotten your version."

Louis shook his head, his face shadowed with memory.

"I kept dreading that he would come to see me, and then when he didn't, I wished I had the nerve to go to him, but I was ashamed and afraid. I couldn't bear to have him tell me to my face all the things I knew he had a right to be feeling about me."

Louis crumpled the empty popcorn bag in his big, strong hands. "I owed him so much. The very fact that I was graduating from high school was in large part due to him. I'd wanted to drop out and work for him full-time as a carpenter, but he bit my head off when I made the suggestion." Louis smiled ruefully, remembering. "He told me, 'Son, if you have hopes of being a contractor some day, you'd better get that diploma. Ain't nobody going to hire some ignoramus who didn't finish high school to build his house for him.'"

Katie smiled along with Louis at his fond mimicry of Red Gamble's rumbling tones and felt none of her old jealousy at the younger man's open affection for her father. That jealousy was gone now, leaving her no protection against her deep regret for what she'd denied Louis and her father.

"You'd probably have become his partner if it hadn't been for me."

Louis linked his arm with hers and squeezed it against him.

"Who knows? Maybe I would have. Maybe I wouldn't. I've done all right, and your father had a good partner, anyway—one who could do all his paperwork for him, too. The thought makes me envious."

Katie smiled up at him through a mist of tears.

"I wish I had your philosophy, that everything happens for the best," she reflected. "I guess there isn't much point in dwelling on what can't be changed. But I still feel bad knowing I deprived you and my father of a close relationship all these years. I think if you're honest, you'll admit you regret what you've missed, too."

"I missed out on a lot more than being friends with your father," Louis replied softly. "I'm just beginning to realize how much."

Katie stared at him, taken completely unawares by his sentiment. She hardly dared believe that his tone of voice and the expression on his face said what she thought they did . . . and that the message was for *her*.

Chapter Eleven

I don't suppose you're just talking about my mother's cookies, are you?" Katie joked hollowly.

"No, I'm talking about you and me. I've been thinking lately that it's a damned shame we didn't get together a lot sooner." Louis bent and kissed the tip of her nose and then smiled into her face. "Thank goodness you took the first step or I'd still be missing out on your company. I like the grown-up Katie."

Katie looked away from him, blinking at a fresh, painful glaze of tears as she struggled with her emotions. She'd been right to keep up her guard just now. His affectionate words warmed and pleased her, yet they weren't enough, not nearly enough. They touched off an old yearning she'd have thought long dead by now, not just buried somewhere deep inside, making her vulnerable.

"I'm glad one of us made a move, too," she said, pretending to take notice of their surroundings. "It's been great being friends with you again."

Wondering what he'd said wrong, Louis watched her give undivided attention to the loudspeaker's blaring welcome to the two returning teams at the completion of the halftime show.

"I guess we should find our seats again," he suggested reluctantly. He felt hope flare as she hesitated.

"I guess it's time," she agreed, and they returned to the bleachers to sit through what Louis knew had to be the longest second half of a high-school football game in history. If her nervous fidgeting was any indication, he suspected Katie was finding it interminable, too. She wasn't still an instant, and he was aware of her every movement.

"Everybody's invited over to our place for coffee and cake," Barb announced at the game's conclusion. "Katie and Louis, are you two coming?"

"No, don't count on us." Louis spoke up quickly before Katie could respond. "We didn't have time for supper before the game. We're planning to go somewhere to eat."

There were laughing comments that Louis didn't want to share Katie for the rest of the evening, and he good-naturedly agreed with the charges. As they walked along with the others toward the stadium exit, he had one arm possessively around her shoulders.

"I guess I should have given you a chance to say whether you wanted to go to your sister's," he remarked apologetically when they'd split off from the group and were heading for his pickup in the parking lot.

"I'm glad you refused," Katie assured him. "It was bad enough sitting through that game without having to listen to more talk about it. I didn't think it would ever end, did you?"

Louis squeezed her shoulders in agreement.

"I'm almost sure they slipped in an extra quarter of play during that second half. Are you as hungry as I am? I feel as if my stomach's caved in."

"I'm starving," Katie lied. The discomfort in her stomach was nerves, not hunger.

"Where would you like to eat?" Louis asked. "Let's go somewhere where the food comes out in a hurry."

"How about just going to a hamburger place? Then we won't have to wait." Katie's heart thudded as she elaborated on the suggestion, trying desperately to sound casual. "For that matter, we could just pick up some hamburgers and French fries and take them back to the Bergerons' house and eat there."

It was intended as an oblique way of letting Louis know she intended to invite him in tonight, but it came out sounding blatantly obvious to her. She felt her face grow hot as Louis gave her a searching glance, but her embarrassment provided some relief from her nervous tension.

"A hamburger and fries sound good to me," he replied. "Although I'll probably make that two hamburgers and two orders of fries."

Faintly disappointed by his response, Katie considered the matter settled. From the Covington High stadium, it was no more than a ten-minute drive to the Claiborne Hill area at the opposite side of town, where most of the fast-food chains had sprung up. When they pulled into the hamburger place they'd agreed on, she expected Louis to pull up to the ordering station for take-out service and was openly surprised when he parked instead.

"You'd rather eat here?" she asked him uncertainly. He smiled at her ruefully.

"I think it would be better for my digestion. If we go back to that house, I'm definitely not going to have my mind on food." He groaned as he took her into his arms and hugged her close. "Lord, Katie, I wish you wanted me just half as much as I want you. We'd never have gone to that damned ball game. It was sheer torture sitting in those bleachers and knowing we could be alone back at your friends' house and making love instead."

The raw passion in his voice combined with the powerful need in his embrace made Katie feel weak and breathless.

"We can go there now," she told him softly, and she felt his whole body respond to her words. He sucked in his breath audibly as he tightened his arms until they held her too tightly for comfort.

"Katie, you won't be sorry this time. I promise you that, sweetheart."

It was the first time he'd used the endearment. Katie's reaction to hearing it was so deep and strong that she was shaken. When he pulled back enough to look at her, she was afraid that he'd sensed her emotion.

"I'm sure I won't be sorry," she said swiftly and kissed him to evade his scrutiny. After a second's hesitation, he returned the pressure of her mouth and kissed her back urgently until they were both gasping for breath.

"Now you've done it to me," he accused her with unsteady humor, squeezing her in a bear hug so that she could feel his shudder of need. "There's no question of going inside the place to eat now. I'd be embarrassed in my present condition."

Taking one of her hands from around his neck, he dragged it to his jeans and pressed, moaning her name softly at the intimate contact.

"Katie...I dream of having you touch me like this," he confided softly. "I want to feel your hands on me without any clothes. I want to touch you all over, kiss you from head to toe, with all the time in the world. When we can't stand being apart a second longer, I want to satisfy you. Don't you want all of that, too, sweetheart? Just a little?" he cajoled, leaving her hand in place and caressing her thigh.

"Yes," Katie whispered truthfully, reacting to his tender endearment again. She stroked him intimately.

Louis closed his hand quickly over hers again, drawing in his breath. Reaching for the ignition with his free hand, he kissed her gently on the lips.

"I feel like a volcano that's long overdue to erupt," he said apologetically. "Two months is a long time for a man to want a woman and not get any satisfaction."

Katie moved her hand to his thigh and sat as close to him as possible while he started the truck and shifted it into gear.

"We've only been going out for six weeks," she pointed out.

Louis scooted her an imaginary inch closer to him before he backed out of the parking lot.

"It was right at the beginning of September when you showed up with the two girls that afternoon I was leaving the Pearson house. This is the end of October. According to my arithmetic, that's two months." He smiled at Katie, meeting her surprised look of inquiry. "My, what big eyes you have," he mocked gently.

"Are you telling me you had an ulterior motive in being so generous in sharing your subs with me?" Katie demanded, pleasure seeping through her.

"I'm afraid so," Louis admitted. "But you must have had that figured out all along."

Katie pressed her cheek against his hard shoulder, contending with her swell of happiness.

"I'm glad you told me, anyway," she said softly.

Louis braked for a traffic light. Glancing down at her, he dropped a kiss on the top of her head and then nuzzled his face in her hair, feeling tender and protective toward her as well as amorous. It felt good to confess his personal motive, laying the foundation for more incriminating revelations at a later date. Not tonight, though. He didn't want to take any risks with tonight.

"These animals you're sitting aren't German shepherds, are they?" he asked her when they had ridden along for several minutes in silence. He sensed that she was thinking ahead to their arrival at the house and wanted to ease any anxiety she might be feeling. "If they are, I hope you fed them well before you left. I'm attached, in more ways than one, to my ankles."

Katie smiled at him. "No, they're two adorable cocker spaniels and a Siamese cat. I can warn you all three are spoiled and demand attention. Tonight when I was getting dressed, they followed every step I took and sat there, watching me."

"It doesn't sound as if we're walking into a very private situation," Louis remarked dryly, pleased at his intuition that he was voicing their common thought.

"Lucy warned me that if I didn't close the bedroom door at night, I'd have company in bed," Katie said laughingly. She met Louis's glance with a sheepish smile. "I know I must have turned red and looked guilty."

Louis raised his eyebrows with hopeful male interest.

"I'm sure you realized when you agreed to sleep in their house that you'd have to barricade the place to keep me out."

"I offered to sleep in the house," Katie confided, telling him what she knew he really wanted to know. "They didn't outright ask."

Louis thanked her with his warm sideways glance. He squeezed her hand resting on his thigh and slid it higher to a more intimate position. "I don't wish any harm to your friends' relative who's having the surgery," he observed with a happy note in his voice, "but I sure wish they wouldn't be in a hurry to come home."

The dogs created a welcoming furor as Louis unlocked the door to the house. He obligingly patted them and spoke a few friendly words to each and to the Siamese cat pacing and emitting yowls several yards in the background. Then he straightened, smiling at his own thoughts, and took Katie into his arms.

"Enough socializing with the pets," he declared and lowered his mouth to hers for a deep, slow kiss. "I'd rather see the house. I remember when you and your dad were building it. You ran into some problems with the skylights, didn't you?"

"How did you ... know about that?"

Katie finished her question weakly, taken by surprise as Louis picked her up in his arms and carried her with ease from the entryway into the main living area of the house, which had a contemporary plan combining the living room, dining room and kitchen.

"I managed to keep up with what you were doing," he remarked, stopping and glancing around appreciatively. He whistled at the massive freestanding fireplace and then gazed up at the vaulted ceiling. "I can see why there would have been a problem with those skylights," he marveled. "Look at the size of them. They must have been a bear to install. Nice house. No wonder you aren't fazed by the Hemphill job." He smiled at Katie, who was basking in his approval. "I can't wait to see how the upstairs came out," he drawled with soft insinuation.

"I can walk," Katie told him unconvincingly, tightening her arms around his neck as he disregarded her words and carried her across the room toward the stairs. Over his shoulder she could see the two dogs and cat following and had to giggle. "The animals are coming along on the tour," she warned him.

At the foot of the stairs, Louis stopped and glanced behind him. Shaking his head humorously, he put her down.

"We'd better make a fast break for it if we don't want company." Clasping her hand, he looked up the stairs. "Which way do we turn up there, right or left?"

"First door to the right," Katie replied laughingly and sped up the stairs with him, holding his hand. "This is so ridiculous!" she gasped, reaching the top and making a sharp turn to the right. Dashing through the door of the guest bedroom, where she was sleeping, she flipped the wall switch, turning on several lamps and softly lighting the room. Whirling around, she was just in time to see Louis closing the door almost in the faces of the two cocker spaniels in pursuit.

"They looked so disappointed!" she exclaimed, laughing and going without hesitation into Louis's widespread arms.

"That was close," he declared, hugging her and lifting her off her feet. "Alone at last. I never fully appreciated that line before. Lord, I was beginning to wonder if I'd ever have you to myself like this, Katie," he added in a low, fervent voice devoid of humor.

Katie's giddiness dissipated, and reality set in abruptly, awakening an odd panicky sensation. She and Louis were alone in a bedroom. They would make love. There was no obstacle now between them and total intimacy.

"You did remember that I'm not taking birth-control pills?" she asked as he put her on her feet just long enough to pick her up in his arms and carry her toward the bed.

"I remembered," Louis assured her, sitting on the edge of the bed with her in his lap. Cradling her head on his shoulder with one big hand, he hugged her. "Don't worry about anything," he urged her. "I came prepared, and I'll be careful to protect you. Trust me. If anything should happen, you know I'll take full responsibility."

"I know. I do trust you." Katie's face was burrowed into his neck, muffling her words. She felt his tremor in response to her warm breath and pressed her lips to his bare skin with a tender impulse, not with any thought of inciting him.

"Katie!" Louis spoke her name in a frustrated groan. His hands were urgent but unsteady as he caressed her shoulders and back. "I want us to make love, but I want you to want it, too."

She raised her head and looked at him, feeling the familiar aching pleasure at the sight of him. With light fingers she touched his soft tangle of black curls, traced the strong, masculine contours of the face she found so appealing and then framed his face lovingly between her hands, smiling into his eyes.

"I do want us to make love, Louis," she told him, speaking with simple conviction because the words were true. She wanted with all her heart what she shied away from because of a vague fear. "That's why I took advantage of this opportunity for us to be alone. That's why I'm staying here in the house."

She brought her lips to his and kissed him with her mouth parted, bruising her softness against the firm shape of his mouth for the sheer pleasure of the contact, not just as proof of her sexual willingness. When she sought out his tongue, it was with a deepening feminine desire for the intimacy, not a deliberate ploy to explode Louis's control, which was the end result. He took over the kiss with a compulsion he expressed with the deep sound in his throat and kissed her more roughly than he'd ever kissed her before, released now from the bounds of restraint. Katie returned his hungry pressure and gave him the full ardor of her mouth and tongue, letting go, holding back nothing.

She felt his hands push beneath her sweater and sucked in her breath with anticipation of his touch on her bare skin. His palms stroking her back and shoulders and then her midriff was an exquisite preparation for the moment when he captured her breasts, delicately, as though taking care not to hurt her. When he released them, she was sharply disappointed until she realized he was simply taking time out to unfasten the front clasp of her bra. She came to the rescue and helped him when he encountered difficulties, his big, strong hands made clumsy by the tremor of his desire for her.

"Louis..." She stopped kissing him to whisper his name in response to the stroking of his fingertips on her bare breasts and then gasped with the pleasure as he took the hardened buds of her nipples between his thumbs and forefingers and gently pinched and rolled them.

"I've been wanting to touch you like this for so long, Katie," he told her huskily. "Take off your sweater for me so that I can see you, too. Please."

Katie obeyed, pulling the sweater over her head and dropping it, heedless of where it fell. All her attention was concentrated on baring her upper body for Louis's view. He gently removed her bra, easing the straps down her arms, and then caressed her breasts reverently.

"You're so soft and firm and pretty," he murmured, bending his head to her chest.

Katie tipped her head backward, her breath quickening with the rush of stimulation as he kissed her breasts and enjoyed them at leisure with his mouth and tongue. The warmth and weak pleasure were almost too much for her to bear and awoke sharper needs lower in her body.

"We need to take off our clothes," she told him, hugging his face against her.

Louis sat up and, taking her by the waist, stood her on her feet. Katie let him take her slacks off while he remained sitting on the edge of the bed, and then she removed her panty hose herself, leaving her naked before him except for her bikini panties.

"You haven't put on a single extra pound," Louis said admiringly, caressing her waist and hips and thighs.

"You still have the same cute figure you had in high school." He smiled up at her as he slipped his hands around and cupped her high, rounded buttocks. "Especially back here. In a pair of jeans, you can drive a man out of his mind."

He kissed her stomach and stood up, unbuttoning his shirt. Katie watched him with unabashed pleasure as he undressed without ceremony until he wore only knit briefs that emphasized more than concealed his arousal. She moved willingly into his arms when he reached for her and caressed his broad shoulders and muscular chest liberally furred with black, curly hair.

"I used to love looking at you stripped to the waist," she told him. "You would get dark brown in the summer, and your muscles would ripple when you were lifting heavy pieces of wood or hammering in nails."

"Don't think I didn't feel your eyes on me," Louis murmured, bending to kiss her neck while he slipped his fingers under the elastic of her panties and took them down her hips. Katie closed her arms around his shoulders as he slipped one hand between her legs, easing her thighs apart and curving his palm to the mound of her womanhood. His possession unleashed a delicious weakness in her entire lower body.

She relaxed her thighs and moaned softly as he stroked with his fingertips, discovering her feminine desire.

"Katie, you want me," he said with deep satisfaction and straightened, cupping her buttocks and lifting her to fit her hips against his, making a declaration of his need entirely unnecessary. "I want you, too," he told her anyway and then laid her on the bed and finished removing her panties. In no hurry, despite her readiness and his, he stroked her inner thighs and hips and stomach before he stripped off his briefs and reached for something from his pants pocket.

Katie lifted her arms to him as he lay down next to her. Pulling his head down to hers, she kissed him with passion, the need in her making her restless and urgent. He kissed her back hungrily, but he was completely unhurried as he slid his palm over every inch of her hips and stomach and thighs, easing close to but never quite touching the melting core of her that demanded intimate attention.

Reaching down, Katie caught his hand and took it between her legs. He stopped kissing her and looked into her face as he stroked her. Katie cried out and arched her body with the sharp pleasure.

"I don't want to wait any longer, Louis," she told him.

He smiled at her tone, a combination of plea and order, looking tender and pleased.

"I don't want to keep you waiting, either," he said softly, reaching to the nightstand and taking a packet from it. "I'd love to have your help, but it might not be a good idea this first time," he said ruefully, looking up to see her watching his intimate preparation.

Kneeling over her, he smoothed apart her legs and kissed her inner thighs. "Are you still on fire for me, sweetheart?" he asked her and tested her with his tongue. She gasped his name as she arched up to him. "I want you to be right at the edge with me, Katie." He kissed her stomach and hips and worked his way higher to her breasts. Katie clutched his head as he bit her nipples gently, setting off spasms of weakness.

"Now, Louis. Please," she begged him.

He rose immediately, letting Katie see the desire written in his features as he braced himself on one arm and positioned himself for the entry he wanted as much as she did. Caressing his shoulders, Katie could feel the hard tremor of his muscles.

"Katie." He whispered her name and closed his eyes with the penetration, going deep carefully and not stopping until he could go no farther. Sheathed in her, he opened his eyes and smiled down at her. "You feel so good to me, sweetheart. It was worth the long wait." Louis knew as he partially withdrew to thrust deep again that he wasn't talking about two months of abstinence. He was talking about all the intervening years. This time the realization didn't bother him.

Katie fought his deep, thorough lovemaking with a desperation she didn't understand. She writhed her hips under him, arched up, wrapped her legs around his waist and urged him to a more frantic pace, but he refused to be hurried. Finally she submitted to the deep union that she craved all the while that she was resisting it. Feeling something turn loose inside her, she gave herself over to his masculine control, tuned her rhythm to his and let him take total possession of her.

It was more than a physical surrender, and as soon as she gave up the struggle she understood why she had tried to hold off making love with Louis. The reason was so obvious. Intimacy with him involved more than sensual pleasure. Uniting her body with his was a matter of the heart as well as the flesh, because she loved him. She'd never stopped loving him.

Admitting the truth set her free to take total pleasure in his lovemaking. It infused physical sensation with a wild, unreasoning joy. She responded with abandon, heightening her stimulation and his.

Her release was a fusion of emotion and senses surpassing anything she'd ever experienced. It left her devastated but filled with a sweet satisfaction. Lying in Louis's arms, she thought of how different this time was, of how it was her first experience that truly qualified as making love.

"Lord, Katie, you're a lot of woman," he marveled in an exhausted voice, smoothing her hair tenderly. "With hair this color and your personality, I knew you'd be as much as any man could handle if you once let go."

Katie kissed his chest and then burrowed her face in the soft, warm fur, breathing in his masculine smell, enjoying the relaxed strength of his embrace and the closeness of their naked bodies.

"It just takes a lot of man to turn me on," she mumbled contentedly, and then chuckled at the sound of scratching and whining at the bedroom door. "I forgot all about the poor animals. Do you suppose they've been out there the whole time?" she mused with faint embarrassment.

"Couldn't prove it by me," Louis replied lazily. Tightening his arms around her, he rolled onto his back, bringing her over on top of him. She raised her head and smiled in response to his rueful grin as his stomach rumbled loudly.

"Me, too," she said. "I'm starving."

He consulted his watch.

"We have time to get dressed and go somewhere to eat. Or we could follow through with your original suggestion and pick up some hamburgers and bring them back here." He smoothed her hair back from her face, making no move to dislodge her.

Katie fully shared his lack of enthusiasm for both options.

"Why don't we check out Lucy's food supply? She told me to help myself to anything she had on hand. Maybe there's sandwich makings in the refrigerator or frozen dinners in the freezer. When I'm this hungry, I can eat almost anything."

"Except mustard greens," Louis reminded her. "Or sauerkraut. Or anything with coconut in it." He grinned and slapped her lightly on her bare rear end as she wrinkled her nose in disgust.

"I said *almost* anything," she countered and looked impish. "Maybe Lucy has a big jar of pickled pigs' feet down there. I'm sure you'd like that."

Louis shuddered. "Now, that's mean of you even to mention pickled pigs' feet. You'll spoil my appetite. You know I can't even stand the sight of those things. How anybody can eat them is beyond me."

"I'm sorry," Katie said contritely. "Then I won't mention boiled okra. I know how you like it cooked whole and slimy—"

"You little devil!"

Louis rolled her over with a powerful twist of his big body, imprisoning her underneath him.

"You haven't changed, have you?" he accused and kissed her hard on the lips. "You still get a kick out of tormenting me."

Katie smiled up at him unrepentantly. Slipping her arms around his neck, she pulled his head back down to hers for more of his punishment, which he freely gave her. The subject of food was dropped and their empty stomachs forgotten as their kisses awoke a new hunger and they made love again.

"I hope there is something to eat in the house," Louis declared afterward, when for the second time they lay together, exhausted and satisfied. "I think I'm too weak to drive. If you don't get me down to the kitchen, I won't be able to leave tonight.''

Pretending that his threat energized her, Katie popped up at once and then giggled at his injured expression.

"Thanks a lot," he told her grudgingly. "I guess you're in a big hurry to get rid of me now that you've had your way with me."

She dropped a kiss on his forehead and climbed out to start getting dressed.

"I wish you could stay all night," she told him with wistful resignation, "but we both know you can't. You have Stephanie and your mother to consider, and I have my parents and family. The news would be all over town by tomorrow that you and I were shacking up."

Louis got up, too, and began putting on his clothes, oddly disgruntled that she was being so reasonable.

"I don't much like the idea of having you stay here by yourself," he observed, frowning.

"It'll be a little strange sleeping in a house alone," Katie admitted. "But this will give me a chance to see what it would be like living by myself. I've been thinking about getting a place of my own for quite some time. For several years," she added when Louis looked at her in surprise. "I doubt I'll get around to it, though, until I finish the Hemphill house and figure out what to do next." She didn't want him to think she was assuming they'd have an affair now, though she would be open to some pressure to make herself more available.

Aware of his eyes on her, she walked over to the door and opened it, letting in the two cocker spaniels, who frisked excitedly around her feet.

"These two guys will protect me tonight if a burglar tries to break in," she said cheerfully, kneeling to pet the two dogs. She wished he'd say something. "And I have a policeman living right next door. You know Andy Hano."

"Sure, I know Andy well," Louis said slowly from behind her. "You've never mentioned wanting to move out of your folks' house. I'd gotten the impression you were perfectly happy with the situation."

"I am happy with it—when I'm happy," Katie said lightly, stung by his reaction. He certainly wasn't very enthusiastic at the notion of her having a place of her own. "But when I'm not happy, I have to pretend I am so as not to worry my parents. It's nice on the one hand to be that important to them, but it gets to be a burden." She rose and turned to smile at him. "It's when things aren't going well—like a couple of months ago, before I got the Hemphill job—that I realized I need to move out. But right now, things couldn't be better. Except that I'm starving to death," she added, pressing her hands to her stomach. "Are you ready to go down and raid the kitchen?"

"You'd better believe I'm ready," he replied agreeably and came over to put his arms around her and hug her. "What you're saying is that I have to want you to be miserable in order to get you into a more private situation. But I'm just like your mamma and daddy! I can't stand to see you unhappy. This is a heck of a predicament." He kissed the tip of her nose. "Let's go down and see what we can find to eat."

His air of warm indulgence was nice, but it didn't ease Katie's disappointment that he seemed so accepting of having her continue to live at home, making it all but impossible for them to have this kind of privacy. When was she ever going to learn her lesson and not leave herself open with expectations? she wondered despairingly. Having admitted to herself that she loved Louis, it was all the more important that she not allow herself to build foolish hopes and risk a heartbreak that would be much more devastating this time.

Chapter Twelve

Louis didn't make it easy for her.

"Call me a male chauvinist, but I'd worry about you living by yourself," he said on the way down to the kitchen, sounding as though he were carrying on a mental debate with himself.

"Covington's not exactly a big city with a crime problem," Katie scoffed, trying not to jump to the conclusion that a protective attitude might be behind his lack of enthusiasm for her living alone. "And you're right. That is chauvinistic. Lots of women my age live by themselves."

"Small towns have their share of crazies," he replied, undaunted. "A single woman attracts attention. Especially a cute one with red hair," he added affectionately, ruffling her hair.

"I won't depend on you for any support when I tell my parents I'm moving out," Katie jeered. "You'll be agreeing with every one of my father's objections."

"Your father and I think a lot alike where our women are concerned."

"Yes, you're both Southern men and terrible male chauvinists," she accused, melted by his joint claim of her.

"Which makes it that much easier for you to twist us around your little finger," he retorted.

Much to her regret, the conversation lapsed as they reached the kitchen and became engrossed in the search for food. They located a pizza in the freezer and put it into the convection oven to cook. Then they foraged in the refrigerator and pantry and found cheese and crackers. Perched on stools at the island counter, they snacked hungrily.

"If you left home, you'd sure miss your mother's meals," Louis remarked. "She's some cook."

"I could still drop by anytime and eat with them," Katie pointed out, delighted that he was picking up the conversation again. "You know how my mother cooks enough for an army. I just dread the actual moving out, when the time comes," she confided. "It's going to be about as cheerful as a funeral. Their feelings will be hurt. They'll see no reason I should move out and live by myself. They'll miss me and worry about me." Katie sighed and munched on a cracker. "It's a mixed blessing, I guess, being the spoiled youngest daughter. If I'd been a boy, it would have been different."

"I, for one, am glad you weren't." Louis cut a chunk of cheddar and put it on a cracker. "Among other reasons, I'd have missed out on a lot of pocket money if your father had had a son," he added teasingly, giving the cracker and cheese to her.

Katie ate his offering, wishing he'd elaborate on the "other reasons," but when he spoke, he seemed to be changing the subject entirely.

"My mother's talking about taking her retirement from the clerk of court's office in June. She'll have thirty years by then."

Katie showed her surprise over his news.

"Why, your mother's an institution down at the courthouse!" she exclaimed. "What will she do if she quits working? She's only about fifty and in good health, isn't she?" Louis, his mouth full, nodded. "I would think she'd get bored staying at home," Katie speculated, visualizing Mildred McIntyre, a trim, well-groomed woman, the model of office efficiency.

"My mother doesn't have the same kind of interests as yours," Louis agreed. "I doubt she'd have enjoyed being a full-time housewife even if my father hadn't gotten killed when I was a baby and she hadn't needed to work." He smiled and shook his head. "She thinks spending hours in the kitchen is a waste of time. Her idea of baking homemade cookies is slicing up the dough you buy in a roll in the supermarket."

"I'm with her. So what will she do with her time if she retires?" Katie asked, curious. "Stephanie's getting to the age where she's more independent and wants to be with her friends. I guess there are lots of worthwhile projects and women's clubs. I can't imagine your mother watching daytime television."

Louis's smile supported her doubts.

"She's more the late-night television type. What she really wants to do is travel. For years now she's read travel magazines and gone to any kind of slide presentation on foreign trips. Now there's really no reason she shouldn't take off and go to some of the places she wants to see. She's saved up quite a bit of money since, naturally, I pay all the living expenses. Plus she'd have her pension coming in regularly.''

"Your mother wants to go off and travel by herself?" Katie blurted out in amazement.

Louis shook his head.

"That's the beauty of it. She has someone to travel with. Her only sister, who lives down in Fort Myers, Florida, is widowed, too, and comfortably fixed. Aunt Mary has the travel bug, as well. She wants my mother to take a Mediterranean cruise with her this summer."

Katie digested that astounding bit of news and Louis's attitude.

"You sound as if you're in favor of it."

"I'd love to see my mother take the cruise," Louis confirmed readily. "Why shouldn't she?"

"How long would it last?"

"Three weeks, and then Aunt Mary wants them to take at least a couple more weeks to traipse around Europe, as long as they're there."

"That's five weeks!" Katie exclaimed. "How are you and Stephanie going to get along for that amount of time on your own?"

"Stephie and I would manage," Louis replied. He put together a makeshift canapé with a cracker and slice of cheese. When Katie refused it, he ate it himself before he continued. "Aunt Mary sold her house recently and is looking to buy a condo. She'd like for my mother to move to Florida and go halves with her on it. She figures that the two of them could take off on trips whenever they wanted to and otherwise take life easy."

"I'm sure your mother wouldn't even consider moving away and leaving you and Stephie." Katie was highly skeptical of the notion.

Louis shrugged. "Floria's not that far away that we wouldn't still see her. She's already more than done her duty. I'm a grown man, not a little boy, and Stephie's my responsibility, not hers. We'd miss her, but we'd get along."

"That's certainly an unselfish attitude on your part," Katie remarked, suddenly feeling awkward at showing too much interest in how he'd fill the gap his mother would leave. "But I doubt seriously that your mother's going to move off and leave you and Stephanie to your own devices. You said she was talking about retiring. It sounds as though she hasn't actually decided."

Louis's smile made Katie's heart race as she realized all of a sudden that he'd been working his way around to whatever it was that he was about to say.

"She's hoping I'll make her decision easy for her and get myself a wife. My mother would like nothing better than to see me remarried," he explained ruefully. "Any time I go out more than a few times with anyone she approves of, she immediately reminds me that she'd never stand in my way. Naturally, she definitely approves of you."

"That's flattering." Katie slid off the stool, went to the wall oven and peered in the glass door with absolutely no interest in the pizza. "I guess your getting married again would solve the problem for her," she said, striving for no expression. "But it's not exactly fair of her, putting that kind of pressure on you."

"It's not just from my mother that I'm getting pressure," Louis replied cheerfully. "I'm getting it from my daughter, too."

Katie turned and viewed him with blank disbelief, reacting not just to his disclosure but to what her common sense told her couldn't be happening. Louis wasn't leading up to a marriage proposal, was he?

"Stephanie wants you to get married again? That really surprises me. I would think she'd be jealous. The two of you are so close." Katie's heart pounded as Louis slid off the stool and stood up, moving at his characteristic unhurried pace.

"If I were going out with anybody besides you, it probably would be different," he admitted. "She likes you a lot." He shook his head, smiling at his thoughts. "It's interesting the way she has things figured out in relation to herself. You know, Betty's folks have never even seen Stephie. They moved to north Mississippi the year after she was born and have never had any interest in being grandparents to her. She's had a shortage of relatives and envies your niece Lisa because she has so many. Stephie asked me the other day, 'Daddy, if I had a stepmother, wouldn't her mommy and daddy be my step-grandma and step-grandpa?'"

Katie's insides tightened painfully at the affectionate mimicry.

"And what did you tell her?"

Louis's smile faded a little at her tone, and he looked uncertain as he stepped toward her, trying to fathom her mood.

"I told her it made perfectly good sense to me." He put his arms around her and hugged her. But when she was stiff and unresponsive in his arms, he released her slowly and looked searchingly into her face. "I know what you're thinking," he said apologetically. "It's a strange turn of events, my daughter trying to get us together. You don't hold what happened with us a long time ago against Stephie, do you, Katie?''

"Of course I don't," Katie denied, too proud to tell him what really bothered her. "Stephanie's a very sweet child. I'm fond of her. She looks so much like you, I never even think of Betty when I'm around her."

The similarity between him and his daughter went a lot deeper than appearance, she was thinking unhappily. They were both attracted to her family—especially to her parents—to the extent that they were willing to take Katie in the bargain.

Louis sighed, regarding her with dismay. "I guess I'm rushing things." He followed Katie's earlier example and peered into the oven. "How's that pizza coming along? Hmm. It looks downright edible, doesn't it?"

Katie wanted to go somewhere and cry. Once she'd have jumped at the chance to marry Louis, however she could get him to agree, and not felt a qualm as long as she tied him to her. And he would have knuckled under to the various pressures, she was sure, if he hadn't gotten Betty pregnant. After Katie finished high school, he would have ended up marrying her, primarily because she was her parents' daughter. If he'd married her, he would have been a member of her family and pleased the person most important to him: her father.

Were his reasons for considering marriage to her still essentially the same? Katie wondered despairingly. And if they were, would she say yes to a proposal, knowing he was simply being swayed into what was convenient and suited everyone?

Of course she would say yes, even if she said it feeling this bitterness and disappointment. There was no saying no to Louis. How could she turn him down, loving him the way she did? Not enough was better than nothing.

Katie had never been good at hiding her feelings. Though she made an effort, she knew her dejection showed. With her appetite destroyed, as it invariably was by unhappiness, she was able to get down only one slice of pizza.

"I guess I ate too much cheese and crackers." She patted her stomach as she offered her fake excuse. "I'm already full."

"Are you sure that's the reason you're not hungry?" Louis asked her gently. "Don't forget, I know you well. You always had trouble eating any time you were upset. I doubt that's changed." He squeezed her shoulder and then left his hand there. "Don't worry your head about the things I said earlier, Katie. Nothing's urgent with us. We have lots of time."

"I won't worry," Katie promised him, feeling immensely better under the soothing balm of his voice and touch, both of which said he did care about her, even if his emotion wasn't as intense as hers.

"That's my girl. Now help me with the rest of this pizza." He put a slice on her plate and added teasingly, "I can't have you losing weight on me. I'll have trouble finding you in bed."

Katie took a bite to please him and proceeded to eat the whole slice.

"I know why you want to keep me strong and healthy," she told him as he served her another piece. "You don't want to lose your volunteer office worker. I guess that desk of yours is loaded down with bills about now, at the end of the month. I can come over in the morning and write out some checks if you want me to."

"I shouldn't take you up on it, but I will." Louis was plainly delighted at her offer. "I have to do some running around in the morning, but I'll leave the door to the office unlocked in case I'm not back when you come over. I'm going to have to get a key made for you," he added, grinning. "That way you can drop in any time you get the urge."

He was reluctant to go when it came time to leave, again expressing his reservations about her staying alone.

"Lock the bedroom door," he ordered her. "If you hear a suspicious sound or the dogs bark, call me and I'll be right over. Don't worry that it's nothing."

He kissed her good-night and then went through the same safety instructions again, with a tender addition. "I can't have anything happening to you, you know."

"You're going to make me paranoid," Katie protested, too touched by his tone and expression to be convincing.

Louis's presence seemed to linger in the house after he'd gone, so Katie didn't feel at all nervous as she turned out the lights and went upstairs. The last-minute sprint in order to close the dogs out of her bedroom brought an amused smile to her face as she remembered the fun of fleeing the dogs with Louis.

Under different circumstances, she might have chanced the novelty of sharing her bed with three animals. But Katie already had a bed partner... Louis.

It felt intimate lying in the darkness in the bed she had recently shared with him for such passionate lovemaking. She imagined him there beside her, holding her, big and strong and masculine. Her love for him welled up inside her, so intense it was painful.

Would Louis ever feel anything this powerful for her? she wondered with longing. Would his emotion for her ever hurt, take away his will and make him helpless?

She yearned for that kind of love from Louis. What she wanted, more than anything, was to matter to him desperately, to be necessary for his deepest happiness.

But she would settle for masculine desire and affectionate caring from him if they were what he had to offer her. A part of a loaf was better than none, even if it didn't satisfy. Affection from Louis was better than declarations of undying love from any other man in the world. He was so special to her, and she could absolutely trust him.

He would never lie to her or deceive her. He was honest and sincere and sensitive, a decent, fine man. Katie was a lucky woman to have him want to share his life with her. She drifted off to sleep on a wave of gladness, thinking that she'd see Louis tomorrow and the next day and the next. . . .

Awakening early, at her usual time, she was briefly disoriented, remembered where she was and then congratulated herself on her sound night's sleep. Eager to start the day, she sprang up and got dressed and, after giving the animals some obligatory attention, drove to her parents' house for breakfast. Imagining Louis's teasing reaction when he learned she hadn't even made coffee for herself, she smiled.

"You went straight home for your mamma's cooking," he'd drawl accusingly and then probably grin and admit, "I can't say I blame you."

Turning the volume of her radio up loud, she sang along with inappropriate cheer to an old song a top male recording star in the country and western field had brought back to popularity. The song's message was a sad one about a cheating wife and the wronged husband's hopelessly shattered life.

"Don't you look in a good mood this morning," her mother declared with a smiling welcome when Katie walked into the kitchen. "You must not have had any problem sleeping in a strange bed. Your daddy and I were just talking about how big this old house would be just for the two of us. But I guess we'd get used to it if we had to."

"Sounds to me as if you're trying to get rid of me," Katie accused, ignoring the broad hint. She could have told Louis last night that his mother wasn't the only one hoping that Katie and Louis were headed toward matrimony. The match wouldn't meet with any objection from her family. Louis was back in solid.

After she'd eaten and visited with her parents a short while, Katie decided it was late enough to drive over to Louis's office. She was hopeful that she might catch him before he left to do the errands he'd mentioned.

But his pickup wasn't in the driveway, she noted at once with disappointment. Her spirits rose with the reminder that he'd be back, probably in an hour or two, and by then she might have caught up on his paperwork. They hadn't discussed plans last night, but she was confident they'd spend the rest of the day together.

Climbing the stairs at the side of the garage, she hummed the mournful tune about the cheating wife and felt warmly complacent at the thought that helping Louis with his paperwork would become a permanent thing. She smiled, visualizing his untidy desk and his grateful wonder when he returned to find it neat.

Halfway to the top of the stairs, Katie heard the phone ring and hurried, thinking she'd answer it and take a message for him. But by the time she'd reached the landing and pushed open the door, his answering machine had been activated. She entered and walked toward the desk, smiling with pleasure at the recorded sound of Louis's deep, slow cadences.

"Louis McIntyre here. If you meant to call me and you're not collecting money or trying to sell something, you can talk to this machine when I'm finished talking. You know the routine. After the beep, leave your name and so on. I'll get back to you when I can. Thank you for calling."

Katie sat down in Louis's chair, shaking her head at the chaos she'd expected to see on his desk. The recorder gave its electronic signal, and she waited with no particular curiosity to see if Louis's caller would leave a message. He or she hadn't hung up.

"Louis, it looks as if you and I can't make contact in person. You get my machine, and I get yours." Katie came alert, recognizing the male caller's familiar voice before he went on to identify himself. *"This is John Hemphill, returning your call. I got your message when my wife and I came in last night, but it was late. We're going out of town for the weekend, leaving in about ten minutes, so you won't be able to reach me until Monday. I trust there's no problem. You sounded rather urgent. From my end, everything seems to be moving very smoothly. I don't regret taking your advice and going with Katie Gamble. It's worked out to my advantage that you owed her father a favor and recommended her. As I've said several times, I'm impressed with her. She's sharp as a tack and seems very competent. It still gives me a little extra peace of mind, though, knowing you personally okay her workmen and are keeping a close*

*eye on progress, as we agreed. Carry on. Talk to you on
Monday if we can manage to make a connection.''*

Katie sat there, stunned and frozen, staring at the
answering machine while she listened to the click as the
man whose house she'd thought she was responsible for
building hung up. After what seemed an eternity, the
tape rewound with a little whirring sound.

Closing her eyes tightly, she tried to muster a denial
of the humiliating conspiracy that had just been acci-
dentally divulged to her.

No. Please, God, no, she begged silently. It was more
than she could bear to think that Louis would do this to
her—trick her, demean her, let her think that she was
proving herself while the credit secretly went to him. He
just wouldn't. But he was. As cruel as the truth was, it
was inescapable.

John Hemphill's message forced an appalling hind-
sight. It explained the man's sudden change of mind, his
choice of her as his building contractor when he'd already picked Louis. It supplied the real motive for
Louis's concern that she make a profit on the job. Now,
dear God, she understood all the trouble he'd gone to
in putting her in contact with his subs, his generosity in
sharing them, his *insistence* that she use them. He
hadn't trusted her to hire competent subs herself and
oversee their work. He'd wanted his own men on the
job.

It was all so painfully clear, looking back. Why, he'd
called her and asked her out the very evening of the day
Hemphill had contacted her. She'd been on cloud nine
over winning the contract and was thrilled over Louis's
friendly overture. Winning the contract became that
much more of a gift from heaven if it led to a new association with Louis, the man she'd never gotten over,

the man for whom she'd harbored an unwilling preference through the years.

The contract hadn't been a gift from above fash-
ioned out of kind circumstance. It had been a gift from
Louis, and not even for her, really, but for her father.
That fact added its own hurt. Apparently Louis had
even explained to Hemphill that it was Red Gamble for
whom he wanted to do a favor, not Katie.

Katie could see the way it had developed. She had
brought Louis and her father together out of the guilty
urge to make amends. Her father had been worried sick
about her because she was unhappy without a house to
build and had no prospects. No doubt he'd confided in
Louis, and Louis had come to the rescue, paying back
old debts to the man who'd been like a father to him.

Did her father know? The question sliced through
Katie, cutting to the quick. Had he and Louis agreed on
the plan? A possible affirmative was too painful for her
to consider. Her mind couldn't dwell on the thought of
the two men she loved most in the world conspiring and
deceiving her. She went on to more tolerable shaming
circumstances, trying to fuel her anger. She desperately
needed some defense.

What about Peewee and Louis's other good subcontractor friends who'd agreed to work for her? Were they
in on the fakery? Were they playing along, smiling with
male condescension behind Katie's back, letting her
think she was the boss while they reported to Louis? Did
they know, as Katie hadn't, that every afternoon when
Louis came around, he was checking on her?

"Oh, God," Katie whimpered aloud, burying her
face in her hands as a wave of anguish washed through
her, drowning the indignation she was desperately trying
to muster. She cringed to think of the eagerness with

which she'd greeted Louis's appearance each day, her confident sharing with him of the builder's problems that had arisen. Unthreatened, she'd solicited his opinion, reveled in the sense of professional camaraderie as well as enjoyed his company.

She could never forgive him. The thought was wrung out of her and flooded her with black despair. Louis had killed her basic trust in him. How was she going to live without it?

Obeying blind instinct that told her she needed to go somewhere besides Louis's office to cope with her emotional devastation, Katie got up jerkily. Louis could return at any time and find her there. She wasn't ready to face him, to make accusations, to have him confirm them.

It didn't seem possible to Katie as she made a headlong rush for the door that she'd ever be ready.

Chapter Thirteen

Louis drove the last eight or ten blocks to his house with growing anticipation. By now Katie would surely be at his office. He smiled, thinking of her sitting at his desk, all redheaded, slim efficiency. Making love to her last night had been incredible. It made him feel deeply possessive, remembering the way she'd responded, the way she'd felt in his arms afterward.

Somehow the intimacy had wiped out all his bachelor's resistance—what there had been left of it. Marriage to Katie. That would be quite an adjustment, but never dull, for sure. She wasn't anything like either of their mothers. Katie was definitely one of a kind, more than he could ever possibly handle, but that was beside the point. He was hooked, and he knew it.

There were problems, but in time they would work out. Katie would have to get over hurt feelings that he'd married Betty and any hidden resentment she might feel toward Stephie. Louis was confident that as the three of them spent some time together, Katie and his daughter would become close. He was prejudiced, of course, but Stephie was a bright, sweet, delightful child, and Katie was certainly fair-minded.

He'd probably have to put Katie's mind at ease about what he would expect from her as a wife. Whether due to her circumstances, living at home, or her personality, she obviously wasn't the domestic type. She wouldn't want responsibility for housecleaning and cooking. Mrs. Evanson could come in more days and perhaps do some cooking as well as cleaning and laundry. They could eat out, bring home take-out food, throw together simple meals. Hell, they wouldn't starve. Katie's mother would probably take pity on them and invite them over often. Louis grinned at his enthusiasm over that latter speculation.

Katie would want to go on working as a building contractor, which suited him fine. She could be his partner. If they could ease by the matter of her pride, there'd be no difficulty keeping her as busy as she wanted to be. Louis could get the jobs for her, just as her father had done. Hell, they'd end up making a whopping income between them.

Before he got the future worked out in too much detail, though, he needed to attend to the present. He had to melt Katie's reservations, overcome her independence. She hadn't exactly jumped at the idea of marrying him when he'd started sounding out her feelings on it last night.

As soon as he managed to get hold of Hemphill and get a release from the promise he'd made the man,

Louis was going to make a clean breast of it to Katie. Lord, how he dreaded telling her, but he hoped she would be soothed by the way she'd impressed Hemphill. Louis wasn't anticipating any problems convincing him that Katie didn't need overseeing.

With just a block to go, he put aside thoughts of the confession that weighed on him and concentrated on the pleasure of seeing her, of giving her a good-morning hug and kiss and probably distracting her from her work if she hadn't already finished. He was in the mood to head straight over to her friends' house and race those dogs up the stairs to her bed.

Louis's broad smile at his vision faded as his driveway came into sight and there was no red Bronco. Katie wasn't there. He was disappointed at the discovery and then vaguely alarmed as he thought about her having spent the night alone.

Pulling into the driveway, he briefly considered driving immediately over to the house on Sixth Street to look for her, passing by her parents' house on the way. But then she might have been to his office and left a message. Perhaps she'd gone off on an errand and would be returning shortly.

Trying to dispel his anxiety, which common sense told him was unreasonable, he took the stairs up to his office two at a time. A quick glance around as he walked to the desk revealed no sign that she'd come and gone. There was no note. The papers on his desk looked untouched.

He'd call her parents and find out if they knew her whereabouts, he decided. He was reaching for the phone when he saw the red light blinking on his answering machine. She'd probably called and left a mes-

sage. Half-relieved with the expectation of hearing her
voice making an explanation, he punched the play button on the machine and sagged at the sound of John
Hemphill's voice.

"Sweet Jesus!" Louis muttered halfway through the
message, horror-struck at the realization that Katie
might have been there when Hemphill called. As soon
as Louis learned the safe, logical reason she hadn't kept
her promise to come by and do his paperwork for him,
he was going to be deeply thankful he'd been so lucky.

Katie's mother answered the phone. With the bare
minimum of pleasantries, Louis asked if Katie had been
by yet that morning, adding, "I'm just checking to see
if I won a bet. I told her she'd be over bright and early
for breakfast."

Edna Gamble's pleased chatter put his fears to rest at
once. Katie was safe and sound.

"Well, now, that's between you two. I can't tell on
Katie, but she was by here this morning. When she left,
she was going to your office."

Louis gazed at the answering machine, suddenly
feeling sick. She had been here.

"That's what I wanted to know, Miz Edna. Thank
you, ma'am."

Louis confronted the appalling likelihood that Katie
had listened to Hemphill's message. She might have arrived, seen the message light blinking and checked to see
if he had called and left a message for her while he was
out running errands.

It was the worst possible way she could have learned
of his arrangement with Hemphill, listening to a
damned recording. Louis cursed violently, thinking of

her shock and hurt and anger, if the scenario he imagined was true.

He tried to cling to a shred of doubt as he left the office and set out on a search for her. The first logical place to look for her was her friends' house, where Louis had anticipated spending a lazy afternoon with her, making love and enjoying her. As much as he wanted to find her, he hoped she wasn't there. Why would she return to the empty house unless she was looking for a place to be alone?

Her Bronco was in the driveway.

Heart pumping with heavy presentiment, Louis rang the doorbell, waited an interminable ten or fifteen seconds and then rang it again.

The dead bolt clicked ominously. Katie opened the door, and Louis could see in a glance that she'd been crying. Her eyes were red-rimmed and bright with the tears she'd shed.

"Damn it, Katie, I'm sorry!"

Full of remorse, he stepped over the threshold, reaching for her, wanting to touch her, to take her into his arms, but she drew back and retreated several steps. He closed the door, feeling helpless.

"I guess you played Hemphill's message," he said regretfully.

She shook her head. "I heard him leave it," she refuted, her voice husky from crying but toneless. "I had just walked in the door."

Louis cursed under his breath. "I feel terrible about this, Katie!" He stepped closer and reached to touch her again. Again she recoiled, moving a little farther away from him. He sighed his frustration. "I've been wanting like hell to tell you, but I was afraid you'd take it like this. Last night, before I came to pick you up, I tried to call Hemphill and let him know that the deal between us was off because it wasn't necessary. I'm sure he'd have agreed, Katie. He thinks very highly of you. He's told me so."

"Is that supposed to make me feel good, Louis? That a man who supposedly hired me to build his two-hundred-thousand-dollar house thinks maybe I can do my job?" Katie said cuttingly. "Does my father know you gave me the contract, Louis? Did the two of you cook up this scheme between you to make poor little Katie happy?"

Louis winced at the raw hurt mixed with her injured pride.

"Honest to God, Katie, your father doesn't know a thing about it," he vowed fervently, clenching his hands to keep from reaching for her again when her face crumpled at his reassurance.

"I'm glad for that, at least," she murmured.

"It was a gentleman's agreement between Hemphill and me," Louis told her humbly. "I haven't told a soul, and I asked him not to, either. He was in a big hurry and pressuring me. I suggested he go with you instead and promised him I'd keep a close eye on his house. If any problems came up that you couldn't handle, I gave him my word that I'd take care of them. There haven't been any problems like that, Katie," he added persuasively. "And there won't be. You're good at your job. Hemphill and I both know that."

"You made sure there wouldn't be any problems," Katie accused bitterly. "You managed to get your own men on the job, giving me that cock-and-bull story about feeling bad that I wasn't making a profit."

"I was sincere about that," Louis protested, knowing he looked guilty as hell. "But I'd gone out on a limb, giving my word to Hemphill, when you and I weren't exactly on the friendliest of terms. Hell, I didn't know if you'd even let me come around on the job. It was my best insurance, seeing that you had men I could trust working for you."

Katie let his lack of confidence in his welcome pass by her.

"You swear to me that Peewee and the others don't know about it. I want the truth," she added reproachfully before he could answer. "Not just what you think will make me happy to hear."

"I give you my word, Katie."

Katie sighed. "It's not as bad as I thought, then," she said bleakly. "If they were all in on it, I couldn't possibly carry on if Hemphill held me to the contract."

Louis frowned at her anxiously. "What do you mean? Katie, you're not thinking of not finishing the house?"

She shrugged disconsolately.

"It depends entirely on Hemphill. If he wants me as his building contractor, fine. I'll finish his house. If he wants you, then he can free me of my legal obligations."

Louis looked relieved. "He'll want you," he stated positively and walked over to put one arm around Katie's unresponsive shoulders and give them a hard hug. "Hemphill knows he has a good contractor. Just say the word, Katie, and I won't come within a block of that house until it's finished, although it won't make me very happy." He was urging her along with him toward the main room. "I was worried when I got to the office and you weren't there, honey," he told her softly. "Then when I started figuring out what had happened, I was sick. I wouldn't deliberately hurt you for anything, Katie."

"Maybe not, but I am hurt," she replied stubbornly, her boots dragging on the carpet. She managed somehow to keep her shoulders stiff within the circle of his arm, although it was difficult. Inside, she wanted so badly just to give in. "Being sorry doesn't change the fact that you weren't honest with me, Louis. How could I ever trust you again?"

"Was what I did really so bad, Katie?" he reasoned, steering her toward the sectional sofa. "Think about it. No harm was done, except to your pride, and don't the plus factors outweigh that? You're having a hell of a good time building a fine house with some of the best people in the business working for you. You're making a good living for yourself, and the Hemphills are getting their money's worth. You and I have gotten together in the bargain. That's the main outcome, for me."

He sat on the sofa, pulling her down next to him. She tried to move away, out of the circle of his arm, but he wouldn't let her.

"Come on, Katie, let's talk it out," he urged. "Put all our cards on the table and be honest. At the risk of making you even madder, I can't say I wouldn't do the same thing again, because otherwise I might not be sitting here next to you now."

Katie crossed one knee over the other and her arms across her chest and gave him a baleful glance.

"Your handy philosophy that if things work out in the end, the pain was worth it," she said scornfully.

"How do you think it makes me feel, Louis, to know that you were coming by every day, checking on me and reporting to Hemphill? I can tell you. I feel like a fool. To think I played right into your hands, asking your opinion on every single little detail." Katie made a disgusted sound and tried to get up, but Louis wouldn't let her. He hooked his arm around her waist and brought her back.

"I enjoyed coming by, Katie, just to see you. Hell, as time went on, it was all I could do to hold myself down to once a day. Among other things, I was hot to get inside your jeans," he teased. He clasped her thigh with his free hand and squeezed it. "I had sense enough to know that you were mainly just stroking my male ego, asking my advice. Now, weren't you? Come on, admit it. You never had the first doubt about what needed to be done in any of the situations we discussed. 'Let's make Louis feel like a big, strong, important man,' you were thinking. And it worked," he admitted, smiling hesitantly.

Katie tried hard, but she couldn't keep her mouth from quirking in grudging response.

"I know how to build a house, damn it. That's what's so humiliating and frustrating about having you go behind my back and give me a contract." She tried to get up again, but he held her, circling her waist tighter and clamping her thigh. "Let me go," she demanded, wanting to put some distance between them before she opened up deeper issues that couldn't be healed with humor.

"Nope," he replied. "You're staying right here. How would it be if I didn't go behind your back from now on?" he asked without a pause.

"There isn't going to be any 'from now on,'" Katie retorted, compressing her lips and glaring at him.

"Sure, there is. How about being partners with me? You're up against an unfair situation, just because you're a woman, and I have more prospects than I can handle. You only have to promise not to show me up too badly," he added cheerfully. "I don't doubt that you can build a house or two more than I can in a year's time. With all that nervous energy, you move a lot faster and don't shoot the breeze as much as I do."

"You're not serious," Katie accused, trying not to even consider what he was suggesting. "You don't want me as your building partner, Louis. You're just trying to smooth things over and patch up my hurt pride."

"I am, too, serious." He hesitated. "Actually, I was thinking along the lines of a husband-and-wife partnership."

Katie meant to get up this time. She kicked Louis's shin with the heel of her Western boot, making him yelp in pain, and struggled against his hold on her.

"Damn it, Katie! What're you trying to do, cripple me?" he muttered, gathering her legs together at the knees and swinging them across his lap. Katie didn't have any choice but to sink backward into the cushiony softness of the sofa. "You're not going anywhere," he told her with grim determination. "I might have a tiger by the tail, but I'm not letting go."

Katie screwed up her face in frustration and fury and landed a solid blow to his shoulder with her fist.

"Go ahead and hit me, sweetheart, if it makes you feel better," Louis urged her gently.

"It won't make me feel any better!" Katie shouted at him, hitting him again. "Damn it! Let me go! You didn't even do it for me! You did it for my father! He's the one you really care about! Not me!''

With a strangled sob, she turned her face and closed her eyes tightly against the sting of tears. It was such a shameful relief to open up finally and let him see her deepest wound.

"So that's it. I thought we'd gotten past that old jealousy."

Katie felt a stab of pain at Louis's gentle, regretful tone. She flinched against his fingertips touching her cheek.

"That's it," she said. "And believe me, apologizing won't solve the problem."

"Katie, you little idiot," he chided tenderly. "I do think a hell of a lot of your father, but I didn't go against my basic policy of being aboveboard and straight because of *him*."

Katie let him turn her face with a gentle palm and met his gaze, seeing his warmth and sincerity.

"So why did Hemphill say in his phone call today that he was glad you owed my father a favor?"

"That was the story I told him." He smiled. "It was the story I told myself, too, but it didn't hold water. I managed to believe it for no more than a day or two. Let's see." He pretended to consider. "As I recall, it fell plumb to pieces during an LSU football game that I didn't see a minute of. That was the afternoon after our first night out. I kissed you and gave myself a good dose of frustration. After that, I was hooked and kept taking swigs. Last night proved I wasn't ever going to be cured of my habit. Will you marry me, Katie?"

Katie closed her eyes, shutting out his face lighted with tender humor. How could she ever resist him?

"It's not going to work, Louis," she said with all the sadness and futility that she felt. Opening her eyes, she looked at his shoulder while she made the difficult explanation. "Pride can be a very serious matter, you know. It's the hardest thing in the world for me to say no to you, but when and if I ever do get married, it's going to be because I'm *me*, not because my name's Katie Gamble."

She looked at him and tried to smile as she touched his cheek, still avoiding his eyes. "You and Stephanie are going to have to figure out another way to get into my family," she said with bleak humor. "And your mother might just have to go on working forever—"

Louis brought her up on his lap and hugged her tightly against him, forcing her head down to his shoulder.

"You can say no all you want, but I won't accept it," he told her, stroking her hair. "And it has nothing to do with making my mother or my daughter happy."

Katie pushed back from him reluctantly and looked into his face.

"But it does have something to do with my being Katie Gamble, doesn't it, Louis?"

"Of course it does," he replied, touching her bottom lip with his thumb. "How the hell can it not, sweetheart? You and I aren't a couple of strangers. I let you boss me around all the years we were growing up. I let you lead me around with a ring in my nose in high school. A couple of months ago, when you showed up in my life again, I realized the ring was still there, waiting for you to take hold of it." Louis took one of her hands and rubbed it against his nose, then kissed it.

"You're impossible," Katie protested softly.

Louis framed her face with his hands.

"Maybe so, but you're still stuck with me." He brought her face to his and kissed her. "I'm nuts about you, Katie," he said softly, without any humor. "It scares me to think you and I might have kept on traveling our separate paths in this same little town. I hate to think of the years I've missed out on with you, but then—"

"I know. You don't have to tell me," Katie interrupted him, incredible happiness spreading through her. She kissed him on the lips with the pretext of cutting off his words and then let herself be drawn into an intimate play of tongues. "Everything worked out in the end," she murmured. "Wasn't that what you were going to say?"

"Well, didn't it?" he murmured, caressing her back and shoulders and then slipping around to her breasts. "Where are those animals you're looking after, anyway?"

"They're out in the backyard. Why?"

Louis answered her a few words at a time between short, deep kisses.

"I can tell...that it's time...to race them upstairs...to the bedroom."

Katie pulled back a few inches and smiled at him.

"How can you tell?"

"Didn't you hear my stomach just growl?" he demanded, sliding his hand possessively along the inside of her thigh. "I jumped up out of bed this morning and rushed off without any breakfast, wanting to get back to you as soon as possible. One of these days I'm hoping to get you into bed when I'm not weak with hunger."

"It's almost eleven," Katie mused, checking her watch without removing her arms from around his neck. "We could go out for some lunch or—"

"I vote for *or*," Louis cut in, leaving no doubt as to the definition of his choice as he kissed her and slid the hand between her thighs higher. "What about you?"

Katie's legs relaxed apart with the delicious sensation he aroused as he stroked intimately along the seam of her jeans.

"Actually, I had breakfast...."

"I know, you rascal. You got up and made a beeline for your mamma's kitchen this morning. You couldn't get by one day without her hot biscuits and homemade jam."

Katie threw back her head and laughed.

"Louis, I *knew* you were going to say something like that! I could just hear you this morning when I was driving over. I could have invited you to meet me there," she reflected. "My mother would have been tickled pink. She always makes a huge pan of biscuits, and there are inevitably some left over."

"Now you tell me," Louis grumbled. "Since you weren't very thoughtful, and didn't invite me, I'll make a meal of you instead."

He put her off his lap, stood and held a hand down to her. Katie went to her fate willingly, grasping the hand of her handsome cannibal.

Upstairs, she sat on the edge of the bed and let Louis take her boots off for her. Then he grasped her waist, stood her up and undressed her, stopping to kiss her breasts when he'd removed her blouse and bra.

"Tender and sweet," he murmured, licking a hardened peak and then nipping it gently.

"I wonder why I feel so weak when you do that," Katie said, stroking his shoulders and back.

Moving over to the other breast, Louis unsnapped her jeans, unzipped them and pushed them down her hips, along with her bikini panties.

"Did I cause this, touching your breasts?" he murmured, stroking between her legs.

Katie moaned softly. "Everything seems to be connected."

Louis kissed his way down her stomach, getting down on his haunches to finish taking off her jeans. When she was naked, he stayed there and caressed her hips and buttocks and stomach. Katie sucked in her breath at the sensation as he bent forward and nuzzled his face high against her inner thigh.

"Mmm. Sweet here, too," he murmured and took a nip.

Katie's knees threatened to buckle with the tide of weakness.

"I felt that all the way to my toes," she told him.

"I felt it, too, but nowhere in the vicinity of my toes." He pressed his lips to her thatch of hair, a mahogany color darker than the hair on her head. "In a place that corresponds to here."

He rose to his feet, holding on to her waist. When he was standing, Katie took charge of undressing him, reaching for the top button of his shirt.

"There's no rule that says you have to start with the shirt," Louis teased her, caressing her breasts. "There's not much of interest from the waist up on a man."

Katie smiled at him saucily, loving the easy intimacy.

"That's false modesty if ever I heard it," she accused. "You know you've got a nice big set of shoulders and a muscular, hairy chest."

"Keep going," he prompted as she took off his shirt.

"That's about it, from the waist up," she said, unbuckling his belt. "I'd be embarrassed to admit I'd taken that much notice from the waist down."

"For someone shy, you know how to get a man's pants off in a hurry," Louis drawled as she took down his jeans. He was silent as she eased his knit briefs free of his aroused body, both of them finding the procedure stimulating. "Notice anything, Katie?" Louis said softly when he, too, was naked. "Go ahead," he urged her when she reached tentatively to touch him. "I'm all yours, sweetheart."

Katie looked at him, struck with emotion by his lover's words.

"Are you all mine, Louis?" she asked wistfully. The whole turn of events was suddenly too good to be true.

He met her eyes with a tender expression.

"All yours, Katie. And we're talking for keeps."

Katie took gentle possession of him and thrilled to his response as he moaned softly, closing his eyes and murmuring her name while he held her by her shoulders.

"What about you, Katie? Are you all mine?"

Busy stroking him and enjoying the intimate liberty of touching his body, Katie looked up at his inquiry. His voice had a hint of yearning that surprised her.

"I don't think I could ever belong to any other man, Louis," she replied, releasing him and slipping both arms around his neck. "I've been hung up on you all

these years. For some reason, no other man has ever
been right for me, like you are.''

Louis hugged her tightly around the waist, drawing
her hard against him, but he seemed to be waiting to be
sure she didn't have more she wanted to say. Taking the
initiative, Katie kissed him and put an end to the talking.

Their lovemaking was more deeply satisfying to her
than it had been the night before. Today there was no
question of holding back anything of herself. Louis belonged to her, and she belonged to him. They were
committed.

"Louis, I love you so much," she murmured, hugging him with all her strength when he lay on top of her
a helpless moment after he'd followed her to release.

He came to life immediately, bracing his arms on
either side of her. Katie blinked at the pleased smile on
his face.

"I was wondering if I was going to have to put the
words in your mouth," he drawled and kissed her tenderly on the lips. "I love you, too."

He rolled onto his side, gathering her close to him,
but it was Katie's turn to pop up and smile into his face.
She was bursting with the sheer thrill of hearing him
speak the words.

"Say it again," she pleaded.

Louis tousled her hair. "I will if you will," he bargained.

"I love you, Louis," she said softly, and they both
knew as she complied that she'd wanted the excuse to
say the words again as well as hear them.

"I love you, Katie." He cupped her head with his hand and brought her face to his to kiss her. "Again?" he inquired as she pulled back to gaze at him.

Katie sighed happily. "I guess we don't want to make it old hat, do we?" she said reluctantly. "Do you think when the newness wears off that we'll say it and it won't mean as much?"

Louis touched her cheek, and Katie caught his hand, holding it against her face while she listened to his answer, which was calm and thoughtful.

"It means just as much to me now for Stephie to say, 'I love you, Daddy,' as it did when she was two years old and first said it. I go all soft inside. As long as the love lasts, I don't think you wear out the words."

Katie kissed his hand, deeply touched by his answer.

"Stephanie's a lucky little girl," she said, her throat closing with her emotion and making her voice husky. "And I'm a very lucky woman. I love you, Louis."

"I love you, sweetheart."

They were saved from the intensity of the moment by the timely growling of Louis's stomach.

"Poor thing. You're starving," Katie sympathized, rubbing his abdomen. "Why don't we go out to eat or—" She broke off, startled, as Louis caught her hand and brought it lower.

He grinned at her expression. "I'm going to waste away to nothing if you keep making me choose," he drawled, pulling her head down for a taste of her mouth and rousing interplay with her tongue. "I'm so hungry I'm weak, but so help me, I can't pass up an *or* with you."

"I was just going to say, 'or pick up some po'boys and bring them back here,'" Katie murmured as he rolled over onto his back, bringing her on top of him.

"It's too late to tell me that now," he stated, stroking her back and caressing her buttocks, moving her against his hard arousal.

Katie moaned softly.

"I'm afraid you're right," she murmured, agreeing with him that lunch would have to be postponed.

*   *   *   *   *

Silhouette Romance™

Legendary Lovers Trilogy

BY DEBBIE MACOMBER....

ONCE UPON A TIME, in a land not so far away, there lived a girl, Debbie Macomber, who grew up dreaming of castles, white knights and princes on fiery steeds. Her family was an ordinary one with a mother and father and one wicked brother, who sold copies of her diary to all the boys in her junior high class.

One day, when Debbie was only nineteen, a handsome electrician drove by in a shiny black convertible. Now Debbie knew a prince when she saw one, and before long they lived in a two-bedroom cottage surrounded by a white picket fence.

As often happens when a damsel fair meets her prince charming, children followed, and soon the two-bedroom cottage became a four-bedroom castle. The kingdom flourished and prospered, and between soccer games and car pools, ballet classes and clarinet lessons, Debbie thought about love and enchantment and the magic of romance.

One day Debbie said, "What this country needs is a good fairy tale." She remembered how well her diary had sold and she dreamed again of castles, white knights and princes on fiery steeds. And so the stories of Cinderella, Beauty and the Beast, and Snow White were reborn....

Look for Debbie Macomber's *Legendary Lovers* trilogy from Silhouette Romance: *Cindy and the Prince* (January, 1988); *Some Kind of Wonderful* (March, 1988); *Almost Paradise* (May, 1988). Don't miss them!

SRT-1

COMING NEXT MONTH

#427 LOCAL HERO—Nora Roberts
Divorcée Hester Wallace was wary of men, but her overly friendly neighbor wasn't taking the hint. Though cartoonist Mitch Dempsey enthralled her young son, convincing Hester to believe in heroes again was another story entirely.

#428 SAY IT WITH FLOWERS—Andrea Edwards
Nurse Cristin O'Leary's clowning kept sick children happy, but her response to hospital hunk Dr. Sam Rossi was no joke. Would the handsome heart specialist have a remedy for a lovesick nurse?

#429 ARMY DAUGHTER—Maggi Charles
Architect Kerry Gundersen was no longer a lowly sergeant, but to him, interior designer Jennifer Smith would always be the general's daughter. As she decorated his mansion, resentment simmered . . . and desire flared out of control.

#430 CROSS MY HEART—Phyllis Halldorson
Senator Sterling couldn't let a family scandal jeopardize his reelection; he'd have to investigate his rascally brother's latest heartthrob. To his chagrin, he felt his *own* heart throbbing at his very first glimpse of her. . . .

#431 NEPTUNE SUMMER—Jeanne Stephens
Single parent Andrea Darnell knew Joe Underwood could breathe new life into Neptune, Nebraska, but she hadn't expected mouth-to-mouth resuscitation! Besides, did Joe really want *her*, or just her ready-made family?

#432 GREEK TO ME—Jennifer West
Kate Reynolds's divorce had shattered her heart, and no island romance could mend it. Still, dashing Greek Andreas Pateras was a powerful charmer, and he'd summoned the gods to help topple Kate's resistance!

AVAILABLE NOW:

In response
to last year's outstanding success,
Silhouette Brings You:

Silhouette Christmas Stories 1987

Specially chosen for you in a delightful volume celebrating the holiday season, four original romantic stories written by four of your favorite Silhouette authors.

Dixie Browning—*Henry the Ninth*
Ginna Gray—*Season of Miracles*
Linda Howard—*Bluebird Winter*
Diana Palmer—*The Humbug Man*

Each of these bestselling authors will enchant you with their unforgettable stories, exuding the magic of Christmas and the wonder of falling in love.

A heartwarming Christmas gift during the holiday season...indulge yourself and give this book to a special friend!

Available now